I0594710

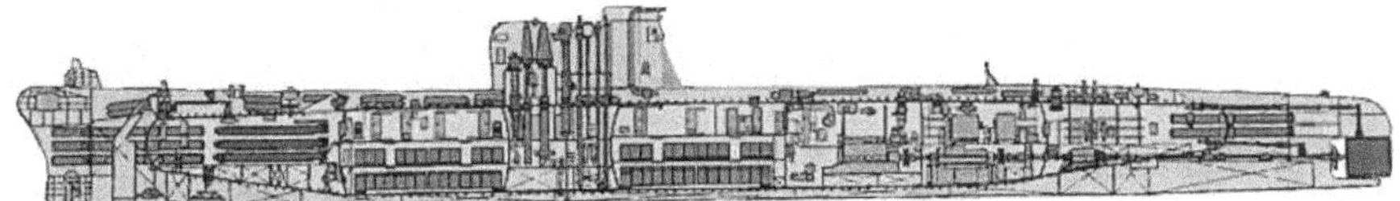

Steven Maffeo's books: naval history and historical fiction

Most Secret and Confidential: Intelligence in the Age of Nelson

*Seize, Burn, or Sink: The Thoughts and Words of Admiral Lord
Horatio Nelson*

The Perfect Wreck: "Old Ironsides" and HMS Java—A Story of 1812

*U.S. Navy Codebreakers, Linguists, and Intelligence Officers
against Japan, 1910-1941—A Biographical Dictionary*

*The Russian Who Saved the World—A Novel of the
Cuban Missile Crisis*

Praise for Steven Maffeo's Books

<u>Most Secret and Confidential: Intelligence in the Age of Nelson</u>

A thoughtful, insightful, magnificent history, exquisitely researched and brilliantly written.
— Stephen Coonts

One of the top three naval/maritime books of the year 2000. — *Seapower* magazine

What a joy it is to review a book that is well-researched, well-written, and put together with loving care. The positive first impression ... grows with familiarity.
— *Journal of Military History*

An exceptional study... a "must read."
— *Naval War College Review*

<u>The Perfect Wreck: "Old Ironsides" and HMS Java—A Story of 1812</u>

A highly recommended "must-read" for every naval enthusiast—indeed, for every American.
— Stephen Coonts

This ripping yarn fascinates, educates, and entertains .... This terrific account is a "must-read."
— *Naval War College Review*

The author does a fine job in writing for the expert and layman alike. The actual battle is superbly written ... in all its bloody and very sad details.
— *Naval History* magazine

<u>U.S. Navy Codebreakers, Linguists, and Intelligence Officers against Japan, 1910-41</u>

Maffeo's book is a great contribution to naval history.
—Vice Adm. John M. Poindexter, USN, Ret., Assistant for National Security Affairs to President Reagan

This volume will remain the standard reference for information about the Navy's intelligence personnel before and during World War II. — Naval Institute *Proceedings*

This book ... will entertain and enlighten today's readers, and perhaps inspire some among them.
— *Journal of Military History*

The Russian Who Saved the World

A Novel of the Cuban Missile Crisis

Steven E. Maffeo

FOCSLE

Annapolis, Maryland

Published by Focsle LLC
509 Schley Road
Annapolis, Maryland 21401

Library of Congress Cataloging-in-Publication Data
Maffeo, Steven E.
   The Russian Who Saved the World – A Novel of the Cuban Missile Crisis /
Capt. Steven E. Maffeo, U.S.N., Ret.
Includes bibliographical references and photographs.
1. Cuban Missile Crisis – Fiction. 2. Soviet Union – Navy – Fiction. 3. Submarine Warfare – Fiction. 4. Arkhipov, Vasiliy A. – Fiction.

Publisher's Note: This book is considerably inspired and informed by true historical events of the Soviet Operation *Kama* in 1962. However some of the story, some names and characters, and some incidents portrayed in this book are fictitious. Thus, many of the characters, names, places, locales, incidents, corporations, institutions, organizations and much of the dialog in this novel are the product of the author's imagination. For those that are or were real, they are used fictitiously without necessarily describing any actual conduct, remarks, or reality.

The Russian Who Saved the World: A Novel of the Cuban Missile Crisis /
Steven E. Maffeo -- 1st ed.
ISBN 978-0-9600391-3-5 (hardcover); 978-0-9600391-4-2 (paperback);
978-0-9600391-5-9 (eBook)

The paper used in this publication meets the minimum requirements of American National Standard for Information Sciences—Permanence of Paper for Printed Library Materials, ANSI/NISO Z39.48-1992.

Basic layout © 2017 BookDesignTemplates.com. Interior design: Steven E. Maffeo

Cover: Tony Mauro Illustration and Design

Printed in the United States of America

This book is dedicated to my mother,
June Augusta Miller Maffeo
(1925 – 2006)

Together, fifty-seven years ago, we watched as President John F. Kennedy delivered his "Cuban Missile Crisis" speech to the American people. On Monday evening, October 22nd 1962, sitting in our living room in southeast Denver, Colorado, our attention was riveted to our *Stromberg-Carlson* black-and-white television. I clearly recall her being extremely apprehensive while trying to explain to her 8-year-old boy the significance of what was going on.

Among other things, in this famous eighteen-minute
Oval Office address, Mr. Kennedy said:

My fellow citizens, let no one doubt that this is a difficult and dangerous effort on which we have set out. No one can foresee precisely what course it will take or what costs or casualties will be incurred.

The cost of freedom is always high—but Americans have always paid it. And one path we shall <u>never</u> choose ... is the path of surrender or submission.

It shall be the policy of this Nation to regard <u>any nuclear</u> missile launched from Cuba against <u>any nation</u> in the Western Hemisphere as an attack by the Soviet Union on the United States, <u>requiring a full retaliatory response upon the Soviet Union</u>.

An accidental nuclear war was not just the stuff of popular fiction. It was within the realm of actual possibility.

— Journalist and historian Michael Dobbs

The odds are even on an H-bomb war within ten years.

— President John F. Kennedy

[The Cuban Missile Crisis is a] trail of mishaps and miscalculations that nearly ended life on earth.

— "American History" Magazine

The Cuban Missile Crisis was the most dangerous ... moment in human history. Because never before had two contending powers possessed between them the technical capacity to blow up the world. This was an unprecedented moment in the history of humankind, and we are lucky to have survived it.

— Historian Arthur M. Schlesinger, Jr.

It was a perfectly beautiful night, as fall nights are in Washington. I walked out of the president's Oval Office and, as I walked out, I thought I might never live to see another Saturday night.

— U.S. Secretary of Defense Robert S. McNamara

In war, the character and personality of the leader is decisive of events much more than [other] questions.

— Novelist and historian C. S. Forester

Let none of us think that he can lead God around by the beard.

— Premier Nikita S. Khrushchev

Операция Анадырь
Операция Кама

In one brief hour of one specific day, in a tiny spot of ocean, the entire course of human events was nearly altered.

Altered ... catastrophically.

This book is dramatically inspired and heavily informed by true historical occurrences which took place in October 1962. In play were the USSR's "Operations *Anadyr* and *Kama*."

It all later became known, in the West, as the

Cuban Missile Crisis.

Part I

What might have happened

CHAPTER I

On board the Soviet Navy diesel-electric submarine "B-59"

Atlantic Ocean, 683 miles northeast of Cuba

Approximately 26° 34' North, 65° 47' West

1737 hours local, Saturday, October 27, 1962

The 12th day of the "Cuban Missile Crisis"

"Tie *Kapitan* Arkhipov's hands behind his back!" Doubting he had heard correctly, the chief warrant officer of the watch stared blankly at *Kapitan* Valentin Savitskiy. The *michman* had just come up from the Control Center into the boat's conning tower. A length of thin rope dangled from his hand.

"Are you f--king deaf?" shouted Savitskiy, the commanding officer of the *B-59*. "Do what I tell you and do it NOW!"

"*Yest', Kapitan!*" Looking frightened and confused, the warrant officer came up to Arkhipov and grasped his left arm. "Your pardon, *Tovarishch Kapitan*," he whispered. Arkhipov decided that there was no point in resisting the poor man and making a crazy situation even worse, so he shrugged and put his hands behind his back. He was grateful that the *michman* tied the cord loosely, his sweat-slick fingers fumbling with the knot.

The *michman* was sweating because the conning tower's air temperature was 104 degrees Fahrenheit. Similar temperatures, along with a humidity level approaching 100 percent, existed throughout the boat. Many of the crew lay in their bunks, on mess tables, or on the filthy and wet decks. Everyone was shiny with sweat. Everyone was gasping in the depleted air—air that was very short of life-sustaining oxygen and very full of dangerous amounts of carbon dioxide.

Just then the telephone-talker caught Savitskiy's eye.

"Tovarishch Kapitan, a new test says carbon dioxide is at two point five percent." At three percent most men would actually pass out. At four percent—even if there were some oxygen still present—the CO_2 would suffocate all. Savitskiy merely nodded.

A few feet from him, appearing outwardly calm, Vasiliy Arkhipov was actually beside himself. Arkhipov, the chief of staff of the 69th Torpedo Submarine Brigade, was groping for ideas and searching for words to stop this madness. Captain Savitskiy appeared ready to give the order to close the torpedo firing switch. If he did, then a massive blast of compressed air would ram the boat's "special weapon" out of Tube Two—with absolutely no way to call it back or stop it.

The special weapon—the *spetsial'noye oruzhiye*—was one of B-59's twenty-two torpedoes. It was the one painted purple. The kind which *Projekt-641* boats weren't supposed to carry. The one with a nuclear warhead.

For one brief moment hope flooded Arkhipov's mind. While the torpedo indeed could be fired right now, in theory and in protocol it still needed to be fed the bearing and range of the American aircraft carrier. Of course the USS *Randolph* was the big target Savitskiy was going to shoot—versus any of the small American destroyers. The *Randolph* was the obvious choice as she was the flagship of the close-by U.S. Navy anti-submarine task force. This was the force that had been aggressively hounding and harassing the *B-59* for the past three days. The *zampolit*—Ivan Maslennikov, *B-59*'s hard-line political officer—had already suggested this choice. But it would take some time to make those targeting inputs—time Arkhipov needed to *puskat' pod otkos* [derail] this horrible scenario.

In fact, next to the FDC-759 radar display in the Control Center, the *B-59* had a computing machine—an electromechanical analog computer—which was essential to the effective firing of torpedoes. For 1962 it was state-of-the-art and incredibly useful. Once fed data from radar, sonar, or periscope readings it would calculate a target's course, speed, and position. It would then send accurate gyroscope angles and other information to the torpedoes as they waited patiently in their tubes. American submariners called their version of this machine the "Torpedo Data Computer." The Russians called theirs the "Weapons Control Center." But, right now, *B-59*'s was not even powered up.

Unfortunately, Arkhipov's hope for more time vanished almost as soon as it appeared. The Americans like to say, "Close only counts with horseshoes and hand grenades." But "close" also counts with nuclear weapons. Captain Arkhipov suddenly realized that Captain Savitskiy needed neither precise analysis nor sophisticated solutions from the WCC. He only needed a couple of pencil calculations from the "torpedo attack crew"—the fire-control party. All that was really necessary was to release the weapon in the approximate direction and distance of the carrier, and it would be good enough. Unquestionably good enough.

As if he were reading Arkhipov's mind Savitskiy turned and shouted down the ladder into the CC.

"Fire Control! You have been plotting the enemy?"

B-59's officers had taken note of the bearings and ranges of the American ships when the boat was last forced to dive. The executive officer and torpedo officer were up in the conning tower, but the rest of the fire-control party—the navigator, a sonar technician, and the idle WCC operator—were packed around the navigator's plotting table in the CC, pouring over the chart with dividers, parallel rulers, and colored pencils. At this moment the OSNAZ Radio Interception Officer, Senior-Lieutenant Vadim Orlov, was also in that group.

"Da, Tovarishch Kapitan," replied Captain-Lieutenant Tsezar Sutulin, the senior navigator. He called up the conning-tower ladder, which was easy to do as the ladder's foot was immediately adjacent to the plotting table.

"You have an estimate for the God-damned carrier?"

"Da, Kapitan. Based on her last observed position, and assuming she has not significantly changed course or speed, *da."* That was a fair assumption. To facilitate her aircraft operations the carrier would likely be cruising steadily and relatively slowly. In contrast, it was not clear where all of her destroyers were as they were dancing around everywhere on the sea looking for

Savitskiy's boat—and for any other Soviet submarines. Of course, the whereabouts of *five* of the destroyers were very clear to the Russians—they were directly above the *B-59*.

"And, *ser*," added the sonar technician, "we have periodically been hearing the carrier on our *Feniks* passive sonar system. We know where she is."

"Excellent! Distance!?"

"*Ser*, estimate three point seven kilometers."

"Bearing!?" Savitskiy actually snarled.

"*Ser*, estimate target bearing two-nine-two degrees." This response was from Lieutenant Orlov. While Sutulin was carefully plotting the movements of the *B-59*, Orlov was employing the skills of his original naval career specialization as a navigator and was tracking the American ship.

The kill radius of the special weapon was just under twelve kilometers. Depending upon what Savitskiy was going to do in the next few minutes, the USS *Randolph*, her destroyers, her support ships, many of her aircraft—and very likely the *B-59*—were all going to die together.

Savitskiy clapped his bloody hands together, apparently not feeling any pain from his lacerated knuckles. "Officer on Deck, make your course two-nine-two, speed four knots!"

"*Yest', Kapitan!*" This would point the *B-59*—and her forward torpedo tubes—at what the Russians estimated was the *Randolph*'s current position.

The navigator handed a scrap of paper to the telephone-talker, who then passed the distance and gyro data to the Forward Torpedo Room. There a torpedoman would manually enter that data into Tube Two's guidance system, which was part of a control panel mounted in between Tubes Five and Six.

The *Ofitser Torpedy*—Senior-Lieutenant Kirill Sluchevski—then said, *"Kapitan,* shall we make a final shooting observation?"

"No! *Konechno net* [Hell no]! And we shall *not* come up to *periskop* depth. We shall *not* raise the scope! For the same reason we shall *not* employ the active sonar. We would betray our exact position. The destroyers would pounce on us before we could shoot. We have enough information, Sluchevski! They cannot escape. The special weapon will destroy them all!"

O Gospodi, Arkhipov said to himself. Oh God of my sainted *Babushka!*

If Savitskiy now merely called out "Shoot!" it was going to happen. Was he going to forget that he needed Arkhipov's agreement? Or was he simply going to ignore the "rules of engagement?" If he gave the order would the torpedo officer refuse—or at least hesitate? Or would Lieutenant Sluchevski obediently reach over to the instrument panel just at his eye level? Would his fingers close around the torpedo firing circuit switch? Would he turn it?

"Tovarishch Kapitan," said Arkhipov, loudly, desperately. He took a step toward Savitskiy. But Savitskiy, raising his arms while simultaneously stepping toward the chief of staff, slammed his bloody fists into Arkhipov's chest. Thrown off-balance with his hands tied behind him, Arkhipov slipped on the wet deck and fell down, hitting his head but able to keep his nose from smacking into the periscope housing. But as Savitskiy moved, so did the chief engineer. Bogdan Pugachev leapt forward and threw his arms around his captain from behind.

"Kapitan," Pugachev said quietly, in the stunned silence of the conning tower. *"Valentin Grigorievich."*

Savitskiy tried to shake him off. "Let me go!" But Pugachev held on firmly.

"God damn it!" Savitskiy screamed, continuing to shake, "why is Captain Arkhipov still in my God-damned conning tower? GET HIM BELOW AND OUT OF MY SIGHT!"

Pugachev continued to hold his commanding officer in a bear hug. Arkhipov shakily got back to his feet, helped by the *starpom*—the executive officer—Zakhar Chernyshev. Despite Savitskiy's order no one seemed interested in moving Arkhipov down the ladder and out of the conning tower, so he started speaking again. Arkhipov was desperate to get Savitskiy thinking rather than fighting.

"Tovarishch Kapitan, the rules of engagement for this mission are clear." Saying nothing, Savitskiy stared past Arkhipov's shoulder. Thus encouraged, Arkhipov went on.

"We are authorized to fire the special weapon *if* we are attacked—either on the surface or under the water—and *if,* as a result of such attack, our pressure hull is damaged. We may also fire it *if* we are so directed by signal from Moskva. But, as of right now, Valentin, *none of these conditions have been met."* With his arms tied behind him, Arkhipov unsuccessfully tried to shake off the sweat pouring into his eyes.

"Despite the infernal harassment the *Amerikantsy* have given us these last three days, they have dropped no fully-armed depth charges upon us. We have to conclude that, at this time, there is no state of war."

"Moreover," Arkhipov continued, "we can fire the special weapon—and let us be clear about this—Captain, gentlemen." He glanced around the compartment, finding all eyes on him once again. Most important, he hoped that the torpedo officer, standing so close to that damned firing switch, was paying attention. "Let us be clear—it is a torpedo tipped with a *nuclear* warhead. Once again, we can fire it *only* if you, and the *zampolit*, and I, all agree. *All-three-of-us.*"

"This is no mere bureaucratic mumbo-jumbo to which we can pay attention, or not. These rules are *inviolate.* We can *not* release a nuclear weapon outside of this protocol. As we all know, those rules came clearly and directly from *Admiral-Flota* Sergey Gorshkov and were relayed to us by *Kontr-Admiral* Leonid Rybalko."

"If we violate these rules we would be subject to court martial. We would doubtless spend the rest of our lives in a Siberian *gulag.* Of course, that would only happen *if* we lived to get home—and *if* there remained a home to go to. Neither of which would be likely." Arkhipov paused for a moment as he tried to catch his breath. For him, and everyone else, it felt as if all the oxygen molecules had been boiled out of the air.

"Again, Valentin, any command on your part to fire the special weapon absolutely requires *Tovarishch* Maslennikov's assent *and* my assent." Arkhipov paused for a few seconds to give his words emphasis. He was speaking to the *zampolit* and the *starpom* as well as the *kapitan,* hoping that all three were turning the issues over in their minds. Arkhipov hoped that *Glavnyy Inzhener* Pugachev was also carefully listening.

"You have the *zampolit's* assent. But, I say again, *Tovarishch Kapitan*, as clearly as I can—*I do not give mine!*"

Savitskiy stared at Arkhipov so intently that Arkhipov feared his eyes might pop out of their sockets. Then Savitskiy drew a deep breath and violently shook his head, scowling. He had been relatively still for the last few minutes but now resumed struggling against Pugachev's "hug." They both slipped on the wet deck and fell down. Breaking from Pugachev's grasp, Savitskiy scooted to the side and pulled himself up using the periscope. Pugachev grabbed him by the leg but Savitskiy savagely shook him off and then kicked him in the head. The chief engineer fell to the wet deck.

Savitskiy took a deep breath of the foul air and then screamed at Lieutenant Sluchevski.

"*STRELYAT*'! God damn you, SHOOT!"

"SHOOT THE F--KING SPECIAL WEAPON!"

Ofitser Torpedy Sluchevski, looking shocked with his eyes popping, hesitated. Captain Arkhipov, looking shocked with his jaws clenched, launched himself at Sluchevski.

"NO, STOP, NO!" Arkhipov shouted. He desperately tried to tackle Sluchevski and throw him to the deck, or failing that he hoped to knock his arm away from the instrument panel. But even in the small conning tower Arkhipov was just too far away. He did not get there in time. As Arkhipov rushed towards him Sluchevski shook off his initial hesitation, reached out, grasped the firing switch, and turned it.

B-59 lurched as a compressed-air charge rammed four-thousand pounds of nuclear-armed torpedo out of her. Already very much off-balance, Arkhipov again fell heavily to the deck.

In both the conning tower and the Control Center there was a moment of stunned silence. Savitskiy and Arkhipov stared at Sluchevski and then at each other. The torpedo officer stuck his fingers in his mouth as if to cool them from the touch of the firing switch.

Chernyshev was the first to recover.

"POGRUZHENIYE! DIVE! NOW! Emergency dive! Take her down! 350 meters! Hard right rudder!"

He looked up and shuddered as if he could feel dozens of fully-armed depth charges—rolling off the racks of the circling destroyers above—dropping down towards the *B-59.*

Then Chernyshev shuddered again—anticipating the massive shockwave of a ten-kiloton nuclear explosion reaching down for him through the depths.

CHAPTER 2

Cabinet Room, West Wing, the White House

Washington, D.C.

1902 hours local, Saturday, October 27, 1962

The 12th day of the "Cuban Missile Crisis"

The thirteen members and a few other advisors of the ExComm were hard at work. The ExComm was the Executive Committee of the United States National Security Council—recently formed to address the Cuban crisis. Most of the men were seated around the huge conference table in tense but quiet discussion. Right now these men included the president himself, the vice president, the national security advisor, the attorney general, the chairman of the joint chiefs of staff, and several others.

Earlier today—a little more than seven hours earlier—an American U-2F reconnaissance aircraft had been destroyed almost 72,000 feet above Banes, Cuba. It was shot down by a Soviet S-75 *Dvina* surface-to-air missile. The pilot, Major Rudolf Anderson, U. S. Air Force, was killed. As a result, the already stressful standoff between the Soviet Union and the United States had now become absolutely terrifying.

The American defense establishment had five levels of "Defense Readiness Conditions," with DEFCON-5 being normal peacetime and DEFCON-1 being set for the most dangerous, severe situations—including imminent or ongoing nuclear war. The current condition, elevated a few days earlier, was DEFCON-3. However, General Thomas Power, the commander of the U.S. Air Force's formidable Strategic Air Command, had secretly been authorized to set his force at DEFCON-2. He had, on alert, approximately 900 strategic bombers, 400 tanker aircraft, and 130 strategic intercontinental ballistic missiles. As of 1100 hours today he had been further authorized to bring all of his remaining forces, including the Air Force Reserve and Air National Guard, to full readiness—such that they would be "cocked, locked," and ready to strike.

The Strategic Air Command controlled 2,900 nuclear weapons.

Five days earlier, seven U.S. Navy nuclear-powered missile submarines had moved to staging points at sea. They carried 112 strategic ballistic missiles armed with nuclear warheads.

Right now, looking around the conference table, President John F. Kennedy called for everyone's attention and began speaking to the group.

"The Soviets fired the first shot today, destroying the U-2." He paused to rub his eyes. "We're now in an entirely new ball game." He looked around the room.

"If worse comes to worse, God forbid, and I had to order the use of nuclear weapons..." He paused for a moment. "I know that the red button on my desk phone will connect me with the White House Army Signal Agency switchboard. I know that they will connect me instantly to the Joint War Room at the Pentagon. But please remind me—if I called the Joint War Room, to whom would I be speaking? And what would I say to them to launch an immediate nuclear strike?"

Secretary of Defense Robert McNamara exchanged a look with the Joint Chiefs' Chairman, General Maxwell Taylor, U.S. Army. McNamara said, "Mr. President, those are good questions which of course we can easily answer. But right now, during a situation like this one with all of us here in your presence, you need do nothing more than make your decision and give the word. We will instantly do what needs to be done."

Kennedy nodded, and then stared silently at the table for a moment.

"Ah, this looks like hell. It looks real mean, doesn't it? And, on the other hand, it's just a question of where the Soviets will go do something next. If they get *this* mean on this one in our part of the world, what will they do on the next confrontation somewhere else?" He thought for a moment, and then went on.

"No choice. I don't think there was a choice. We had to do something. I didn't want airstrikes against Cuba, or for God's sake, an invasion. Declaring the quarantine line seemed—seems—a good choice, though it's risky in its own right."

"Well, there wasn't any choice," replied Robert F. Kennedy, the attorney general, the president's brother—and the president's closest advisor. "You had to do something serious. You had to take action. If not, I mean, you would have been, well, you would have been impeached."

"That's what I think," said the president. "I would have been impeached. I think the Congress would have moved to impeach. And, even so, I wouldn't be surprised if they don't move to impeach me after the coming November elections. They'll impeach on the grounds I said we'd take strong action and they don't think I've done enough."

"Jack, I don't think that will happen," said the attorney general. "If you'd done nothing, or taken some other step that wasn't necessary, then you'd be in trouble."

"OK, yeah," said the president.

"But now, the fact is you couldn't have done any less, and I think you shouldn't have done any more. The quarantine was a good solution—and it seems to be working. Despite this U-2 incident. As you said, this may well change the game."

President Kennedy nodded his head, and looked around the room, and focused upon the wall clock. "Gentlemen, I'm sorry, I didn't mean to keep you this long. It's been a hell of a long day after a long and stressful week. We've been hard at it this session for, uh, three and a half hours. We need to finish the message to Khrushchev. But let's break right now, everybody get a bite to eat, and then come back and we'll see what we can do. So, can we get back together at nine and..."

The door slammed open and a Central Intelligence Agency watch officer flew into the room. He was out of breath, having sprinted from the recently created White House Situation Room and communications center located in the basement of the West Wing.

"Sir! Mr. President! 'FLASH' message from Commander, ASW Task Group 83.2, USS *Randolph*! A Soviet FOXTROT-class submarine—which we'd previously designated as Contact C-19—just fired a torpedo apparently at the *Randolph*!"

President Kennedy and the other ExComm members literally jumped to their feet.

"God in heaven!"

"Mr. President!" exclaimed Air Force chief of staff General Curtis LeMay, "you must order that submarine destroyed—RIGHT NOW!" LeMay was not a full member of the ExComm but he was present as a senior advisor.

"Hold on, dammit," replied Kennedy. "Where is this happening, exactly?"

"Sir, the *Randolph* is about eighty miles northeast of the quarantine line. Her destroyers and aircraft have been aggressively pursuing Contact C-19 for over two days."

"Okay. Now, we do know for certain it's a Soviet diesel-electric submarine?" asked Kennedy.

"Yes, Mr. President."

"According to Wednesday's briefing, this class of submarine does not carry nuclear weapons. Tell me again, is that right?"

"That is correct, Mr. President. FOXTROTs are not missile-firing boats and they do not carry nuclear weapons of any kind. They do carry conventional torpedoes or, on occasion, naval mines."

"Sir, you must...." began General LeMay.

"How far away was this goddam submarine?" interrupted Kennedy. "I mean, how long will it take for this torpedo to reach the *Randolph*?"

"Sir, we don't know precisely, but a fair estimate from last-known positions would be about three minutes."

Kennedy's eyebrows shot up. "Well hell, those minutes must be up by now! You know, I used to shoot torpedoes. From what I remember three minutes is a damned long run. Damned long. And the *Randolph* can take evasive action. Surely the damn thing will miss."

As if on cue another CIA watch officer charged into the room through the same still-open door.

"MR. PRESIDENT!" he shouted. "'FLASH' messages from the USS *Essex* and also ASW Task Group 81.5 at Bermuda! A nuclear explosion has been detected at the location of the carrier *Randolph*!"

The room was silent with shock and surprise. Every member of the ExComm was completely stunned. No one expected this news. No one.

The second CIA officer, catching his breath, continued. "Sir, the first assessment of the detonation is ten kilotons, sub-surface. Not huge—appears similar to the Hiroshima bomb. That still needs to be verified. But the *Randolph* cannot be raised on any comm channel, nor can any of her destroyers."

"Good God!" exclaimed Dean Rusk, the secretary of state. "Can a naval torpedo carry a nuclear warhead of that force?"

No one spoke, but McNamara and Taylor both nodded their heads.

President Kennedy had been pacing in a small circle to the side of the conference table. "Just what the hell is going on?" he exploded. "What are those Soviet bastards doing? They've put nuclear torpedoes on submarines which aren't supposed to have them!?" He paused for a moment.

"It's been said that the Russians are great chess players," mumbled Ken O'Donnell, the president's special assistant and appointments secretary. "When they wish to execute a plot they execute it brilliantly. The game is planned minutely. The gambits of the enemy are provided for. They are foreseen and countered."

"Where did you get that, Kenny?" asked the president.

"Ian Fleming," O'Donnell replied, looking sheepish.

"Well, I'm not seeing any brilliance or great planning here," said President Kennedy, looking annoyed. "They shoot down aircraft of the U.S. Air Force? Then out of the blue they shoot nuclear torpedoes at the U.S. Navy—all this practically in our back yard?" He slammed his fist into his padded, leather chair.

"And they do all these things on a high-stress day? A day that's already so tense we don't know whether to shit or go blind!" He paced a few steps and then paced back.

"No sir. No. Khrushchev is a goddam mystery. Why has he put nuclear missiles in Cuba in the first place? What's the advantage in that? And why does he attack us with a nuclear weapon while we're in the middle of an intense standoff. While we're trying like hell to negotiate? What does he expect us to do? What 'gambits' does he think we'll come up with in the face of this horrendous action? It makes no sense. I know Khrushchev's a tough and ruthless son of a bitch, but until now I never thought he was totally nuts."

"This shows that the threat never has been Castro or Cuba. This underscores that the threat is the Soviet Union. And so far," said Theodore Sorensen, special counsel to the president, "in this mess, the Soviets'—and Khrushchev's—motions have been inscrutable."

"Well, no shit, Ted," said Robert Kennedy.

"So what should we do? What can we do?" asked Vice President Lyndon Johnson from across the conference table.

"Do?" bellowed General LeMay, smacking his hands together. "Do? We respond immediately! We attack! We have to, with all we've got. Obviously the Russkies have decided to go for the whole thing! So it doesn't matter whether they think they're playing world-class chess or whether they've just gone nuts. They've started a God-damned nuclear war! And we've gotta get off our asses and get with it right f--king now!"

Former secretary of state Dean Acheson cleared his throat. "Mr. President, I'm afraid that I have to agree with General LeMay. None of us wanted this, but the die has just been cast. A war has been thrust upon us. We must quickly respond, and we must respond with full measures."

"What if it's an accident?" asked the president.

"Sir! We don't know—and it doesn't matter," said LeMay impatiently. He gave Kennedy a sour look. "We have to assume it is not! We must assume it's the first nuke they've deployed which will be rapidly followed by all they have. So, we need to retaliate with everything we have!" LeMay took a deep breath, and slowly exhaled it.

"They've started it. We need to stop it! The quicker we stop it the more lives we'll save!"

"I'm sorry, Mr. President," he said in a quieter voice, "but there's just no two ways about it. You are in a pretty bad fix right now."

"What? What did you say?" replied Kennedy.

"You're in a pretty bad fix."

"Well, General, you're in there with me. Personally."

After a long pause while Kennedy and LeMay glared at each other, Kennedy turned to the secretary of defense.

"Bob, what do you advise?"

"Mr. President," replied McNamara slowly, "sometimes in order to do good, you may have to engage in evil." Kennedy gave him a long, hard look in turn.

"Mac?"

"Mr. President," said McGeorge Bundy, Kennedy's national security advisor, "I'm horrified at what you're asking. But I don't see that we—you—have any choice. You said as much in your T.V. speech to the world on Monday. You said, 'any use of a nuclear weapon against any nation in the Western Hemisphere will instantly cause a full retaliatory response from us upon the Soviet Union.' We all agreed. We helped you craft that position." He paused for a moment.

"Of course, at that point we envisioned a strike coming from Cuba itself, but this is actually worse—it's clearly a Soviet Navy warship directly striking warships of the United States Navy. And I too am afraid it's likely the beginning of a full Soviet nuclear attack, as crazy as that would seem."

"Well, goddam it, that's what I'm saying!" exploded LeMay. "We have to assume it's the beginning of a full-blown Soviet nuclear attack against us! Maybe the jackass C.O. of that rust-bucket submarine jumped the gun and fired prematurely. Or maybe he was actually supposed to start things off. Or maybe he's just gone bat-shit crazy. IT DOES NOT F--KING MAT-TER—we've got to attack, and RIGHT NOW!"

"General....."

"What the f--k—pardon me—are you waiting for, Mr. Presi-dent? More f--king evidence? You want another gray-suited CIA clown to burst in the room and tell you *another* FOXTROT has just vaporized the *Essex*? Or maybe that the other couple of Russkie subs down there—which right now the Navy's appar-ently 'misplaced'—have nuked the *Enterprise* and the *Independence*? Or the goddam Cubans have put a nuke missile or artillery shell into Naval Station Guantánamo? Sir, every minute we wait works against us!" He spit out some tobacco from the unlit cigar he was furiously chewing.

"Like I said before, we need to get on this fast, and end it fast. Are you going to wait around until more spooks rush in— this time announcing that they've detected the launch of the full Soviet ICBM and bomber force? And they're all coming OUR WAY at the speed of heat? Come on, come on—we need to respond, NOW!" He thought for a moment.

"And, by the way, we've also gotta cream the Cubans as well as the Soviets. You know that f--ker Castro won't miss this chance to throw some of his new Russkie missiles at us. We need to get them on the ground before they get in the air."

The room was silent for a moment as everyone digested the situation.

Finally, General Taylor said, "I think General LeMay is cor-rect, Mr. President. I just don't know how else we can interpret this event. I think we have to assume the worst, and time is not in our favor."

Secretary Rusk said, "I've long believed that the first side to use nuclear weapons would carry a very grave responsibility and endure heavy consequences before the rest of the world."

"For Chrissake, Mr. Secretary," shouted LeMay, "they—the Russkies—already have struck first! So fine, they are gravely responsible! Indeed, they are very bad people. Somebody get a pencil. Let's write that down and issue a memorandum." He spit more tobacco.

"But now we must stand up to our responsibilities! Now we must throw everything we have at them—before everything they have hits us. And, with any luck, maybe we can destroy a lot of their weapons before launch or at least in the air before they get to us."

"I can see you politicians are hung up on the morality of all this. But I think it's more immoral to use too little than it is to use too much. If you dilly-dally with indecision, and go light rather than heavy, you'll end up killing-off more of humanity in the long run—because you'll be merely delaying and protracting the struggle."

Dean Acheson nodded his head. "Yes. We can't wait until we detect their missiles launch or see their bombers up on radar. It will be too late at that point. In order to maximize our chances of survival we must strike immediately." He looked at the Air Force chief of staff, who was half-way finished chewing through his cigar. Acheson went on.

"I'm heartsick to say it, but I think the Russians have brought Secretary Rusk's heavy consequences upon themselves. Sorrowfully, they have brought them upon the world."

General Taylor said, "If we move now, and decisively, we might be able to save the situation." He threw up his hands. "Well, of course by that I don't mean save—I mean minimize our casualties."

The president furiously rubbed his eyes. He had slept very little this week and not much at all in the past two days.

"Gentlemen. Under the present circumstances does anyone here believe that there is any other reasonable course open to us?" He slowly looked around the room. Most of the ExComm members met his gaze with distraught expressions; a few stared at the floor; some had buried their faces in their hands. But no one spoke.

Kennedy looked from side to side. He was trapped, and he felt trapped.

"My God! God! How can this have happened?" The president sat down in an armchair and massaged his right temple. "Am I to be the greatest mass-murderer in history?"

"It isn't murder," said Bundy, "it's war. It isn't murder if you're fighting for your country's existence. If you're fighting to save your citizens' lives."

"Yes!" interjected LeMay.

"Mr. President, of course as you know, this isn't a new concept," said McNamara. "We've been worried about such a scenario for fifteen years. We've war-gamed such things a hundred times. In the fear of nuclear war we've built a huge defense and strike capability—hopefully to deter, but also to act if necessary."

"He's right, sir," said Ted Sorensen. "We've gamed it over and over. We're not kids in a schoolyard fistfight which all of a sudden just broke out to everyone's surprise. We've thought these scenarios through and studied angles and options. If they do A, we do C. If they do M, we respond with P. If we do X, then they'll do Y." He paused, started to speak again, but then looked away with his thought unfinished.

Seconds passed. Finally, Bobby Kennedy cleared his throat and addressed his brother.

"Jack." he said slowly and sadly. "Jack, there's nothing else to do. Ever since the U-2 shootdown earlier today, I haven't been able to shake the feeling that the noose was really tightening—on we Americans, on mankind—and that the bridge to escape was crumbling. At this point I think any such bridge is gone." He paused for a moment, thinking. "There's nothing else to do."

As a sophisticated student of history, John F. Kennedy knew he was cornered by an outrageous and unlikely twist of fate. He now had to make the most incredible decision that any leader could ever hope *not* to face. He stared at the famous portrait of George Washington which hung over the mantel on the north wall of the room. He was quiet for a long, long moment. Then he quietly began to speak.

"Mr. Secretary of Defense. Mr. Chairman of the Joint Chiefs of Staff. This is an order. I, John Fitzgerald Kennedy, President of the United States of America, do hereby direct you to set Defense Condition One."

"I further order you to immediately implement the Single Integrated Operational Plan. Commence a full-scale nuclear attack upon the Union of Soviet Socialist Republics, the nations of the Warsaw Pact, and the Republic of Cuba." He was silent for almost a minute.

"God help us. God help me."

As he spoke, the president turned very pale. He then covered his mouth with his one hand, made a fist with his other hand, and stared bleakly at his brother.

CHAPTER 3

After thirty-six hours, and the detonation of the final nuclear weapon, the war was over.

As it began American strategic forces were many times larger and much more reliable than their Soviet counterparts. The United States possessed over 3,500 nuclear weapons of different sizes—including small artillery shells owned by U.S. Army units in Europe and small depth charges owned by the U.S. Navy. All of these weapons totaled a combined yield of some 6,300 megatons. At the time of the attack the Air Force's Strategic Air Command was organizing and readying everything it had—regular, reserve, and National Guard—which was close to 1,480 bombers, 1,000 refueling tanker aircraft, and 180 ICBMs—altogether capable of delivering 2,900 nuclear weapons. In addition, the U.S. Navy's strategic submarine force brought to bear over 100 nuclear ICBMs.

Despite the USSR's boastful propaganda, there was a much smaller Soviet arsenal facing the American force: 40 ICBMs carried a combined yield of some 200 megatons. Only 140 bombers were available. A handful of submarines carried only 80 missiles with a combined yield of less than 100 megatons. In fact, it was believed that Premier Khrushchev and his military advisors had recently estimated that US strategic nuclear forces outnumbered the USSR's by a factor approaching 17 to 1.

Thus, nearly 2,000 megatons of American nuclear fire struck the Soviet Union, Eastern Europe, and Cuba. Those nations were effectively destroyed. They essentially ceased to exist.

Relatively few Soviet nuclear weapons were able to reach the United States—perhaps only around thirty—but the impact was still terrible. Millions of people died. Yet the country, and the civilization, were not destroyed. Many states and cities were not hit. Many parts of the government, the military, and the infrastructure survived.

So the exchange went substantially in favor of the United States—if it really could be considered in those terms. But large swaths of Western Europe and North America lay in ruins

The expected radiation clouds and overall world-wide fallout were terrible, but thankfully were significantly less than earlier war games had suggested they might be. This was due to both sides predominantly using high-altitude air bursts rather than ground bursts. This minimized the amount of radioactive dirt and other debris being thrown into the atmosphere.

However, it is estimated that over 500 million people died from the explosions, radiation poisoning, and eventual starvation. Millions more were displaced and became homeless refugees.

It was, perhaps, not a holocaust beyond all imagination. It was not, literally, the end of the world. But, depending upon your perspective, it certainly appeared that way.

Part 2

What may have happened

 # CHAPTER 4 

Revolyuzia Café
Zheleznodorozhny, Russian Federation
21 kilometers east of Moscow
June 19, 1998

"*Zdravstvuyte!* Hello! Hello there, my young friend. Come closer. Please do not be shy of an old man.

My associates tell me that you wish to hear my story. Certainly. Certainly. Can you sit with me for a while? This is a nice corner of this wonderful café, do you not think? If you look through this window you can see the blue dome of the Savvino Church of the Transfiguration. I like to look at it. The beautiful blue of the dome reminds me of the sea in the morning, lit by the early sun.

So, you have heard that some people call me "the man who saved the world." Well, I ask you, is that not a *dramatichnyy* title? The man who saved the world. Or, perhaps you will like this other one, "the man to whom you owe your life."

So. Perhaps I did save the world. Perhaps you do owe me your life. On the other hand, perhaps these are exaggerations. Whatever it was that happened, it was a long time ago. I have never actually told my story before, except to my wife. I suppose I could tell you the story today and you can decide for yourself.

But before we begin my particular tale, shall I relate to you the general setting? Are you comfortable? They have wonderful *kofe* here, as good as in the Bosco Café in Moskva, just down from the Cathedral of St. Basil. You will have some? Good! The waitress will bring it.

I shall call you *Tovarishch Slushatel'*. May I call you that? "Comrade Listener." I like that, if it is all right with you.

Now, are you ready to hear the story? Yes? *Otlichno* [Excellent]!

 **CHAPTER 5** 

Well then, for you, here is some background *infor-matsiya*. I shall tell you that in mid-1962 the leaders of the *Soyuz Sovetskikh Sotsialisticheskikh Respublik*—of course, that is the Union of Soviet Socialist Republics—decided on an extremely bold action. Their intent was to counter what they thought to be certain disadvantages for the *Sovetskiy Soyuz* in the "Cold War" struggle with the West. Perhaps they hoped to create some advantages as well. Of course that struggle was mainly the conflict with the *Soyedinennyye Shtaty Ameriki*—the United States of America. I am told that the initial plan was secretly presented to the *Prezidium Verkhovnogo Soveta*—Presidium of the Supreme Soviet—in May 1962. As you may know, that institution was the *Sovetskiy* version of the British parliament or the American congress.

The bold action was this: the *Sovetskiy* leaders decided to move a large quantity of ballistic missiles, medium-range bombers, and a division of motorized infantry to *Kuba*. Of course, *Kuba* is a large island in the Caribbean Sea—and a communist country—just a few miles from the U.S. state of Florida. These missiles and bombers were "nuclear capable." So, many nuclear warheads and bombs were also to be brought to *Kuba*. The code name for this ultra-secret and extremely dangerous plan was Операция Анадырь [Operation Anadyr].

There was a cover deception put in place for the operation. It was publicly stated to be an enormous *Sovetskiy* "humanitarian and economic assistance" operation for the poor and suffering people of *Kuba*. Thus, starting in July, some 85 cargo and transport ships—originating from ports all around the *Sovetskiy Soyuz*—began bringing many tons of military material and equipment, as well as thousands of troops, to that island. This deception seemed to fool the West, which did not pay much attention to the actual cargos in these ships and thus did not appreciate their military nature.

Secrecy was paramount, and indeed the key to the operation. Our leaders hoped that the movement and establishment of strategic arms in *Kuba* would be accomplished before the *Amerikantsy* could discover the plan and take any action.

I have read that—in April 1962—*Prem'yer* Nikita Sergeyevich Khrushchev, the First Secretary of the Communist Party of the Soviet Union, joked with the *Sovetskiy* defense minister, Marshal of the Soviet Union Rodion Y. Malinovskiy.

He supposedly said, "Rodion Yakovlevich, what if we were to throw a hedgehog down the pants of Uncle Sam!"

That was meant to be a humorous remark. Premier Khrushchev was like that, you know. A colorful speaker, with a peasant's sense of humor.

However, he and other top *Sovetskiy* leaders had some very serious goals in mind. That is why they sent ballistic missiles, nuclear weapons, and 40,000 troops to *Kuba*.

First, they hoped that these missiles and troops would deter the *Amerikantsy* from trying another attempt to invade or otherwise attack *Kuba*. You will recall the failed "Bay of Pigs" invasion attempt in April 1961? This was executed by a force of non-communist Cubans, backed by the *Amerikanskiy* "special services," which is to say the U.S. Central Intelligence Agency. As I said, the attempt failed. But our leaders, and the communist *Kubinskiy* government led by Fidel Castro, were certain that another U.S.—or at least a U.S.-sponsored—attempt at an invasion was just a matter of time.

Second, this significant force placed in *Kuba* would help equalize the "balance of power," creating a large *Sovetskiy* presence close to the United States. Would you not agree that would be fair? Just as large western North Atlantic Treaty Organization—NATO—forces were stationed close to the USSR?

Third, it might teach the Western *imperialisty* an important lesson. Khrushchev is said to have later written, looking back from his retirement, that

> it was high time *Amerika* learned what it feels like to have her own land and her own people threatened. We *Russkiye* have suffered three wars over the last half century: World War I, our own Civil War, and World War II. America has never had to fight a war on her own soil—at least not in the past fifty years.

By the way, my friend, you do know that for decades we *Russkiye* considered the United States to be the главный противник [Main Enemy] of the USSR? That is how we often referred to the United States: "the Main Enemy or the Main Opponent." Oh yes, it is so. And this was certainly true in 1962.

Well, I must also mention to you, Comrade Listener, there was a simultaneous naval part to this Operation Anadyr. It was called Операция Кама. This plan called for the forward deployment of a significant *Sovetskiy* naval force to *Kuba*. This was to include four diesel-electric submarines, seven strategic-missile submarines, two squadrons of mine-warfare craft, two gun-armed cruisers, and two missile-armed destroyers.

Indeed, by early September, the *Voyenno-Morskoy Flot* [Soviet Navy] had already secretly shipped an enormous amount of parts, ammunition, and other supplies into Mariel Bay—including twelve 25-meter *Projekt*-183R fast-attack boats equipped with *Termit* anti-ship missiles.

The most significant part of Operation Kama, as you may have already concluded, was the permanent basing and support for those seven ballistic-missile submarines close to the United States.

Well, this large deployment of ships was to be preceded by the movement of the four long-range diesel-electric submarines armed with conventional weapons. All of these vessels were to be based at Mariel Bay. Mariel is, as you may know, a deep-water port around forty kilometers west of Havana.

Of course, you also may know that these plans were well underway, and some of the land-based missiles had actually been made fully operational, before they were discovered by the *Amerikantsy.*

We had done well. Ha! What a surprise it was to the американцы [Americans]!

But now the world faced an extraordinarily dangerous confrontation.

In the West, it is widely known as the "Cuban Missile Crisis" of October 1962.

Comrade Listener, forgive me, but it is past time to introduce myself!

My name is V. A. Arkhipov—Vasiliy Aleksandrovich Arkhipov. Here is how it is written on my birth certificate: Василий Александрович Архипов. You did know that Russians do not use the Roman or Latin alphabet? We use the Cyrillic alphabet as do other Slavic peoples. However, it is common to transliterate Cyrillic script to Latin script, which enables Westerners to more easily read and sound out the words. In my story I have already given you examples of both, and will continue to do so.

Surely you will not be surprised when I tell you that I am *Russkiy* [Russian] and perhaps, in your eyes, worse—a Советский Коммунист [Soviet Communist]! For 41 years I proudly served the *Rodina* [Motherland] as a naval officer. In fact, in my 55th year I became a Вице-адмирал [Vice-Admiral] in the *Voyenno-Morskoy Flot, SSSR*, which as you know was the Navy of the Union of Soviet Socialist Republics.

Do not be intimidated that I was a vice admiral in a powerful navy. If it makes you more comfortable, just consider me as a family friend, or perhaps even your uncle—*Dyadya* Vasiliy!

In any event, most of my career was as a submariner, a *podvodnik*. I flatter myself to think that I was a good officer and a good submariner and I am very grateful to have long served the *Rodina*.

In any event, in 1962 I was a *Kapitan Vtorogo Ranga* [Captain 2nd Rank]. *Amerikantsy* and *Britantsy* call that rank "Commander." In the fall of that year I was serving as chief-of-staff of the 69th *Torpeda Podvodnaya Brigada* [Torpedo Submarine Brigade]. The brigade was part of the *Severnyy Flot* [Northern Fleet], stationed at Pol'arnyi, near Murmansk. That is extremely far to the north, in Kola Bay, off the Barents Sea.

But before I go into more detail of that time—which is, after all, the time and the mission about which you are interested— let me tell you a little more about myself.

I was born on January 30th, 1926, into what we used to call a крестьянский [peasant] family. I am not sure what that would be called in the West. Are there peasants in the West?

My home town was Staraya Kupavna—very close to where we are sitting right now in this beautiful café—and as you know not very far from Moskva. I was very lucky to have a good early education—that is, good for some of the more fortunate people in the *Sovetskiy Soyuz* of the 1920s and 1930s. I later attended the Pacific Higher Naval School in Vladivostok.

I entered active service at the very end of the Великая Отечественная Война [the Great Patriotic War]. Of course, that is the Second World War as it is more commonly known in the West. I was assigned to a minesweeper. I saw a little service against Japan. Very little, actually, as the war was essentially over by that time.

So, I then was sent to the Caspian Higher Naval School at Baku, from which I graduated in 1947. Because the *Sovetskiy*

Soyuz no longer exists, I might mention that Baku is now in the Republic of Azerbaijan.

I shortly transferred into the submarine force. I served in the Soviet Black Sea Fleet, the Northern Fleet, and the Baltic Fleet. Over the years I gained considerable experience and received several promotions in rank.

In June 1961 I was a staff officer at the *Severnyy Flot* headquarters, and I was one of four liaison officers temporarily assigned on board the *Projekt-658* Class submarine *K-19*. You possibly would recognize the NATO designation for this class, which was "HOTEL." It was the first *Sovetskiy* nuclear-powered boat fitted with nuclear ballistic missiles as weapons.

It occurs to me that you might know of this specific submarine. This is because you may have seen the *Amerikanskiy* Hollywood motion picture called "K-19: The Widowmaker." In reality, much as depicted in that movie, *K-19*'s first operational mission ended with a nuclear reactor disaster while she was in the North Sea conducting an exercise. This catastrophic equipment failure did not create an explosion, but the accident immediately—or within days—killed 22 men with nuclear radiation. For the rest of us on board—well, let us just say we were considerably irradiated. As a result, while many of us survived, almost all of us had to contend with long-term health issues.

I might add that some ill-informed people have said that I was second-in-command of the *K-19*. Others have said that I was the officer portrayed by the Irish actor Liam Neeson in the movie. Nothing could be further from the truth! As I told you, I was not part of the permanently assigned "ship's company," as it is said in the West. I was an observer, a supernumerary, merely temporarily attached.

Regardless of my status on board, during *K-19*'s disaster I tried to be as helpful as possible. For much of the time the *komanduyushchiy ofitser* had me serve as one of the conning officers, or the "officer on deck." I was, after all, an experienced naval officer, although at that time I was officially a diesel-power submariner—rather than nuclear-power. So, when performing the duty as conning officer on *K-19*, I and others controlled the movements of the boat. The commanding officer and some others focused upon regaining control of the nuclear reactor and trying to save our lives.

The commanding officer was *Kapitan Pervogo Ranga* [Captain 1st Rank] Nikolai Vladimirovich Zateyev. He was portrayed in that Hollywood motion picture by the *Amerikanskiy* actor Harrison Ford. However, for some reason, the Hollywood people changed Zateyev's name to Alexei Vostrikov.

I might also mention that I was one of only five officers that Captain Zateyev armed with *pistolety* [pistols]—right before he had all the other small arms thrown overboard. He feared that members of the crew might make an attempt against his authority due to the incredible and deadly stress of the situation. It was a wise precaution.

By the way, we survivors of the incident do not call *K-19* the "Widowmaker" as the Hollywood people did. We simply call her "Hiroshima." Perhaps you see the black humor in that?

As a result of the dose of radiation I received, I was treated for a short while in the *Severnyy Flot*'s naval hospital and then at the Sergey M. Kirov Military Medical Academy in Leningrad.

After my treatments were completed I was sent home to recuperate. I was fairly lucky. Many of the crew sustained much more serious harm than I did.

The higher authorities did say some nice things to us, such as "Родина будет вечно благодарна за вашу службу, товарищ" ["The *Rodina* will be eternally grateful for your service, Comrade]." Perhaps they could have done more.

Your pardon, Comrade Listener. I have wandered from my subject. The story of poor *K-19* and her crew is its own tale, and it is a tale for another time.

So, after a period of medical convalescence at home, under the loving care of my beautiful wife Olga and our little daughter Yelena, I was returned to active duty and was made chief-of-staff of *69 Torpeda Podvodnaya Brigada*.

 CHAPTER 7

*S*o, Comrade Listener, let us now begin my story in earnest! This is the tale for which you have patiently been waiting. Are you comfortable? Is the *kofe* good? *Otlichno!* Then come with me in your mind.

We go to Gadzhiyevo at Sayda Bay, not far from the submarine base at Pol'arnyi, near Murmansk. As I mentioned earlier that is where the *Sovetskiy Severnyy Flot* was based, extremely far to the north, in Kola Bay off the Barents Sea.

It is shortly after sunrise on the morning of September 28th, 1962. The personnel of the entire *69 Podvodnaya Brigada* have been brought together on board our "mother ship"—the 9,000-ton submarine-tender *Dmitriy Galkin*.

There, to brief the crews, is *Kontr-Admiral* Leonid Filippovich Rybalko, the commanding officer of *20 Operativnaya Podvodnaya Eskadril'ya* [Operational Submarine Squadron]. Our *brigada* is subordinate to *20 Eskadril'ya*. In addition to *Kontr-Admiral* Rybalko there are a number of other very senior officers present. I think it is very logical to see *Vitse-Admiral* Anatoliy Ivanovitch Rassokho, Chief of Staff of the *Severnyy Flot*. He is stationed nearby at Severomorsk and is also in our direct chain of command.

But I am frankly amazed to see *Admiral* Vitaliy Alekseyevich Fokin, the First Deputy Commander of the entire *Voyenno-*

Morskoy Flot, walk in. He clearly has come a long way north, all the way from Moskva, perhaps 1,900 *kilometrov*. He is a man of large build, brown eyes, a pleasant, round face and short and thinning white hair.

Then, a young officer accompanying the admirals looks around the room. He barks out a command.

"*Vstat' SMIRNO!*" All hands snap to attention.

Well, Admiral Fokin wastes no time and gets right down to business. He makes a brief speech to the assembled crews. I share it with you to the best of my recollection:

"*Tovarishchi! Dobroye utro!* [Comrades! Good morning!] *Vol'no!* [Stand at ease]!

I congratulate you! 69 *Brigada* of long-range diesel torpedo attack submarines is poised to take part in a special mission for the people and the government of the *Sovetskiy Soyuz!* This assignment is vital and filled with great responsibility. And upon completion of your *sekret* transit across the *Atlanticheskiy Okean*, you will be stationed permanently in a friendly country. Your families will join you shortly."

"I just said '*sekret*.' Of uttermost importance to the success of the mission is that we maintain the *sekretnost'* of your deployment. Your *brigada* will make the best speed while remaining undetected, arriving as soon as possible in the allied country sometime in late *Oktyabr'*."

"I wish you happy sailing and successful accomplishment of your mission!"

Well, I think it is interesting that he did not specify the location of the new base or even the country.

In addition, and this I must emphasize to you, Comrade Listener, he made no mention to us officers or our crews of the enormous *Sovetskiy* expedition to the *Sotsialisticheskaya Respublika Kuba,* which as you know was already well advanced. No mention of the huge numbers of soldiers and quantities of weapons and equipment that were already there. No mention of the *very* many nuclear weapons which were being staged there.

In short, nothing about *Operatsiya Anadyr', Operatsiya Kama*—or about our specific mission. What do you think about that?

CHAPTER 8

The next day, *Sentyabr'* 29, 1962, *Kapitan Pervogo Ranga* Vitaliy Naumovich Agafonov was called to the Military Council of the *Severnyy Flot.* There he was given a commission as the new commanding officer of 69 *Podvodnaya Brigada.* 69 *Brigada* was actually a relatively new unit, having just been formed in the summer of 1962.

By the way, as part of his 20 *Operativnaya Podvodnaya Eskadril'ya,* Rear Admiral Rybalko commanded seven ballistic-missile submarines. I have already mentioned that these were later to be sent to *Kuba* as part of Operation Kama. They were *Projekt*-629 diesel-electric boats—called the "GOLF I" class by NATO—each carrying three *R-13* missiles tipped with nuclear warheads. These boats were designated as *18 Podvodnoye Podrazdeleniye* [submarine division] within *20 OPE.*

You may wish to know that the Северный флот [*Severnyy Flot*; Northern Fleet] was, and still is, responsible for the defense of northwestern *Rossiya.* The fleet headquarters and administrative center are located at the main base at Severomorsk, with secondary facilities nearby in the Kola Bay. The *Severnyy Flot* has access to the Arctic and Atlantic Oceans from those bases. This fleet, and its submarines, executed active as well as training missions predominantly in the Barents and Norwegian Seas.

Well, Vitaliy Naumovich had barely two hours to pack and report to *20 Eskadril'ya*'s location. On *Sentyabr'* 30th, at two o'clock in the morning, he arrived at Sayda Bay and the village of Gadzhiyevo, twenty kilometers northwest of Murmansk.

At that time all four submarines of *69 Brigada* were completing weeks of intense preparations. This was for our very special, very *sekret* mission.

Of course, Comrade Listener, I have already told you about these boats! These submarines were the ones assigned to be the advance element of *Operatsiya Kama*. We were to spearhead the main *Voyenno-Morskoy Flot*'s movement to Mariel Bay in Cuba. I say spearhead because I do not count the small, non-ocean going *Projekt*-183R fast-attack boats which were already there. All four submarines had been in the Sevmorput Naval Shipyard outside Murmansk, during the spring and summer of 1962, for overhaul and repair operations. Now, for the last four weeks each boat had been loading huge quantities of fuel, supplies, and stores of all kinds. The stores included warm-weather clothing and khaki-colored short-sleeved uniforms. We crammed supplies everywhere. They took up seemingly every square *santimetr* of space in each submarine.

Our boats were part of the *Projekt*-641 class of *dizel'-elektricheskiy* [diesel-electric] submarines. People in the West might know them as the "FOXTROT" class, using the NATO designation. I have no particular national pride in names, so for your convenience during the rest of my tale I shall often use the term FOXTROT.

These four boats were usually berthed in the base at Pol'arnyi. However to increase security, and under cover of darkness on *Sentyabr'* 27th, they had been moved a few *kilometrov*. This was to the more secluded former fishing port at Sayda Bay. It was more secure and secluded, that is, from eyes of large numbers of civilians and even many naval families inhabiting Pol'arnyi. You see, it was not so much that we feared *Amerikanskiy ili Britanskiye shpiony* [American or British spies]. Rather, we mostly feared the loose tongues of our own families and coworkers!

I might add that there was some irony in now trying to cloak our activity from the local people. This is because before the mission was designated as "covert" the *brigada*'s officers and their families had been kept fairly well-informed. They were even helped with preparations for the relocation to *Kuba*. Some people had already started to study the Spanish language! They were all excited about the prospect that they would be moved to a new home port in a faraway land with a tropical climate. After all, Christopher Columbus himself had called *Kuba* "the most beautiful land that human eyes have ever seen." Who would not be excited about that, after living at the top of the world in the harsh and cold climate of the Kola Peninsula?

The change to a "covert mission" designation actually placed us in a difficult position. It also added a number of challenges. As I just mentioned, the boats moved from Pol'arnyi to Sayda Bay and into restricted berthing. Now access to our piers was only by special pass. All work had to be done by our own crews with no further support from *20 Eskadril'ya* personnel. All supplies and materials had to be inspected before placement on board the boats. All the boats' existing provisions were replaced by fresh stocks. Extra care was taken to ensure we stowed a comprehensive collection of spare parts and accessories. Greater than usual supplies of fuel and drinking water came aboard.

Oh, and there were fresh tests of "loyalty" for the crews by any number of "political officers." This added considerably to our general stress and anxiety as each man made extra efforts to show his best work to his own officers—and to these extra *politikany* who were poking around.

I was already aware that I would be embarked on board the FOXTROT submarine *B-59* for the duration of the mission. Others of **69** *Brigada*'s staff, including Captain Agafonov, were assigned to other boats. I lost no time in going on board the *B-59*, introducing myself, and getting situated.

The afternoon I came on board I was escorted to the commander's stateroom where I was politely received by *Kapitan Vtorogo Ranga* Valentin Grigorievich Savitskiy. Although small, the compartment was nicely finished in chest-high, honey-brown wooden paneling and with upgraded wooden furnishings. The metal bulkhead above the paneling was painted with a pleasant beige color—as was, actually, much of the interior of the boat. Looking at the overhead, the curvature of the upper pressure hull was evident but did not really threaten headroom. The steel deck was of course covered in the *Voyenno-Morskoy Flot*'s ubiquitous dark-green linoleum. Like the beige paint such linoleum was found almost everywhere in the boat—but for his stateroom Savitskiy had brought on board a rich, dark-red rug. A small amount of built-in shelving on the aft bulkhead held various books and *bezdelushki* [knick-knacks], as well as richly framed photos of who, I assumed, were his family. On the long bulkhead over his built-in bunk were other framed photos, in black metal and glass, containing the dour visages of Admiral Sergey Gorshkov and Premier Nikita Khrushchev. Attached to the forward bulkhead was a cream-painted instrument panel featuring a compass, depth gauge, clock, and communications handset.

I surmised that my quarters would be slightly smaller and not as nicely furnished. FOXTROT boats had a number of individual staterooms, some in the vicinity of the captain's in Compartment Two, and some aft of the Control Center in Compartment Four. I hopefully would not displace the boat's second-in-command from his stateroom; but, whomever I displaced was going to have to crowd-in with someone else. Naval service is hard service, and submarine service even more so.

"*Dobroye utro* [Good morning] *Tovarishch Kapitan*," I said. Savitskiy gave me a formal smile, holding out his hand.

"Good morning, *Tovarishch Nachal'nik Shtaba* [Comrade Chief of Staff]," he said. We had met once before, years ago, but really did not know each other. He was a little older than I with wavy black hair cut short and rugged features—features which, I was to learn, were often set in a stern if not sour expression.

"It seems I shall be traveling with you on this mission," I said. "I hope having another captain second rank on board will not be a problem—other than finding me a berth, of course. After all, as it is said, *nezhdanny gost' khuze Tatarina* [an uninvited guest is worse than a Tatar]."

"No, no, of course there is no problem, *Kapitan* Arkhipov," Savitskiy replied courteously, looking a little surprised. "It will be a pleasure to sail with you."

"I am delighted, *Kapitan* Savitskiy," I said. "I was concerned that it could be a little awkward or difficult. But I assure you that I will never forget that you, and not I, are the boat's commander."

"Thank you, but I am not at all worried," Savitskiy replied. "Shoulder-to-shoulder, with distinguished and professional colleagues, it is never difficult to do one's patriotic duty in the service of the *Rodina*."

I was wondering if we were always going to be speaking this formally, but just then we were interrupted by the boat's chief engineer who needed the commanding officer's immediate attention.

As I have told you the *B-59*, along with the rest of our boats, was in the midst of considerable frenetic activity as we prepared the *brigada* for sea. But I must mention, Comrade Listener, that shortly there occurred a couple of remarkably unusual things.

On *Sentyabr'* 29th a lorry, or a truck—whichever word you prefer—had rumbled to a stop on the pier alongside the *B-59*. A dozen men jumped out, five of them heavily armed. They began to unload several crates from the back of the vehicle and stack them on the pier, while one man approached our pierside sentry. This man displayed a handful of papers and, after a minute's deliberation, our guard saluted the stranger and allowed him to pass.

At that moment Savitskiy and Zakhar Chernyshev were sitting in the Control Center—the CC—discussing operational details. I believe that in Western navies this compartment is usually referred to as the "control room." The CC is located immediately below the conning tower.

Chernyshev was the boat's second-in-command—the *Starpom*. The *Amerikantsy* call this position the "Executive Officer." As it turned out he fortuitously had not been required to give up his stateroom for me; that misfortune happened to a more junior officer.

I was in the CC as well, sipping tea and listening to their conversation. Remember, I was more or less just a passenger—well, perhaps a slightly distinguished passenger—for this upcoming voyage. My real job would begin after we arrived at Mariel Bay and set up our new headquarters.

Amidst all the noise of routine ship's work and preparation, a *michman* [warrant officer] called down from the conning tower.

"*Tovarishch Kapitan*, an *ofitser* has come aboard to speak with you."

"Very well," Savitskiy replied. "Send him down."

A slightly rumpled, dark-haired young man—unusually equipped with a pencil-thin moustache—came down the ladder. He was somewhat hampered by a bulky briefcase handcuffed to his wrist. He safely alighted onto the deck, looked at the three of us, and drew himself to attention. Unsure as to which one of us was *B-59*'s captain, he addressed one of the many green-glowing gauges attached to the bulkhead just behind us.

"Tovarishch Kapitan, I am *Starshiy-Leitenant* [Senior-Lieutenant] Vadim Pavlovich Orlov. I am the officer-in-charge of the OSNAZ Special Purpose Radio Interception Unit assigned to the *B-59* for this mission." He held out several of the partially crumpled papers in his hand, which Savitskiy reluctantly took from him.

Valentin Grigorievich quickly glanced at them, but obviously re-read one particular paragraph twice if not three times. He looked up at the newcomer.

"Tovarishch Starshiy-Leitenant Orlov, am I to understand you are bringing nine men—NINE GOD-DAMNED EXTRA MEN— on board my already overcrowded and overloaded boat?"

"Da, Tovarishch Kapitan." He hesitated for a moment, and then added, "And I am sorry but we also have several crates of specialized and *sekret* equipment we need to bring on board."

"Oh, of course you do," replied Savitskiy, "and I suppose you will want me to assign you a half-dozen compartments for your men and your *sekret gadzhety* [gadgets]."

"Da, Tovarishch Kapitan," Orlov said with a smile. "Well, no, not that many, but I am afraid you will have to berth us somewhere. Anywhere convenient to you."

Savitskiy looked at him impassively. After a moment Orlov continued. "Um, I will need one small compartment, *ser*, for the equipment and to work in—and it will need to be apart from the boat's standard radio room."

Rather than the explosion of temper which I—and young V. P. Orlov—expected, Captain Savitskiy merely looked down at the handful of papers with an expression of what almost looked like sadness.

"It says here that each boat in the *brigada* is assigned an OS-NAZ group such as yours."

"*Da, Tovarishch Kapitan.*"

"Why so many men? Do you really need that many?"

"*Nyet, Tovarishch Kapitan,*" Orlov replied. "I can operate the at-sea mission with just a few. But the rest of the men are being sent so that we can establish permanent signals-intelligence ground posts once we reach *Ku*—once we reach the country of our destination."

"Perfect. That is wonderful. It also says that your group is to 'ensure the security of the submarine for the length of the mission.'"

"*Da, Tovarishch Kapitan.*"

"Well, that is all very interesting. Tell me, *Leitenant* Orlov, are you really a naval officer, or are you KGB?" Savitskiy referred, as you might know, to the Soviet Union's powerful *Komitet Gosudarstvennoy Bezopasnosti*, or the Committee for State Security. This huge and feared organization provided the *Sovetskiy Soyuz* internal security, intelligence, and secret police.

"I am a naval officer, *ser,*" replied Orlov with another smile.

"Are you qualified in submarines?" asked Savitskiy.

"*Nyet, ser.* Not formally qualified. But I have been deployed on board submarines in the past as have most of my men. And before I became a signals-intelligence officer I served as a navigator at sea."

"What makes you qualified to take this assignment?"

"*Ser,* I and my group are *radisty* [radio men]. But beyond that we have had lengthy training in signals intelligence. Very likely your regular radiomen have had no such training. And some of us have a good amount of operational experience including service on board *tral'shchiki.*" Orlov referred to the *Voyenno-Morskoy Flot*'s surveillance trawlers which ranged all over the world—posing as fishing vessels—equipped with sophisticated sensors and communications equipment.

He went on. "*Tovarishch Kapitan*, most of us are conversant in *Angliyskiy*. As you know, *ser*, communications interception is useless unless you can understand the language."

"How is *your* English, *Leitenant* Orlov?" I asked. Orlov, totally focused upon Savitskiy, was momentarily surprised that I had spoken. He turned to me and proudly raised his chin.

"*Tovarishch Kapitan*, my father was also a naval intelligence officer. He was attached to foreign military intelligence—as of course you know, the *Glavnoye Razvedyvatel'noye Upravleniye*—the GRU. When I was eight years old he was assigned to work in the United States. So, he and our family spent several years there. As a result I am told that my *Angliyskiy* is excellent."

"Fine," said Savitskiy. "Fine. But tell me, Orlov, how shall you ensure my security at sea?"

"*Ser*, my men and I will do many things for you," replied Orlov. "We will take care of your communications with Moskva as well as with the other boats of the *brigada*. We will intercept the radio signals of the potential or actual enemy. We shall conduct radio surveillance of NATO and *Amerikanskiy* forces at sea as well exploit radar detection. We shall process intelligence gleaned from high-frequency direction-finding. And we will do surveillance of *Amerikanskiy* commercial radio." He thought for a moment.

"*Ser*, we are limited in our capabilities regarding *deshifrovaniye* [decryption], but experience tells us that much of what the adversary will transmit will not be encoded. Using those interceptions we will supply you with reliable reports as to the tactical actions of any NATO or *Amerikanskiy* antisubmarine forces that might try to track us. In addition—"

"Interesting. How nice," Savitskiy interrupted. "Well, *Tovarishch Leitenant*, I shall be the judge as to the reliability—and the usefulness—of your reports."

"Of course, *Tovarishch Kapitan*."

"Fine," said Savitskiy. "Go collect your men and your toys. Stow your equipment out of the way of my crewmen. Do not leave any of the packing crates on board my boat." He turned to the *starpom*.

"Zakhar Yanovich, please find *our* radio officer, *Starshiy-Leitenant* Rodzyenko, and have him take *Starshiy-Leitenant* Orlov under his wing."

"*Yest'*, *Kapitan*," replied Chernyshev. Motioning Orlov to follow him, the executive officer walked forward and out of the CC.

"Oh, by the way, welcome aboard, Vadim Pavlovich Orlov," called Savitskiy with a contemplative look on his face.

After they had gone Savitskiy turned to me.

"Is not "OSNAZ" a KGB term? I think he is KGB. Damn them! *Synov'ya suk* [sons of bitches]! I do not need a squad of KGB goons on board my boat snooping around making my crew nervous. Making me nervous!"

"He says he is not KGB," I replied. "OSNAZ indeed might be a KGB term, but it also might just simply be the abbreviation for *osobogo naznachneniya* [special detachment]." Savitskiy snorted and shook his finger at me.

"*Kapitan*," he replied. "By his own admission his father was GRU."

"Yes," I said. "But *Kapitan*, what difference does it make? What do you care? I cannot really imagine them snooping around the boat all the time. I am quite sure they will be very busy with their own technical duties."

Unable to help myself, I smiled. "You know, if you really wish to worry about someone snooping, you already have *Tovarishch* Maslennikov on board."

"Huh," was Savitskiy's only reply.

I was referring to our *Zamestitel' Komandira po Politicheskoy Chasti* [Deputy to the Commander for Political Affairs]—the Political Officer. All *Sovetskiy* military and naval units had a political officer—abbreviated as *zampolit*—to keep an eye on all personnel. This was to ensure that everyone remained, at all times, good and loyal communists with proper discipline and high morale. *Kapitan Tret'yego Ranga* Ivan Semonovich Maslennikov was *B-59's zampolit*. I assure you, Maslennikov had wasted no time in making my acquaintance when I first came on board. Tall, slender, and with black hair slicked back and with a non-regulation handle-bar mustache, the *zampolit* was as nosy, opinionated, and self-assured as one might expect of a person in his position.

Well, all of that aside, Comrade Listener, I must tell you that things got even more strange the next day!

On the morning of *Sentyabr'* 30th all of the *brigada's* submarines were visited by a senior staff officer and his entourage.

This ranking person said he was from the *Severnyy Flot*'s Special Weapons Directorate. This worthy individual deposited one of his men, a uniformed *kapitan-leitenant*, with each boat.

Right after that a floating crane approached our piers simultaneous to the arrival of a heavy truck with an enclosed trailer. They were both heavily manned by seamen and guards armed with *Avtomat Kalashnikova*—AK-47—automatic rifles. The seamen methodically lashed the crane to each of the FOXTROTs in succession. From the trailer the crane raised and lowered a single torpedo to each submarines' forward deck. The men proceeded unusually slowly and carefully. They coaxed the purple-tipped cylinders into the torpedo loading hatches and then down into each boat's forward torpedo room.

Purple-painted tips on torpedoes were unusual. Normal service torpedoes had gray-painted noses.

During this process each boat's new Special Weapons Directorate captain-lieutenant stood on the deck beside the hatch. Each one filled the chilly air with voluminous orders and instructions. These officers were all neatly dressed in submariner's coveralls and *pilotka* [garrison caps]. Each of them, judging from the pronounced bulges on their hips under their coveralls, was armed—another unusual thing.

I was standing on *B-59*'s bridge, next to Captain Savitskiy, watching this procedure. I was both alarmed and a little amused as Valentin Grigorievich interviewed the officer that had been assigned to *B-59*. He had come up to the bridge immediately after the "special torpedo" was securely stowed.

"I am sorry, *Kapitan-Leitenant*, I did not catch your name from when you came on board earlier," Savitskiy said.

"Tovarishch Kapitan, I am Dmitriy Konstantinovich Pavlov, *Spetsial'noye Oruzhiye Ofitser* [Special Weapon Officer]. As my superior from the Special Weapons Directorate briefly informed you when we first came on board, I shall accompany you on this voyage and I shall need to be berthed in close proximity to the weapon." He was a little stiff and pompous, I thought.

"Does it have a nuclear warhead?" Savitskiy asked.

"Kapitan, I cannot say."

"Is the torpedo an operational asset for my boat? Or am I just ferrying it to our destination, to then turn it over to the *Kubintsy?"*

"Ser, I really cannot say."

Standing right next to him it was clear to me that Savitskiy was about to lose his temper. Apparently Pavlov, a few feet away, sensed it as well. He had the good grace to look a little sheepish, and tried to make amends.

"Tovarishch Kapitan, I am sorry. I mean no *neuvazheniye* [disrespect]. In my work I am bound to *sekretnost'.* It is often excessive *sekretnost'.* All I can tell you right now is the weapon is not to be loaded in a tube—rather it is to be stowed as a service-ready torpedo. It is my understanding that you will receive more information in the commanders' briefing later today. And there should also be full information in your sailing orders—once you are authorized to open them."

"Very well, *Kapitan-Leitenant* Pavlov," Savitskiy replied. "Report below to my *Sotrudnik Shakhty i Torpedy* [Mine and Torpedo Officer]. His name is *Starshiy-Leitenant* Sluchevski. He will give you your berthing assignment and anything else you might need." Pavlov saluted smartly and left the bridge.

Savitskiy turned to me.

"*Chto za chert* [What the hell]!" he exclaimed. "Vasiliy Aleksandrovich, these 'special' torpedoes obviously have nuclear warheads."

"It seems likely, Valentin," I replied. "I do not know." At that point I did not. As *brigada* chief-of-staff I should have known about something like this, but I had heard nothing. I wondered if the *brigada komanduyushchiy ofitser* knew about it.

"If they do have nuclear warheads," he continued, "it is *bezumiye* [madness]. *Projekt-641 dizel'* boats do not carry nuclear weapons. We do not have the necessary safeguards. We have not been trained on them." His face lit up as he thought of something.

"Wait! Our friend over there, Captain Shumkov, has been trained and has experience." He jerked his head in the direction of *B-130*'s berth, one pier over from where we were.

"I read a report about it. A year ago he was ordered to test-fire two of them off Novaya Zemlya in the Arctic Ocean. One was a subsurface explosion and the other was surface. He used *T-5* torpedoes with some kind of nuclear warheads. They exploded with around ten kilotons of force. The test was successful, and for it Shumkov got the Ushakov Medal."

"So I understand," I replied. I had seen the same report.

"I think the warheads were designated '*RDS-9s*.' Shumkov wrote that the torpedoes ran eleven and twelve kilometers respectively and that after firing he had to quickly maneuver to gain shelter behind a small island."

"Nevertheless," I added, "the shock waves moved through the water quite a distance. They tossed *B-130* around like a toy in an overturned bathtub."

"Well, *der'mo* [crap]!" Savitskiy exclaimed. "Have they really given us such weapons? How would they be used? On whose authority would they be used?" A grave look came over his face.

"You know," I replied, "I wonder if they will have Shumkov brief us on his experience before we sail."

"*Der'mo!*" Savitskiy repeated. "If we use them in a tactical situation the blast will wipe out everything—in what?—at least within an eleven-kilometer radius. In a tactical situation we would probably be within that radius!"

"Well, Valentin Grigorievitch," I replied, smiling. "Let us hope we do not have to use them."

CHAPTER 9

Comrade Listener, there was another pre-mission briefing I must tell you about. This one was the "commanders' briefing" which had been mentioned by Captain-Lieutenant Pavlov. It happened on that same afternoon, *Sentyabr'* 30th, in a poorly heated and tiny building not far from our piers. On this occasion there were the same three admirals who had met with the *brigada*'s crews on the 28th, but now the audience was much smaller.

Before the briefing started, *Kontr-Admiral* Rybalko introduced *Kapitan Pervogo Ranga* Agafonov to me, to the rest of our small staff, and of course to the commanders of the four boats—which naturally were now *Tovarishch* Agafonov's four boats. You will recall that Agafonov had just been appointed to the command of the *brigada* and had just arrived? I was not myself acquainted with V. N. Agafonov, but I had heard that he had a superb service record and a solid reputation as an efficient officer.

The four boat commanders were all *kapitany vtorogo ranga*. Their names were Ryurik Aleksandrovich Ketov, commanding the *B-4*; Aleksei Fedoseyvich Dubivko, commanding *B-36*; as you already know Valentin Grigorievich Savitskiy, commanding *B-59*; and Nikolai Aleksandrovich Shumkov, commanding *B-130*. For the duration of this mission Captain Agafonov was to be embarked on board *B-4*, while—as you already have heard—I was to be carried on board *B-59*.

In retrospect it might have been better had the *komandir brigady* and I switched billets for this operation—that is, he be assigned to *B-59* and I to *B-4*. Vitaliy Naumovich was an old comrade of Valentin Grigorievich, and I was a long-standing friend of Ryurik Aleksandrovich. My reasoning for saying this will become clear later on, but at the time these "travel arrangements" seemed unremarkable.

In any event, Admiral Rybalko opened the meeting with the usual greetings and pleasantries before quickly getting down to business. You are surprised by pleasantries, Comrade Listener? Well, *Russkiye* can be pleasant. We are not all gruff *Russkiy* bears!

Mostly for the benefit of Captain Agafonov, who had not heard the first briefing on board the *Dmitriy Galkin*, Rybalko introduced the other flag officers. At that point Admiral Fokin took the floor.

Fokin immediately called Agafonov forward and handed him a package of documents. I could see that this package was encased in a binding with a shiny black cover, and a thick white stripe ran diagonally across it from the top right to the bottom left. On the top left was written "C.C." in large white letters, while underneath them were the words Совершенно Секретно [Top Secret]—also in white. *"Operatsiya Kama: 69 Torpeda Podvodnaya Brigada "* was printed across the center.

The package contained five separate and sealed envelopes, one for Agafonov and one for each submarine's commanding officer. These envelopes were not to be opened until the boats were in the open sea.

Admiral Rybalko then addressed us. He spoke hesitatingly, appearing somewhat uncomfortable. To the best of my recollection, he said:

"*Dzhentl'meny* [Gentlemen], I am now going to relay to you verbal instructions from our Navy's commander-in-chief, Admiral Gorshkov. I met with him in Moskva three weeks ago."

Rybalko was a very handsome man who could easily be mistaken for an actor in motion pictures. He looked considerably younger than his fifty-three years. I was not at all surprised that he had been given this important command. He had achieved a brilliant record in the Great Patriotic War and had subsequently shown a remarkable ability to, as it is said in Western countries, "get things done." Though far inferior in rank he was a close friend of the *Sovetskiy* defense minister, Marshal Malinovskiy—they had served together during the fighting at Stalingrad against the Germans. Rybalko was a very cultured and *kul'turnyy* [cultivated] officer. Interestingly, he could speak Spanish.

The admiral referred to some notes which he had retrieved from a pocket. "This is what Admiral Gorshkov said to me."

'*Kontr-Admiral* Rybalko, your assignment is to get your four *Projekt*-641 *dizel'* submarines to the *Kubinskiy* port of Mariel undetected on or about 20 *Oktyabr'*. Once there, they will prepare for the subsequent deployment of your seven *Projekt*-629 ballistic-missile submarines, which will follow with their support ships. The 641s are to reconnoiter the waters surrounding Mariel and ensure they are free of *Amerikanskiy* forces or fixed acoustic arrays, and to survey and report the hydro-acoustic conditions of the area.'

'Communication code-words are all set and will be broadcast in parallel on low-frequency schedules and on high-frequency single sideband, so your captains will have to keep one boat near the surface at periscope depth to monitor the HF. Obviously, that will be particularly challenging if the *Amerikantsy* deploy any antisubmarine warfare forces.'

'Admiral Rybalko, you are in no way to allow *Amerikanskiy* antisubmarine forces to discover your submarines during their transit.'

'Beyond that, the new and unusual element for this mission is the nuclear *torpeda* warheads your *dizel'* submarines will carry. Your new *komandir brigady*, Captain First Rank Agafonov, and his individual submarine commanding officers have advance authorization to employ the special weapons without specific permission from fleet headquarters or the ministry in Moskva. That is if they are attacked by *Amerikanskiy* ships or aircraft.'

'This is very important. This must be totally clear. Your submarine captains will use their special weapons if *Amerikanskiy* forces attack and damage them while submerged, or force them to surface and then attack, or—of course—upon receipt of orders from Moskva.'

'Additionally, prior to firing the special weapons, the individual commanding officers must have the full agreement of their embarked *zampolit*. And, in the case of the two boats carrying the *komandir brigady* and the *brigada nachal'nik shtaba*, those commanding officers must also have the full agreement of those two officers.'

'These special weapon operational rules have been approved by the *Politbyuro* and by *Prem'yer* Khrushchev and that is enough for us. As true socialist patriots all of us will of course follow orders.'

Rybalko stopped speaking and looked down at the floor while he secured his notes back into his pocket. After a few seconds, and in a quiet voice, he said, "*Tovarishchi Kapitany*, during the time of your transit it is considered highly unlikely that *Amerikanskiy* or NATO anti-submarine warfare forces will be any more than at their usual state of alert. Normally this usually is not much of a threat."

"Once at sea, open and study your mission orders closely. They are outlined in great detail." He again looked down at the floor. He then raised his eyes and briefly stared at each submarine commander in turn.

"You each possess the capability of inflicting considerable lethal damage to *Amerikanskiy* forces, but with all my heart I urge you to use great discretion! Each of you has in your hands the potential to start the next world war. *Tovarishchi*, do try and *not* do that!"

Months later, Rybalko told me that he had been stunned by the concept that his individual submarine *komanduyushchiy ofitsery* were—in essence—being given personal authority to begin a nuclear war with the United States. Authority given by the top *Sovetskiy* leaders. I have no doubt this is why he seemed so uncomfortable during this meeting.

"I say again, my friends," he repeated, "do try to keep us out of total nuclear war."

Rybalko stepped back, glancing at the other *admiraly*, whose expressions gave away nothing. Once more there had been no mention of *Operatsiya Anadyr'* and no mention that our *brigada's* mission was part of a much larger expedition which was already far advanced. In fact it appeared that we had come to the end of the briefing.

However, my old friend Captain Ketov, commanding the B-4, stepped forward with a question. He could be stern and even grim with his hawk-like features—features which could instantly relax in a grin and be accompanied with a twinkle in his pale blue eyes. Right now he looked a little grim.

"I have some concerns, *Tovarishch Admiraly*." All three admirals looked at him with raised eyebrows.

"Firstly, as we all know, *Projekt*-641 submarines are not designed for extended runs in warm, tropical water. They are designed for anti-surface and anti-submarine warfare operations in the cold water and cold air temperatures of northern latitudes. I am therefore worried that some equipment will operate poorly, to say nothing of how uncomfortable the boats' internal *temperatura* may become when we get close to the equator."

The admirals merely looked at him. Finally Rybalko, again shifting his gaze to the floor, quietly said, "Your boats are what are available, *Tovarishch Kapitan*."

"I understand, *Tovarishch Admiral*," Ketov replied. I am sure he knew there would be no good response or discussion. Perhaps he just wanted to speak his mind. He nodded and carried on.

"I expect that our sealed orders will provide more mission details." He paused.

"Yes, *Kapitan?*" said *Vitse-Admiral* Rassokho.

"*Ser*, I believe I speak for all of us," Ketov said. "I am afraid that we are still somewhat unclear as to our 'rules of engagement' and particularly in regard to the 'special weapons.' Admiral Rybalko just spoke of the incredible responsibility you have given us by placing nuclear weapons on board our boats. *Projekt*-641-class boats have never carried such weapons in actual service." He paused for a moment, and then continued.

"So, might we please have a little more detail as to when and under what circumstances we can—or we should—use them?"

Admiral Rassokho caught Ryurik Aleksandrovich's eye and held it for a few seconds. He stood silent, apparently gathering his thoughts.

"*Tovarishch Kapitany.*" He paused, I thought a little theatrically, as if to ensure that he had everyone's undivided attention. After he looked around the room at each officer he seemed to be satisfied.

Continuing, he said, "Each of you will write down the following specific instructions into your logbooks when tonight you return to your boats: the use of the Special Weapons is authorized for only three situations. One, naturally, upon explicit orders from Moskva. Two, you are submerged and are depth charged or torpedoed and your pressure hull is ruptured. Three, you surface your boat—or you are on the surface and there attacked—and enemy fire ruptures your pressure hull." Rassokho paused for a moment.

"I suggest to you, *kapitany*, that if necessary you use the nuclear weapons. After that you will figure out what to do next." He nodded and pretended to smile. I say pretended because his eyes and face were very hard.

"So. That should be clear enough. Are there any other questions?"

There were none. The silence in the room was heavy, palpable. After a few seconds Admiral Rybalko mercifully broke it with the traditional *Russkiy* seaman's benediction.

"All right. Good! Well then, *Khoroshiy parus—Derzhis' sem' futov pod kilem* [Good sailing—and keep seven feet beneath your keel]!"

After the admirals departed, we—the four submarine commanders, Captain Agafonov, and I—stayed in the cold and tiny building and attempted to develop a tactical plan for the passage. Everyone except Agafonov fished *sigarety* out of their pockets and Captain Dubivko shared his lighter.

The discussion was limited to only a few major issues. We agreed that specifics of speed and stealth had to be open to each commander's discretion, as well as some flexibility concerning the designated course. We decided to maintain communications with each other as best we could in regard to tactical cooperation.

I have to tell you, Comrade Listener, that "as best we could" was not, as it turned out, going to be very good. Or even, perhaps, good enough.

By the way, on the topic of "good enough," our Admiral Sergey Gorshkov is often associated with the phrase "'Better' is the enemy of 'Good Enough'" (лучшее—враг хорошего), a framed version of which hung on the wall of his office in Moskva. I do not believe that he invented the saying because similar remarks have been attributed to previous philosophers and military theorists.

And I am not sure Gorshkov really meant it. Serving as commander-in-chief of the *Voyenno-Morskoy Flot* for thirty years, he forcefully set extremely high standards as he built our Navy from a relatively small coastal fleet into a "better" first-class world seapower.

Anyway, as we continued our meeting in the chilly building, my friend Ketov continued to grumble about the situation.

"*Tovarishchi,*" he said, "it is one thing to move ships openly and on the surface—proceeding to a new permanent area for subsequent duty while presumably carrying out routine at-sea training exercises. But it is quite another to try to move covertly which means slowly and quietly with the majority of time spent under water. I do not see any way we will be able to meet the timeline that they have set for us."

"Can we possibly make it?" asked Captain Shumkov.

Shrugging my shoulders, I replied with an old Russian saying. "*Babushka skazala; to li dozhdik, to li sneg, to li budet, to li net* [Grandmother said that we shall see what we shall see; maybe rain or maybe snow, maybe yes or maybe no]."

CHAPTER 10

You know, Comrade Listener, since we are shortly going to be "shipmates"—living on board and very close together for the rest of this story—I think I should introduce you to our submarine boats.

As I have already told you, all four boats of *69 Brigada* were of the *Projekt*-641 Class—which the U.S. Navy and the NATO navies called the FOXTROT Class. This was a group of around fifty-eight boats, all of which were long-range *dizel'-elektricheskiy* submarines and all of which were built in the Sudomekh Shipyard—Yard 196—in Leningrad.

The *B-59* was launched on June 6th, 1960, so you can see she was fairly new at the time of our voyage. Actually, all of our *brigada*'s boats were fairly new. *B-4* was also built in 1960, *B-130* in 1959, and *B-36* in 1958. These boats displaced 1,950 tons while on the surface and 2,400 tons when submerged. Each submarine was 91.4 meters in length, had a beam of 7.6 meters, and drew 6.1 meters of water when on the surface.

The boats were moved by three turbocharged *Model'* 37-D marine *dizel'* engines, producing 6,000 horsepower which drove three *propellery*. When running underwater each boat used three *elektricheskiy* motors producing 5,300 horsepower. Maximum range was 32,000 *kilometrov* at economical speed.

Maximum safe depth was 300 *metry*. Crews consisted of twelve commissioned officers, ten warrant officers, and 56 enlisted men.

Armament was twenty-two "53-centimeter" *torpedy*—the 53 cm representing the diameter of the *torpedo*. They were about eight *metry* long, had an effective range—versus maximum range—of at least three *kilometrov*, and had a speed of around 40 knots. Except for our single and *sekret* "special weapon" and two "decoy" models, our *torpedy* had warheads containing 560 *kilogramm*—or 1,250 pounds—of conventional high explosives.

I am proud to tell you that the submarines also had state-of-the-art electronics. This included a surface-search radar, our FDC 759. NATO forces had early identified this radar, calling it "SNOOP TRAY." As with all electronic emissions, NATO had built a catalog such that, when they detected an emission, they could quickly associate it with specific types of *Sovetskiy* ships. Of course, we did the same thing regarding identifying and cataloging U.S. Navy and NATO equipment.

We had an active sonar, the *Gerkules*, which NATO named "WOLF PAW," and a passive sonar, the *Feniks*, which NATO called "TROUT CHEEK." Finally, we had an electronic surveillance measures system, *Nakat*, which NATO called "STOP LIGHT B." I always found the NATO names for our ships and equipment somewhat amusing. I particularly like "TROUT CHEEK," do you not as well?

On a more negative note, I should repeat Captain Ketov's remarks that *Projekt*-641 submarines were designed to operate in cold air and sea *temperatura* in trans-polar latitudes. Similarly, 641 crews were trained and accustomed to work and service equipment in such cold conditions. Beyond that—designed for such low *temperatura*—these boats were not equipped with high-capacity freezers and refrigerators for keeping large supplies of provisions cold through long-duration missions. Likewise, while they had basic fans and blowers, the boats were not furnished with actual air-conditioning equipment or other interior air-cooling systems. As you will hear later on in this story, these issues were to become very serious when we reached latitudes of high air *temperatura*, high water *temperatura*, and high humidity levels.

Another concern, which will become very significant later on, was that the three *dizel'* engines driving three *propellery* made 641s noisier than most contemporary Western designs.

Lastly, the 641s had an enormous interior space dedicated to their *akkumulyatory*—or heavy-duty batteries. This gave them an underwater endurance of around ten days. However, if the goal of ten days were to be achieved a boat could move at no more than a speed of two or three knots. And due to the *akkumulyatory* taking up so much space the onboard conditions were very crowded. One nice thing about FOXTROTs, however, is they had unusually good headroom throughout the main interior deck. Even men slightly taller than six feet almost never banged their heads on anything.

The FOXTROT class all had the prefix "B," taken from the word *bol'shoy*. In *Russkiy*, the word *bol'shoy* means big, or large, and indeed these were pretty large boats for the time.

In those days the *Voyenno-Morskoy Flot* did not generally give actual names to submarines. You were hoping for something very historic and striking such as *Krasnyy Oktyabr'* [Red October], I suppose? Alas, no. Sorry. In this time period—with rare exceptions—we simply referred to them by their permanent numbers. And those numbers usually were not the same as the "tactical" numbers we sometimes painted on the exteriors of the boats. Such tactical numbers were often changed to create confusion and enhance deception against NATO navies. How well that worked against NATO I do not really know. I know it often confused us!

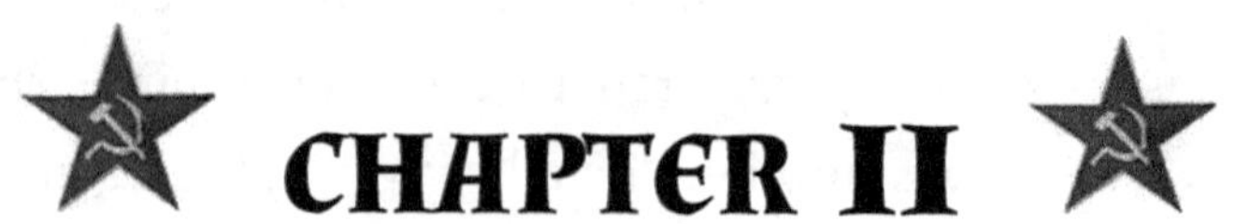

CHAPTER II

So, my friend, back to the story. The morning before we were to depart I went to post last-minute letters to my parents and to my wife and daughter. The post office was officially closed for some reason, but I was able to persuade them to take my letters—and I also managed to get them to release some correspondence which had come in for *B-59* crewmembers. Charm—and rank—usually helped to persuade people in the *Sovetskiy Soyuz!* I dropped into the barber shop and got my hair cut fairly short—it would be easier to take care of on the voyage, and there would be no one on board that I needed to impress with my dapper good looks! The barber had a *telefon* which he let me use to try to call my wife but, unsurprisingly, it was not working that day.

Lastly, I stopped by the little "floating store" that was docked alongside our boats and bought two kilos—about four pounds—of apples to take with me. Later that afternoon, as I have already told you, I attended the "commanders' briefing" given by Admirals Fokin, Rassokho, and Rybalko.

On the morning of our departure all of those admirals came down to the piers to see us off. Comrade Listener, I use the word "see" somewhat loosely. At four o'clock in the morning the darkness was total and, for security, there were very few lights in the area.

I expected to hear more inspirational speeches, but no. Apparently all that sort of thing had already been done and finished on board the *Dmitriy Galkin* as well as on the day before. The admirals contented themselves with walking among the piers—escorted by guards armed with rifles and flashlights—and exchanging a few brief, mostly ceremonial words with each captain.

As they stopped alongside the *B-59*, *Kapitan* Savitskiy brought to attention the few of us on the bridge and the few line-handlers on the deck. He saluted the group of flashlights below us and called down to them.

"*Ser*, request permission to carry out our assigned task in defense of the *Rodina!*"

Admiral Fokin gave the expected reply, intoning loudly and deeply, "Carry out your patriotic duty!"

CHAPTER 12

The *starpom*, Captain 3rd Rank Chernyshev, was standing with us on the small bridge—just behind Captain Savitskiy. Consulting his pocket watch Chernyshev came to attention and touched the brim of his cap.

"*Tovarishch Kapitan*, the crew was mustered on deck half an hour ago. All men are on board and correct. They have been sent to their action stations and are wearing life vests. Upper deck cleared. Lower decks cleared. Engine room ready. All watertight doors sealed. Sir, *Sovetskaya Podvodnaya Lodka* [Soviet Submarine] *B-59* is ready for sea and ready to leave port."

"*Spasibo* [thank you] *Starpom*," Savitskiy replied, touching his cap in turn. "*Bol'shomu korablyu, bol'shoye plavaniye* [For a big ship, a big voyage]." He smiled. "Start the engines, if you please."

We heard the three *dizeli* cough to life, mutter and chortle to themselves for a moment, and then settle into a reassuring rumble. Their large exhaust pipe was not at the stern of the boat as perhaps you might expect, but rather came out of the deck directly above the engine room—only 25 meters behind the bridge. Thus, clouds of foul-smelling exhaust fumes filled the air, mixing with the thick fog.

Standing to the side on the bridge I was warm in several layers of clothing topped by my felt-lined lambskin coat. My heavy

boots, cork-lined, were also very warm. It really was not particularly cold this morning but I knew the boots would come in
handy later at sea, shielding my feet from icy-cold water and
the equally cold steel deck. I had been given a life vest but, for
right now, I was holding it under my arm rather than putting it
on.

Before our engines awoke and filled the air with their strong
voices I had heard at least one other boat, over on the next pier,
start up.

"Take her out, *Starpom*," Savitskiy ordered.

"*Yest', Tovarishch Kapitan*," replied Chernyshev. He pulled
himself above the bridge's bulwark to better see the entire boat
bow to stern—or at least as much as the black morning would
allow. The *starpom* raised his voice to ensure the seamen on
deck and the pier heard him.

"Cast off all lines! Let go bow and stern mooring lines!"
Several dockworkers on the pier cast them off. Several crewmen on the deck hauled them in.

"All engines slow astern! Rudder amidships!" These orders
were directed to the speaking tubes leading into the conning
tower and the Control Center.

Soviet Submarine *B-59* noisily cleared the pier and glided,
stern first, about 100 *metry* into the black morning and into the
deep channel. Suddenly there was foam swirling around the
stern amidst a surge of water, and then this phenomenon
moved forward along both sides. This was the buoyancy or ballast tanks being blown out until they were completely filled
with air.

"All engines stop! All engines slow ahead!"

Chernyshev, a very experienced ship handler, coolly directed the boat into the center of the channel. I was glad, Comrade Listener, that the *starpom* was in *kontrol'*! I, for one, could not see a damned thing—and I was not particularly familiar with Sayda Bay. There was only about three *metry* visibility. This made for perfect conditions regarding getting underway covertly—despite the noise of the *dizeli*. It was also perfect for running aground despite Sayda Bay being generally blessed with fairly deep water. As an added factor of safety the senior navigator, Kapitan-Leitenant Sutulin, sat below us in the conning tower, his eyes fixed upon the radar console. He watched as the radar slowly traced the sides of the channel, ready to advise the *starpom* regarding any necessary course corrections.

So, in total, foggy darkness and showing no lights, at 4:20 a.m. on *Oktyabr'* 1st, 1962, *Sovetskiy 69 Torpeda Podvodnaya Brigada* officially began its mission. It was a relief to get to sea. Frankly, the officers and crews were exhausted from the many weeks of unusual and intense preparations. I might mention that having your personnel mentally and physically exhausted is not an ideal way to start a long and arduous voyage. Alas, I am afraid it happens all too often.

At that moment most of the men in our crews did not know that it was to be the longest deployment ever made by *Sovetskiy* submarines in history. Certainly the senior officers were aware of the destination, but right then the majority of the crewmen were not.

I am happy to say that FOXTROT submarines *B-36*, *B-59*, *B-130*, and *B-4* all departed Sayda Bay without incident. The destination was, as you already know, Mariel Bay in *Kuba*. And, as you know, our orders were to sail covertly for the entire voyage—if at all possible—and it was our patriotic socialist duty to ensure that it was possible.

Kapitan Dubivko in *B-36* led the way, and as it turned out he was going to lead the way across much of the *Atlanticheskiy Okean*. As we left port we, in *B-59*, were second in the line. *Kapitan* Savitskiy, the *starpom*, and I remained on *B-59*'s bridge surrounded by a handful of lookouts and other watch keepers. The lookouts were very much at leisure for the time being as the darkness was completely impenetrable. On *B-59*, for the moment, we trusted the charts and the familiarity of Savitskiy and Chernyshev regarding the bay—and the sparing use of our radar. The other boats proceeded similarly.

Dubivko and *B-36* sped along at ten knots over a remarkably smooth surface. So calm and flat was it that the windscreens to the front of the bridge cockpits were not really deflecting any spray. We followed Dubivko, 75 *metry* astern and slightly to his port side, each boat's three *Model' 37-D dizel'* engines rumbling pleasantly. As we reached the mouth of the bay the other two boats trailed well behind us. I was a little surprised that on board the *B-4* the brigade commander, *Kapitan* Agafonov, seemed content in bringing up the rear. I thought he might wish to, as people in the West like to say, "lead from the front." No matter. It was really not important. After all, this was neither a parade nor a cavalry charge!

CHAPTER 13

It was not long, Comrade Listener, before the sun blessed us with his presence—although he perversely glared at us without providing much warmth. That was all right because, as I already mentioned, it was actually not very cold. Most of us on the bridge were wearing dark blue *karakul'* wool greatcoats and our fur *ushanka* winter hats, but they really were not necessary this morning. You might be surprised to know that the average *temperatura* in the Pol'arnyi area for *Oktyabr'* is around 48 degrees *Farengeyt*—although the average *temperatura* is consistently below freezing from November through April.

In any event we on the bridge marveled at the beauty of the Barents Sea all around us. There we were, our little *voyenno-morskaya flotiliya* [naval flotilla] underway at the veritable top of the world.

We were sailing in a *kil'vaternaya kolonna* [formation in line] on a sea almost as smooth as it had been in Sayda Bay. Behind us the land began to disappear and ahead the blue-green sea melded with a gray sky full of clouds.

From the instant we left the pier we ran with our technicians closely monitoring our radar detection gear and other electronic counter measures—ECM—equipment. You are amazed that we should worry so, only a few minutes away from one of the Soviet Union's greatest *voyenno-morskiye bazy* [naval bases]?

Well, I must tell you that we were in very close proximity to the northern tip of *Norvegia*. In fact, Pol'arnyi is only 125 kilometers from the northern Norwegian border. Are you further surprised that we should worry about the Norwegians? You should not be. You must remember that *Norvegia* was a member of NATO and every country in NATO rightfully feared us *Russkiye*! Due to Norvegia's border actually touching ours, they were even more fearful and thus watched us very closely.

However, you also need to know that the Norwegian air force and navy were well-equipped and well-manned. Oh, we certainly did not fear them. Rather, we held them in high esteem as fine airmen and seamen—competent, aggressive, and tough. And they had earned a strong reputation for their proficiency in anti-submarine warfare skills. By the way, in *Russkiy* antisubmarine warfare—ASW—is *bor'ba s podvodnymi lodkami protivnika*. A mouthful, yes? Therefore, perhaps you and I for the rest of this story shall simply say "ASW."

So, I will now tell you that all of our *brigada*'s boats had detected traces of Norwegian electronic pulses even before we cleared our piers. Is that not remarkable? And they were increasing with the passing of every minute. It was only going to get worse. At this point we needed to sail north about 240 *kilometrov*. We would then curve around to the west in order to round the northern coast of *Norvegia* and to continue our mission into the *Atlanticheskiy Okean*. Thus, to be prudent, and to conform to our navy's standard operating procedures, it was time to submerge and hide.

Indeed, ahead of us we saw the *B-36* execute a perfect, smooth dive.

"*Dzhentl'meny* [Gentlemen], it is now our time to *pogru-zhat'sya* [submerge]," Savitskiy said. "*Starpom,* dive the boat."

"*Yest', Tovarishch Kapitan,*" Chernyshev replied. He leaned toward the voice tube. "Prepare to dive!" He waited a few seconds and then spoke again. "Lookouts, below! Clear the upper deck." The lookouts disappeared into the conning tower. The seamen remaining on deck scurried about with final preparations: they took down the flagstaff; they retracted several bollards—to which the mooring lines had been fastened—into the deck; they lashed down the boat hooks; they finished stowing the mooring lines into built-in compartments; and then they stowed themselves down into the boat, dogging the hatches as they went below.

"*Ser,* upper deck cleared for diving!"

Chernyshev was taking intercom reports that confirmed each of the boat's seven interior compartments was prepared to dive. He then called out, "Clear the bridge!" And following that, "*Pogruzheniye* [Dive the boat]!"

In the conning tower the telephone-talker repeated these orders which, over the intercom speakers, were heard all through *B-59.* The dive bell began to sound, further demanding everyone's attention. I dropped hastily down the hatch into the conning tower, followed by Savitskiy, the lookouts, and lastly the *starpom.*

"Rig out bow planes!"

Throughout the boat many other orders and much machinery noise filled the air. The *dizel'* engines growled to a stop as the air induction and main engine exhaust valves crashed to a close. Down in the Control Center the *starshina* [petty officers] at the ballast-tank vent controls called out their reports to the chief engineer.

"One ready!"

"Two ready!"

"Three-and-four—ready!"

"Five ready!"

"All vents ready!" *Kapitan Vtorogo Ranga* Pugachev called up to us in the conning tower. Pugachev was the *glavnyy inzhener*—chief engineer.

"Open Kingston valves in bow and stern group ballast tanks." Named for their inventor—an early nineteenth-century British engineer—Kingston valves are arranged so that the pressure of the sea forces the valve on its seat or closes it, thus differing from most valves which are arranged so that the pressure is in the direction of the opening of the valve. Submarines world-wide use them. Too technical, Comrade Listener? My apologies!

"Flood!" Chernyshev called back down to the CC.

"Flood!" Pugachev ordered the *starshina*.

The ventilation valves in the ballast tanks opened and tons of seawater rushed in, literally flooding the spaces between the pressure hull and the outer hull. Then the three big *elektricheskiy* motors came to life with their unique whine, drawing power from the boat's many heavy *akkumulyatory*.

"Extend forward diving planes." The retractable bow planes were now fully rigged out and the *inzhener*, Pugachev, moved to stand behind the hydroplane operators. To his side was a *michman*—a warrant officer—studying a rectangular panel displaying some thirty-five circular lights. These lights indicated the open or closed status of every valve and hatch in the boat's pressure hull. With the final closure of the bridge hatch—usually the last to be closed—the panel indicated everything was properly sealed. The chief engineer looked hard at the *michman*, who then elaborately touched his ear.

"Bleed air!" Pugachev ordered. Immediately I—and everyone else—felt a slight pressure in my eardrums. That meant that a small amount of compressed air, released into the boat as a test, was holding pressure. This confirmed that everything was indeed water and air tight.

"*Ser*, there is pressure in the boat!" Pugachev called up to Savitskiy and Chernyshev. Pugachev then turned back to the hydroplane operators.

"Bow planes, ten degrees down. Stern planes, level," he ordered. The deck tilted forward—too much! "Easy on the bow planes!" As you might know, submarines alter their specific underwater depth by using the bow and stern planes. The ballast tanks are essentially used to create overall positive buoyancy (which brings the boat to the surface), or overall negative buoyancy (which sinks the boat below the surface).

"All ahead one-third," ordered *Kapitan* Savitskiy, taking conning authority from the *starpom*. "Take her down to twenty *metry*." At fifteen *metry* the engineer reported, "Negative tanks!" and at twenty *metry* he leveled the dive. "*Tovarishch Kapitan*, we are stable at twenty *metry*. All vents are cycled and shut."

"*Otlichno* [excellent]. Now make the depth forty *metry*," Savitskiy ordered. "All ahead, dead slow. Trim the ship."

Working the trim-tank controls Pugachev, with the help of the plane operators, stabilized the boat on an even keel. When

B-59 reached forty metry Pugachev gave authority to the plane operators. They then worked independently by watching the differential pressure gauges and making minor corrections to keep her steady. Those gauges, as well as the myriad of other ones in the CC, cast an eerie green phosphorescent glow into the compartment.

Thus, the dive was complete. Gradually the orders, noise, and activity stopped. It became very quiet. Now the predominant sound throughout the boat was just the faint whine of the electric motors. Having just been up in the fresh sea air, now to me the interior of the submarine noticeably smelled of food stores, hydraulic fluid, machine oil, and diesel fumes. Experience told me that after a few more days these and other odors would increase—dramatically.

I apologize, Comrade Listener, if I have gone into too much detail! Such activities often look simple in Hollywood movies. I merely wanted to make sure you understood that taking a submarine under the water is a very complicated evolution.

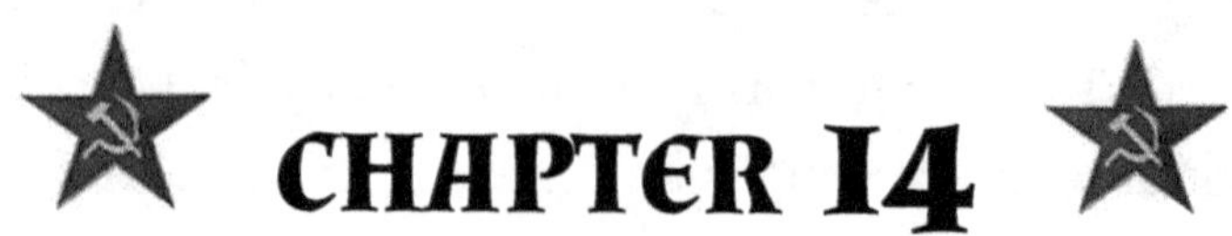

CHAPTER 14

In the conning tower Captain Savitskiy lowered himself onto one of the small metal stools next to the *periskop*. As an aside, may I tell you that those stools were not nearly as comfortable as their dark-green padded covers suggested they might be?

"I need to address the men," Savitskiy said, looking at me as he pulled some crumpled notes out of his uniform coat pocket. At the beginning of a voyage it was the custom in the *Voyenno-Morskoy Flot* for a ship's *komanduyushchiy ofitser* to proclaim the mission—and to motivate the crew to do their socialist duty. I have no doubt other navies have similar customs.

"Of course, *Tovarishch Kapitan*," I replied, nodding my head. "Do you want to read your sealed orders first?" I knew those orders were still locked in the small safe in his stateroom, only to be read now that we were at sea.

"No. I can tell the men enough detail to content them. The orders no doubt have *sekrety* which I do not need to share with everyone—at least not today."

"What about the "special weapon?" I asked. "There are many rumors passing among the crew, of course."

He seemed to hesitate for a moment.

"No," he said again. "I will wait on that as well."

Savitskiy reviewed his notes and then picked up a handset, thumbing two switches. A metallic click sounded from speakers throughout the boat. He began to speak.

"*Vnimaniye* [Attention]. Attention in the boat. This is the captain speaking. *Tovarishchi* [Comrades]! Officers and men of Soviet Submarine *B-59*! I congratulate you on the beginning of this important voyage! And I congratulate you for the honor you have been given to be part of the crew of *B-59*—just as it is my honor to be *B-59*'s *komanduyushchiy ofitser*."

"*Tovarishchi*, we have orders directly from the Navy's high command in Moskva! A few days ago you received some details from Admiral Fokin. I shall now tell you more. The *B-59* and the rest of our *brigada* of attack submarines are taking part in a special mission. A mission for the glory of the *Sovetskiy Soyuz*. As the admiral said, this assignment is vital and filled with great responsibility."

"Right now we are heading north, and soon we shall head west to round the *Nordkapp* [North Cape] of the imperialist NATO country *Norvegiya*. We shall then turn southwest and proceed into the *Atlanticheskiy Okean*. We shall avoid the cowardly reconnaissance aircraft and underwater acoustic arrays of the *imperialisty*. We shall not be detected! We shall continue southwest, and upon the completion of our *sekret* transit across the *Atlanticheskiy Okean* we shall be stationed permanently in a friendly country. You may now officially know that country is the *Sotsialisticheskaya Respublika Kuba*. There we shall enjoy that tropical island's warm breezes. And, soon, our families will be allowed to join us to reside in our new base at *Kuba*'s Mariel Bay!"

"First, we will reconnoiter the waters surrounding Mariel. We will ensure they are free of *Amerikanskiy* forces or any of their new fixed acoustic arrays. We will then survey and report the hydro-acoustic conditions of the area. Then, we shall be the first ocean-going units of the *Voyenno-Morskoy Flot* to be established at this base!"

"We have the proud duty of ensuring all is ready for the *Sovetskiy* vessels which will follow us. These will be seven strategic-missile submarines, two squadrons of mine-warfare craft, two gun-armed cruisers, and two missile-armed destroyers. Later there will also be support ships joining us including our own submarine tender, the *Dmitriy Galkin.*"

"*Tovarishchi*, I repeat, it is vital to the success of the mission that we maintain the *sekretnost'* of our deployment. Thus, we shall make best speed while remaining undetected."

"*Tovarishchi*! Officers and men of *B-59*! That part will be a challenge! The ASW patrols of the NATO countries, and particularly the *Amerikantsy*, are noteworthy. Thus, we will have to spend a great deal of the voyage—certainly most daylight periods—submerged. This will be difficult—but for a *Sovetskiy* seaman it is never difficult to do his duty! We shall arrive at Mariel sometime in late *Oktyabr'.*"

"*Tovarishchi*, much is expected of us, but we are part of the *Zashchitniki Rodiny* [Motherland's Defenders]. We shall not fail! This voyage will demand our best efforts. We must all do our socialist duty and we must do it well. That is true for me, the *kapitan*, as well as the most junior *matros* [seaman] on board. Many of you seamen are young and new to the Navy. So, I tell you, work hard and keep alert! Instantly obey the orders of your superiors. Our lives depend upon each other. Remember, *distsiplina mat' pobedy* [discipline is the mother of victory]!"

"*Tovarishchi!* We shall make this voyage a memorable one. It will be the longest deployment ever made by *Sovetskiy* submarines in history! We will wipe the noses of the *imperialisty*. They will soon understand that they cannot play 'ducks and drakes' with the men of the *Voyenno-Morskoy Flot*. *Tovarishchi*, I wish us all happy sailing and the successful accomplishment of our mission! That is all."

Savitskiy clicked the handset to "off" and replaced it in its cradle. He looked at me with a raised eyebrow. I smiled at him, clapping my hands softly together. I thought it was a good speech. Perhaps an inspired speech. Frankly, I did not think the gruff Valentin Grigorievitch had it in him. What do you think, Comrade Listener?

CHAPTER 15

So, there we were, off on our great patriotic adventure. Captain Savitskiy got up from his stool and stretched. "Well, no use putting it off any longer. Let us see about those *sekret* orders." Slightly raising his voice he called, "Officer on Deck, send my secretary to my stateroom, if you please."

Savitskiy, the *starpom*, and I dropped down the ladder into the CC where we encountered the *zampolit*, Maslennikov. We all then walked out of the CC heading forward, shortly arriving at Savitskiy's stateroom. It was on the port side close to the Forward Torpedo Room. Even that far forward, the stateroom was still reasonably close to the CC and the conning tower, so the commanding officer could quickly be available in case of any emergencies. Savitskiy's *sekretar'*—a burly petty officer— arrived out of breath, having sprinted from the ship's office in Compartment Four, aft of the CC. Savitskiy posted him outside the stateroom to guard against any crewmen who might accidentally—or purposefully—eavesdrop on our conversation.

We all crowded in and let me tell you it was very difficult to fit in the tiny space. The *starpom* and I sat closely together on the gray navy-issue blanket covering Savitskiy's narrow bunk, while everyone struggled to make themselves as small as possible. Maslennikov tugged the narrow wooden sliding door shut, in so doing banging his head and pinching his fingers against the communications handset on the stateroom's forward bulkhead.

Leaning over his small desk, Savitskiy fiddled with his compact safe which was bolted to the aft bulkhead. He pulled out an envelope and I could see that it was black and had a white stripe and white lettering on it. It was similar to the large package that *Admiral* Fokin had handed *Kapitan* Agafonov in the commander's briefing just before our departure. The words *Sovershenno Sekretno* [Top Secret]—also in white—were very apparent across the bottom.

Savitskiy turned around, sat on the desk, and waved the envelope at us. "You can see, *dzhentl'meny*, that the seals are unbroken." We could and so we all replied, "*Da, Tovarishch Kapitan.*"

He took a letter opener from his desk and cut the envelope open. The opener was gold—in least in color—and shaped like a miniature naval officer's sword. Inside were two smaller envelopes which he also opened. Extracting a sheet of paper from the first envelope he began to read the main points out loud as he ran his finger down the page.

"Ummmm ... as to the overall operation, *Operatsiya Anadyr'* ... mmmm ... this internationalist intervention mission by the *Soyuz Sovetskikh Sotsialisticheskikh Respublik* is designed to equip the *Sotsialisticheskaya Respublika Kuba* with sufficient resources and support to undermine further Western aggression."

"*Khorosho* [Okay]. *69 Torpeda Podvodnaya Brigada* is tasked with a special mission for the *Sovetskiy Soyuz*, which includes transiting the *Atlanticheskiy Okean* in *sekret* to a new home port in our allied country. Ummmm ... this transit must remain undetected by enemy forces, and the *brigada* must arrive at Mariel Bay, *Kuba*, not later than 20 *Oktyabr'*."

"This is *der'mo!* 20 *Oktyabr'*!" Savitskiy exclaimed, looking up from the paper. Lowering his voice he continued. "If we could run the whole way on the surface, not caring if we were detected, it might be possible. But proceeding submerged for over half the distance to hide our movement will eat up a lot of time. Were these orders written by a *sukhoputnyy zhitel'* [a landlubber] for God's sake?"

We all looked at him impassively. What could we say? What could I say? Was he really surprised, I wondered. Had he expected the written orders to be more *realisticheskiy* than what we—at least he and I—had already been told by the admirals in Sayda Bay? Why would he have thought things would have improved?

Chernyshev ventured to agree with his captain as a good executive officer should. "*Ser*, it does seem, all too often, that orders written at headquarters make no account of wind, tide, weather, or distance."

For a moment Savitskiy looked sourly at Chernyshev, then shook his head and continued to read.

"The naval aspect of all this, called *Operatsiya Kama*, specifically tasks the submarines of *69 Brigada* with performing reconnaissance of all seaward approaches to Mariel. Acoustic area conditions are to be logged for port entry. This is in preparation for seven ballistic-missile submarines of *20 Operativnaya Podvodnaya Eskadril'ya*, as well as for several cruisers, destroyers, and mine-warfare craft—*da, da, da*—which will be sent at a later date to be determined."

He then read us parts of the attached pages, rapidly skipping through them. These vaguely referred to the *Sovetskiy* military forces which had already been sent to *Kuba* and also mentioned the naval forces assigned to *Operatsiya Kama*. He tossed the papers onto his desk and then extracted a single sheet from the second envelope.

"Right! Here are the *pravila dlya bitvy* [rules of engagement]. Ummm ... mmmm ... rules of engagement for the use of weapons." He read them first to himself, silently, and then aloud.

"One: Weapons during transit will be in combat readiness for use."

"Two: Conventional weapons are to be used as directed by the Main Navy Staff; however, they may be used at the discretion of the individual *komanduyushchiy ofitser* in case of attack against his submarine."

"Three: Torpedoes with nuclear warheads may be used only as directed with *instruktsii* from the Ministry of Defense and the Main Navy Staff."

Savitskiy picked up the contents of the first envelope and then handed me the papers with a small, polite bow. As he did he also gave me a puzzled look, but said nothing further. I slowly read through the papers to make sure I fully understood what they said and that Savitskiy had not missed anything crucial in his quick review.

How curious, I thought, and how confusing.

The rules of engagement seemed clear and logical considering the incredible responsibility for using nuclear weapons. Not to mention the potential consequences of such use.

But they were totally at odds with the verbal orders we had heard just prior to our departure. And those were from the mouth of *Vitse-Admiral* Anatoliy Ivanovitch Rassokho, the Chief of Staff of the *Severnyy Flot.* All those present had heard them clearly. No wonder Savitskiy looked puzzled.

And they were also contrary to the immediate and apparent endorsement of those orders which we all, again, had clearly heard. Those words were spoken by *Admiral* Vitaliy Alekseyevich Fokin, the First Deputy Commander of the *Voyenno-Morskoy Flot.* Clearly, we had been authorized to use the nuclear torpedoes under certain conditions—without necessarily informing Moskva.

With great emphasis Fokin had said, "If they slap you on the left cheek, do not let them slap you on the right."

Well, Comrade Listener, I ask you: what do you make of that?

CHAPTER 16

The four submarines of the *brigada* proceeded north, just as Captain Savitskiy had told the crew we would. *B-59* then changed course to the west to round the *Nordkapp*. We could only assume the other boats were doing the same thing for we were not in continuous communication with them.

So, we began to settle into our necessary routine of surface sailing at night, using our *dizel'* engines, and submerged sailing during daylight, using our *elektricheskiy* motors. When running at night we also used the *dizeli* to recharge the many heavy-duty *akkumulyatory*. These batteries were, of course, vital to us. Whenever we could not operate the *dizel'* engines—which is to say when we wished to be quiet or when we were submerged— we had to draw a lot of power from the *akkumulyatory*. This was to run the *elektricheskiy* motors for propulsion—as well as run everything else. Thus, it was crucial that we kept them charged to the fullest for we often did not know when or how long we might be forced to use them.

I must refresh your thinking, Comrade Listener, concerning this notion of traveling unseen and unnoticed. Keeping our mission secret and undetected was grossly and overly optimistic. It was a pipe dream on the part of our higher commanders. An *illyuziya* [illusion]! As it turned out *Amerikanskiy* and NATO electronic warfare resources did pick us up early. It was perhaps when we rounded the coast of *Norvegia* and entered the Norwegian Sea. Or, it may have even been earlier as I already mentioned. Now, when I say "picked up," that essentially means they found some early indicators of our presence. That does not mean they achieved any sort of solid identification or location.

The *Voyenno-Morskoy Flot* was of course aware that *Amerikanskiy* and NATO capabilities were good. However, at that time we did not know just *how* good. In addition, while we had some awareness, we did not have a complete understanding of the new *Amerikanskiy* fixed underwater acoustic arrays. I will tell you more about those arrays a little later in the story.

But right at this point we became aware of how challenging our voyage was going to be regarding discovery.

Shortly after we had rounded the *Nordkapp* and were proceeding on a course roughly west-southwest, *B-59* came up to *periskop* depth. We were just off the Vesterålen Archipelago along the coast of northern *Norvegia*, approximately 69 degrees north latitude and 15 degrees east longitude. We wanted to take several visual bearings of the shoreline—through the *periskop*—to confirm our position. We also elevated our electronic countermeasures—ECM—mast and tuned to known Norwegian frequencies.

Well, much to our dismay we instantly discovered sweeps of surface-search radars! And our broadband receiver also recorded several other sources of electromagnetic radiation.

Kapitan Savitskiy was in the conning tower, desiring to take the *periskop* bearings himself. The executive officer, along with

Kapitan-Leitenant Sutulin and I, were there as well. I think I have mentioned that Sutulin was the *starshiy navigator*.

Both the *B-59*'s assigned radio-electronics officer, *Starshiy-Leitenant* Rodzyenko, and our new "special" radio-intelligence officer, *Starshiy-Leitenant* Orlov, were closely monitoring their respective sets of equipment. The former was in *B-59*'s radio room one deck down, just aft of the CC in Compartment Four. The latter was crowded into his small, makeshift radio room, right across the passageway from Rodzyenko's. Suddenly, both *radisty* shouted similar warnings into the intercom.

"*Vnimaniye* [Attention] Conning Tower! Detecting surface-search radar, believe it to be an *Amerikanskiy* or NATO AN/APS-20!"

Savitskiy instantly slapped the *periskop* handles flat. "Down *periskop*! Down ECM! Where is it coming from!?" he shouted.

"Cannot determine exactly where, *Tovarishch Kapitan*, but it appears to be from an aircraft. Possibly a P2V *Neptune*." P2Vs were American-manufactured land-based ASW patrol airplanes. They were flown by several NATO countries, including the United States, Denmark, and Norway.

"Make depth fifty *metry*!" Savitskiy ordered. A minute passed as the boat swam downward. We grimly stared at each other. The intercom came alive again.

"*Kapitan*, quick analysis of the ECM tape indicates *Amerikanskiy*-type passive-listening sonobuoy radio transmissions—the kind they call JEZEBEL. We must also assume that they have on board and are using an *Amerikanskiy*-type magnetic anomaly detector—probably the AN/ASQ-8."

"Damn!" Savitskiy exclaimed. "Did they pinpoint us?"

"*Ser*, we may or may not be precisely discovered. We cannot determine if they sensed *B-59* individually, or one of our sister boats, or several of our boats—or perhaps—none of our boats."

"*Kapitan* Savitskiy," I said, "we must, of course, conclude that they did." I should not have said that. Savitskiy was *in komande*. He was calm and in *kontrol'*. He did not need any meddling from a person who was essentially a passenger. The *Amerikantsy* have an amusing expression for this: *zadneye siden'ye voditelya* [a backseat driver].

"I concur, *Kapitan* Arkhipov," Savitskiy replied. Fortunately he showed no irritation at my unsolicited advice.

We had to assume that the aircraft had observed indications of at least one of our boats' presence. If not, they would not have dropped sonobuoys from the aircraft—after all, like everything else, sonobuoys are expensive pieces of equipment, not to be wasted even by the rich *Amerikantsy* or their allies! And if the airplane's *komandir* truly felt confident of his discovery he would be climbing to altitude to transmit a *situatsiya* report. This would be directed to the underground Norwegian and NATO headquarters at Mount Jåttå, near Stavanger.

If it were a P2V, it likely was working with one or more nearby surface ships in the so-called "hunter-killer" *model'*. In addition, if their radio reports were convincing, their headquarters might even move other ASW ships or aircraft toward our position.

As of 1962 we *Russkiye* really had no significant history of Cold War encounters. That was to become common in the future. But even then we clearly understood that NATO hunter-killer ASW forces had become the major threat to our submarine operations. An ASW aircraft carrier—most likely *Ameri-kanskiy*—could be extremely dangerous once informed of a submarine's general location. Such information usually came via underwater acoustic sensors or long-range air patrols. The aircraft carrier could skillfully coordinate its accompanying destroyers, which were generally equipped with the powerful *Amerikanskiy* high-frequency SQS-23 sonar. It could also coordinate its own carrier-based ASW aircraft—particularly SF2 *Tracker* airplanes and SH-3 *Sea King* helicopters. These all presented formidable challenges.

As I mentioned earlier, our *radisty* predicted the use of a magnetic anomaly detector against us. Allow me to explain, Comrade Listener. A magnetic anomaly detector, or "MAD," is an *Amerikanskiy* term, and for simplicity I shall use MAD for the rest of my narrative. A MAD is an electronic instrument that can sense small variations in the earth's magnetic field—such as that caused by a cruising submarine's mass of steel under water.

A report came up from the CC telling us that *B-59's* bathythermograph was showing a layer of very cold water at ninety *metry* depth. Savitskiy nodded in satisfaction. "Well, there is some luck."

Extremely cold water, presenting a different thermal density, would basically lay a protective cover over our boat. This would hopefully deflect any more active or passive listening in case the Norwegians came back above us.

Savitskiy called down to the CC. "Make our depth 120 *metry*, and make our speed eight knots."

Every *minut* was taking us farther from the Norwegian shore as we headed for our next goal—the seaway between the Danish-owned Faroe Islands and the NATO-member country of *Islandiya* [Iceland]. Of course, this we intended. Crossing that line would bring us into the *Severo Atlanticheskiy Okean*, a significant milestone as we made our way toward our far southern destination in the Caribbean Sea.

This close-call with the Norwegians was a very early and very sobering alert to us. It was going to be very difficult to execute an undetected journey. It was a poor beginning. And it occurred to us that this encounter could very well cause the NATO forces to increase their efforts if they thought they had discovered a group of *Sovetskiy* submarines on the move.

I need to make something very clear to you, Comrade Listener. Of course we had no fear that the *Amerikantsy* or NATO forces were actually going to attack us! No state of war existed at this time and so any such action would be completely unjustified. It would be unlawful in the eyes of the world.

And, if an actual state of war came about we certainly were not defenseless! Indeed, submarines such as FOXTROTs had, as a specific wartime mission, the destruction of NATO ASW aircraft carriers. Once we found ourselves in the vicinity of such a ship—and its hunter-killer group—we could listen with our sensitive passive sonar and track the enemy.

As I told you earlier, we had on board the excellent *Sovetskiy Feniks* passive sonar as well as our *Nakat* electronic support measures equipment. Again, the NATO navies had amusingly named these systems TROUT CHEEK and STOP LIGHT B—just as they named our *Projekt-641* boats FOXTROT.

Anyway, regardless of what you or I wish to call these equipments, we operated them with highly trained technicians. These men were good at listening to and then identifying NATO ships and aircraft. Our technicians could analyze the intensity, bearings, and other characteristics of NATO sonars and propeller noises—as well as aircraft sensors. Thus, we *Sovety* could differentiate between the aircraft carrier and its destroyers without having to use our fine *Gerkules* active sonar or our FDC 759 surface-search radar. By not using the active sonar, the search radar, or raising our *periskopy* for visual identification, we minimized the chances of giving away our positions.

We were also heavily armed. I think I already mentioned that each FOXTROT boat carried twenty-two torpedoes which could be fired out of six torpedo tubes in the bow or four tubes in the stern. There was also our single and *sekret* "special weapon."

I could also point out that two of the *torpedy*, loaded into tubes in the Aft Torpedo Room, did not carry explosives. They were "noisemaker" torpedoes, designed to emit sounds similar to the noises of the boat only somewhat louder. If we detected an enemy submarine or destroyer in our vicinity trying to attack us, we could fire a noisemaker *torpeda* which would immediately turn to the side and move away at around fifteen knots. Then, with any luck the enemy would be decoyed by this torpedo and begin to follow it, rather than us.

But these were principally wartime issues and we were not at war. That aside, we had every fear that the imperialist *Amerikantsy* and their NATO vassals would try very hard to track us and pursue us. We feared that they might pin-point us and even make efforts to force us to the surface if we were submerged—or harass us if they found us on the surface. If these things could be accomplished then the ASW air crews or the ship crews would gain valuable experience. They would also likely be recognized and rewarded by their superiors. More important, if these things happened we would be reprimanded—and likely punished by our superiors.

Assuming that they were aware of us, one of the areas in which they might *kontcentrat* their forces would be the Faroe-Iceland line. This was, Comrade Listener, an historic naval "choke point," and we were heading right for it.

CHAPTER 17

As I have said, we were now into the required routine of surface sailing at night and submerged sailing during daylight.

When not on the bridge or in the CC, I spent a lot of my time in my small stateroom to be out of the way of the crew performing their duties. Essentially just a passenger, I had no specific job. Thus, not being underfoot was important. Space is always extremely tight in a submarine and the addition of myself, the "special weapon officer," and the nine radio-intelligence people made it uncomfortably cramped inside the *B-59*.

I know that you can imagine that the crowded conditions on a submarine are unlike any other vessel. Depending upon the class of submarine, you will find a very large number of men in a very small space. There were 78 crew plus 11 extra "passengers" on board the *B-59* on this mission. Relatively speaking we were all packed pretty tightly. When underway, when the boat is closed up and under the water, no man can get very far from any other. Indeed, on many boats there are not enough cots or bunks for everyone, so many of the enlisted men have to share. In the *Amerikanskiy* navy this is called "hot-racking"—two men assigned to one bunk or "rack," sleeping in shifts. One man uses the bunk while his shipmate is at his duty station.

Such was the life of a *Sovetskiy podvodnik*. By and large you worked, slept, ate, read, and smoked. You may find it strange that we smoked on board a submarine but it was very common in those days. When we were on the surface and constantly drawing fresh air it was of no concern. When submerged smoking was still authorized for we knew, in normal conditions, we would surface and ventilate within a few hours.

Submariners may well sleep more than other sailors because recreational opportunities are severely limited. Freely moving about is very restricted, and there are virtually no spaces to, as the *Amerikantsy* say, "hang out." Thus, lying down—out of the way—is both comfortable and efficient.

I did spend a lot of time on the bridge at night, but always mindful to yield space to the officers and crew actually on duty.

Aside from the *insident* with the Norwegian ASW aircraft, the first five days of the voyage saw everything fairly serene, and the weather was auspicious.

During this period, with light from the moon and stars, the sea looked beautiful at night. The water is luminescent at that time of year, especially in the Norwegian Sea. It is quite a sight.

On a number of such evenings the *ofitser kolody* [officer on deck, or OOD] was a young man, just a junior *leitenant*, named Anatoliy Petrovich Andreyev. He was the boat's *ofitser snabzheniya* [supply officer]. He had recently qualified as a submariner and Captain Savitskiy was giving him opportunities to gain more OOD experience during this period of relative calm. I took an instant liking to him and he to me. I felt a little sorry for him. New to the boat, and very junior in rank, he was somewhat intimidated by his superior officers. He was also constrained by regulation and custom from being friendly with the warrant officers and enlisted men. Although I was far older and senior in rank I was not in his chain of command, so I allowed a friendship to develop.

He particularly amused me one evening.

"*Ser*, is not the sea especially beautiful tonight? Is not the view wonderful?"

"Yes, Anatoliy Petrovich," I replied. "It surely is."

"At such moments," he said, "I wish we were on board the *Rossiya* [a famous Soviet luxury liner]. I wish, next to me, might be my wife Sofia—my dear Sofochka—instead of this burly signalman in his rubber protective suit. Or even instead of you, *ser!*" He looked at me to see if I were bored or annoyed with his babbling. Reassured, he went on.

"Sofia is in a light summer dress and feels chilly. We stand with our arms around each other, admiring the beauty of the sea at night."

"You paint a pretty picture, Anatoliy."

"*Da, Kapitan*, it is. Ah, well. So, in my crowded berth, surrounded by *foto* of my wife and daughter, I devote a great deal of time on a diary—a serial letter, if you will, which I will post to them when we reach *Kuba*. But in the short run, as it stands, I do the next best thing. I send her greetings via the Constellation of Orion, which is currently visible both here and in *Rossiya*. I pretend that if she and my little daughter Lyalechka also see Orion, we will be able to send messages to each other via those stars. I know—it is silly."

I just smiled at him. I was thinking of my wife Olga and little daughter Yelena, and I could not help looking up at Orion.

CHAPTER 18

As I mentioned earlier, Comrade Listener, we had great concerns as the *B-59* approached that Faroe-Iceland line. Via our *elektronica* and also due to the occasional visual observation, we were very aware of flights of NATO reconnaissance aircraft. Our "OSNAZ" *radist*, Senior-Lieutenant Orlov—along with his technicians—began to steadily intercept NATO long-range ASW air-patrol radio communications. This was in the brief hours when we were surfaced or when the ECM mast was elevated from its housing in the conning tower. Orlov was hearing considerably more than he had anticipated. He even wondered if we were somehow expected to be in the area. I can tell you that Captain Savitskiy and I wondered the same thing.

As best that Orlov could determine from the aircraft-to-shore radio "chatter," the American, British, and Danish ASW units were thinking that there might be a half-dozen *Sovetskiy* long-range *dizel'* submarines deploying into the area. The *Amerikantsy* were flying P2V *Neptunes* from Iceland, the Danes were flying *Neptunes* from Jutland, and the British were flying Avro *Shackletons* out of Scotland. Later we suspected that we might also encounter Canadians flying Canadair *Argus* aircraft out of Nova Scotia.

Orlov thought perhaps an intelligence source in Pol'arnyi may have compromised us, or maybe it had been the earlier first encounter with the Norwegian PV2.

It is important to tell you, Comrade Listener, that back then neither *Leitenant* Orlov nor any of the rest of us had any real or meaningful knowledge of the *Yanki* SOSUS ASW system. In *Angliyskiy*, SOSUS stands for Sound Surveillance System. This was a newly developed and widespread chain of passive underwater listening posts located around the world. It was in such places as the ocean near Greenland, Iceland, the United Kingdom, and along the east coast of the United States. It was a very new system and very *sovershenno sekretno*. Even the abbreviation SOSUS was classified and known only to small numbers of people in the U.S. Navy who actually needed to know. By 1961 there were nine arrays of this system in the *Atlanticheskiy Okean*.

The SOSUS was specifically aimed at the *Sovetskiy* submarine force. The Americans had anticipated that our submarines were going to be a true threat in the future, and therefore had found a lot of money to develop this system. SOSUS monitored low-frequency sound using large numbers of bottom-mounted underwater listening devices. These devices were equipped with hydrophones. Utilizing underwater cables, data was collected at multiple processing facilities. A single facility, we learned much later, could determine approximate submarine positions by triangulation over hundreds of miles. A *dizel'-elektricheskiy* boat, running on her *akkumulyatory*, was very quiet and thus was very difficult to detect. However, SOSUS could be very effective if the submarine surfaced—or came close to the surface and deployed its *shnorkel'* [snorkel]—and ran its *dizel'* engines.

The *Amerikantsy* had established such facilities at Newfoundland, Nova Scotia, Massachusetts, New Jersey, Delaware, North Carolina, Bermuda, Puerto Rico, Barbados, and three more sites scattered through the islands of the Bahamas.

Again, please note that this was all unknown to us in 1962. It was years later that we learned that, in early 1962, SOSUS for the first time detected a *Sovetskiy dizel'-elektricheskiy* submarine.

And by mid-*Oktyabr'* 1962 the SOSUS network system indicated that several *Sovetskiy dizel'* submarines were apparently in the western *Atlanticheskiy Okean.*

Comrade, I am afraid those several boats were us—*69 Torpeda Podvodnaya Brigada!*

And in a few more days SOSUS was going to precisely detect one of our boats, and that was going to aid the *Amerikanskiy* navy in accurately locating the rest of us as we neared *Kuba.*

Of course we did understand, even then, that the *Amerikantsy* were placing here and there some sort of ASW underwater acoustic arrays. Unfortunately, we had no specific details.

Indeed, and as you already know, the orders of *69 Torpeda Podvodnaya Brigada* mentioned this. They required us, when we reached *Kuba,* to determine if there were any such systems operational down there—and in particular operational near Mariel Bay.

But it was not all bad news for us *Sovetskiy* submariners! I am pleased to tell you that as early as 1959 the *Sovetskiy Soyuz* had actually found and cut a few of these new *Amerikanskiy* seafloor cables, using deep-sea fishing trawlers to do so. The

Amerikantsy were very unhappy with this activity, but could not actually prove that we had done it.

Be that as it may, I do not know if this SOSUS system had good capability near the Faroe Islands and Iceland at the time of our approach. Whether it did or did not does not matter, for we encountered a stroke of luck! As we approached the area we found several hundred small commercial boats busily fishing along a wide stretch of that Faroe-Iceland line. We maneuvered through them, at night and on the surface, at around fifteen knots. We apparently got by without being identified by SOSUS—and if we were identified by the fishermen, they kindly chose to not inform the NATO forces!

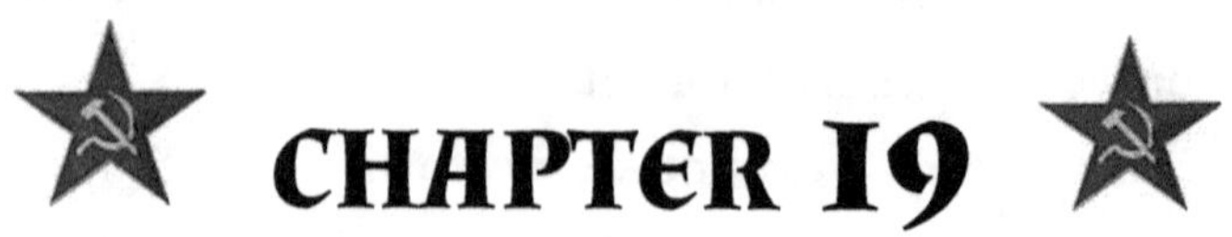

CHAPTER 19

Well, I am sorry to tell you that our pleasure at getting through the Faroe-Iceland line was short-lived. This is because we very soon encountered heavy weather in the form of a very strong gale. The winds grew in strength to be as much as eighty *kilometrov* per hour—sorry, that would be fifty miles per hour. And this came with seas occasionally more than ten *metry* high—around thirty-three feet. In fact, the sea conditions deteriorated to the point that, for a protracted period of time, we were struggling with a "Force-Nine" gale. Through necessity we rode out this rough weather mostly on the surface. And, on top of the unpleasant motion, we had to go several days with no good navigational fix to verify our position. We could not see the sun or the moon, and we could not "shoot" a single star. Remember, my friend, this was long before navigational satellites. Seamen—and airmen, for that matter—were constrained to use the ancient practice of celestial *navigatsiya*, involving instruments such as sextants, quadrants, and slide rules to determine position. But this could not be done if we could neither see the sun nor the stars.

That aside, you might well ask me why did we not just submerge and avoid the gale? Would it not be peaceful under the water, leaving the shrieking wind and mountainous waves on the surface? Certainly, my friend, running submerged would be more comfortable. We would have had to go fairly deep to evade the swells—which can be felt as far down as twenty *metry* below the surface. If our boats had been nuclear powered we certainly would have done just that. But in a *dizel'-elektricheskiy* boat, running submerged required us to go very slowly using our *elektricheskiy* motors, and the *elektricheskiy* motors consumed an enormous amount of *akkumulyator* power. And, of course, we would frequently have to come up to refresh our air and run the *dizel'* engines to recharge the *akkumulyatory.*

So we had to run on the surface much of the time for such practical reasons. Thus, for the most part, we stayed there. In stormy weather we were unlikely to be discovered by any aircraft. In extremely rough weather no aircraft would even be flying.

Moreover, trying to surface in the face of heavy seas was actually very dangerous. Trim settings which are ideal for the tranquil depths instantly became incorrect. The unstable roll, pitch, and yaw—presented by those shrieking winds and mountainous seas—often create overwhelming *problemy* to all but the best ship-handlers. Of course, surface vessels are also very much affected by heavy seas and forceful winds. But, while they may roll steeply from side to side, they usually do not stand on their heads or tails. Submarine boats are very sensitive to many factors and can be difficult to keep on an even keel. A submarine can pitch as much as forty degrees even when underwater. This is why the regulator tanks and the trim tanks are so important. By skillful and constant adjustment of these tanks the crewmen standing watch hope to keep the boat exactly at "trim state zero"—or at least very close.

An example, if you will permit me? The second night of the storm, before we realized how severe it had become, saw us attempt to surface as normal. The *ofitser* on deck was my new young friend, the relatively inexperienced *Mladshiy-Leitenant* Andreyev.

Even before *B-59*'s bridge and conning tower broached the surface we were laid over to starboard, jolted upright, and then rolled over to port. The lookouts and other personnel in the conning tower, heading for the bridge, clung desperately to the ladder and other solid things—momentarily unable to open the hatch. That was just as well because then the bow fell away. The *starpom*, Chernyshev, shouted at Andreyev.

"*Ostorozhno, Leitenant* [Watch out, Lieutenant]!—hold the boat above three *metry*! Lookouts!—do not open the hatch!"

B-59 sank even more.

"*Chert* [damn it], Andreyev, catch her and hold her nose up!"

Well, the boat did leap up—and at that point I suddenly found myself thrown to the deck.

"You are relieved, *Leitenant* Andreyev," the exec shouted. "I assume the watch as conning officer."

Barking out a series of orders, *Kapitan Tret'yego Ranga* Chernyshev had conning tower and Control Center crewmen adjusting valves, working the hydroplanes, modifying steering, and caressing the trim-tank controls. Every man's efforts were complicated by the necessity of clinging to wheels, pipes, and any handhold as they performed their duties, trying to stay on their feet. Gradually the boat stabilized, no longer rising and falling like a child's see-saw. But, I hasten to add, that *stabil'nost* was relative. The boat still rocked severely as the momentous waves tossed her about.

For several *minut* the electrical humming of the *periskop*'s motor filled the air. Chernyshev was having a lot of trouble with the scope and was moving it up and down trying to coordinate with the rise and fall of the sea. He wanted to take a quick look around before we fully surfaced.

Then surface we did and the bridge hatch was finally opened, admitting cold, wet, wonderful fresh air along with considerable salty *sprey*. The air induction valves slammed open and the *dizel'* engines took over from the *elektricheskiy* motors, firmly pushing the boat forward as well as starting to recharge the *akkumulyatory*.

"*Tovarishch Starpom*, I am very sorry," began Andreyev, looking miserable.

"*Zabud' eto* [Forget it]," replied Chernyshev. "I should have taken over sooner. Surfacing into a storm requires considerable experience—and even then it is difficult."

Captain Savitskiy spoke up from a seat at the CC's after bulkhead from where he and I had been watching the event unfold.

"Agreed. In fact, we shall remain on the surface— unpleasant as that will be—until the storm abates. Surfacing, and even submerging, in such conditions presents extra *problemy* which none of us relish."

Just then I noticed that the assistant navigator, *Mladshiy-Leitenant* Mikhailov, had a huge grin on his broad and always-cheerful face. He was seated at the CC's navigation and chart table.

"What is so amusing, Viktor Sergeyevich?" I asked.

"*Tovarishch Kapitan*, I love this kind of thing! For us submariners perfect weather is when there are waves—when there is a storm. We can stay on the surface, running the *dizeli*, and the *imperialisty* cannot find us."

I grinned too, with the notion that this junior officer—of very little experience himself—thought he knew all about deepwater sailing.

"Well, my young friend," I replied, now trying to look serious. "I wonder if you will sing the same song after a few days of these conditions. After a few days when you cannot stand on your feet. When you have to put your legs against the bulkhead and keep your back pressed against the fittings just to keep yourself stable. When you have to triple-strap yourself into your bunk. If you do not do that, and the sea suddenly swings the boat around, you will fly about and break your head—or damage something even more important."

"*Da, Kapitan*," Mikhailov said cheerfully, rubbing his blond and bushy eyebrow. He opened his mouth as if to continue, then closed it and looked away. Well, what else could he say, with Savitskiy and I both fixing him with steely eyes?

Indeed, Comrade Listener, that is how we spent the next few days, trying to keep on our feet—trying not to break our heads—miserably tossed about as *B-59* pushed herself forward on the roiling surface.

Nor could we effectively utilize our *shnorkel'* because those same rough seas would likely overwhelm it.

Of course, I should explain the *shnorkel'* to you, Comrade. You probably have one! It is a small piece of individual recreational swimming gear, yes? A wonderful device which allows you to keep your face and mask continuously down in the water while still breathing.

Well, a submarine's *shnorkel'* is similar though a great deal larger. It was a device mostly used by German U-boats late in the Great Patriotic War, and then became widely used in all navies. It is a reinforced steel tube that can be raised like a *periskop* while the boat is submerged. But, as with using a *periskop*, the boat has to remain somewhat close to the surface. Through the tube, air comes into the submarine to feed the *dizel'* engines. This allows the boat to use its *dizeli* rather than its *elektricheskiy* motors—yet still remain almost entirely concealed by the water. Also, coming up from the engine room—but contained inside the submarine—is another larger tube allowing the engines to get rid of their considerable exhaust smoke and fumes. On FOXTROT boats this exhaust tube vents into the water, just below the surface, from a port behind the rear of the conning tower.

But, there are some drawbacks to the *shnorkel'*. The boat must proceed very slowly—perhaps only five or six knots—to avoid bending the intake tube. In addition, the tube is equipped with an automatic valve to prevent sea water from being sucked into the engines. This of course will happen if the *shnorkel'*'s head should even briefly be dipped underwater, and thus must be vigorously prevented. When this does accidentally happen the valve slams shut and the engines immediately and forcefully suck air from inside all the boat's compartments. This causes a *vakuum* which, even if it only lasts a few *sekund*, is extremely painful to the ears of the crew, and can even rupture eardrums. So, you can see why utilizing our *shnorkel'* was impractical during these rough seas and why we needed to remain on the surface.

The unmerciful and incessant wave action resulted in many minor injuries and also many cases of *morskaya bolezn'* [seasickness], even among the veteran sailors.

Regardless of this particular gale, I must emphasize to you that the *Atlanticheskiy Okean* is very turbulent in general—which was no real surprise to us considering that it was *Oktyabr'*. In fact, stormy weather continued off and on for the rest of the voyage until we were well into the Sargasso Sea and nearing *Kuba*.

Moreover, before we approached *Kuba* the tail of a hurricane was going to catch us. It would make this storm that we were experiencing now, just south of the Faroe-Iceland Gap, seem relatively tame. I will describe to you our troubles with that hurricane a little later.

One day, shortly after young *Leitenant* Andreyev's unsuccessful attempt to surface *B-59* in the storm, I encountered him in the officers' wardroom at dinner—which is to say the midday meal. Officers and enlisted men ate in shifts, for neither the wardroom (just forward of the CC) nor the enlisted mess compartment (several spaces aft of the CC) could hold very many people at one time. Due to a fluctuation in the watch rotation there were, unusually, just the two of us this time—which encouraged Andreyev to talk more freely than he otherwise might.

The mess steward brought us our meals on trays from the galley, which was far aft in Compartment Four. Shall I tell you the *menyu*? We had *borscht*, pork with rice, vegetables, and a half-glass of *vino*. We had three full meals each day, and tea with cookies or pancakes at ten p.m. As in most navies, submariners generally received the best food in the navy as a small compensation for the arduous living and working conditions.

In addition to his duties as the boat's supply officer, at night when we were on the surface Andreyev was standing many bridge watches. As I mentioned earlier, this was in order to hone his skills in that aspect of our profession.

"Oh, *Kapitan* Arkhipov, I love being on the bridge in the fresh air. Yesterday we were accompanied by a group of tuna fish for at least an hour. They were actually able to keep up with us. I am amazed they have the strength. They only dive in for a second and then surface again with a powerful push. And I saw a flying fish for the first time in my life." He smiled. "I was just telling my wife and daughter about it." I looked puzzled.

"*Da, ser*. My stateroom has three "families" sharing it. Photos of the OSNAZ radio officer's wife and daughter are under the glass of the desk, pictures of the assistant *inzhener*'s wife and two little boys are on the bulkhead, and photos of my wife and daughter are on my headboard." I had to smile.

"But, *Kapitan*, right now the boat's pitching and rolling is terrible. It is all we can do to stay on course and make headway. And it seems like everyone is feeling very funny. Most are finally past being actually seasick, but are now simply tired-out by all the tossing. As I am sure you know very well yourself, I do not think anyone is getting good rest—you have to hold onto something even in your sleep, or else you will fall out of your bunk. And it does not matter whether we are in a gale or not; the ocean's surge alone can do it."

"It is very challenging, Anatoliy Petrovich," I replied. "We feel this more here than when we operate in the far north—in our usual patrol areas."

"*Da, ser.* And though I do like being on the bridge, we feel the waves and *sprey* continuously. Of course you know this—you are often up there. Most of the time the binoculars are of no use. Our eyes get so full of salt they hurt. In fact, the water is often whipped into a milky froth. It really crusts our eyes and noses with salt. Often the bridge is half-filled with water. You can dodge one wave, but not all. Even the rubber suits are not totally protective—we still have to dry our clothes after the watch! We have a salty taste in our mouths all the time, and there is no getting rid of it since you get to swallow a lot of it. And, unless you want to be thrown overboard with no chance of recovery, you must always keep your steel belt fastened to a clamp."

I just nodded, to encourage him to go on.

"You know, *Tovarishch Kapitan,* the smell I have come to hate most is rubber. I was not too crazy about it to begin with, but now—eewww! All the time we are up on the bridge we have to wear the rubber suits, and at times you cannot even enjoy the fresh sea air because of the rubber stench. Yesterday I revolted and came onto the bridge wearing just my raincoat. Twenty *minut* later I was soaked to the bone. I guess from now on I will have to suit up properly!"

CHAPTER 20

Well, again I must mention our requirement to try and make the passage within the timetable established by Moskva. Whatever the conditions, we had to maintain a fairly high average speed. As I have said this meant we had to sail on the surface as much as possible, *shtormy* or no *shtormy*. At least—and on the positive side—the rough seas, rough aviation weather, and the poor visibility all severely degraded the capability of the NATO ASW aircraft and helped to hide us. Yet, the rough seas were very hard on us and made our lives extremely difficult.

Comrade Listener, I cannot emphasize this enough! Much of the time we were, in fact, absolutely *neschastnyy* [miserable]. Of particular concern was the strong current which for days steadily pushed on our starboard side. This caused the boat to roll as much as forty and even fifty degrees. And the associated pitch and yaw forced us to go very slowly—only six to eight knots—versus a normal surface speed of perhaps fifteen knots. You can visualize this, my friend, as we occasionally faced wave heights as much as fifteen *metry*!

But not for a moment could we forget the time schedule. Again, this problem—this incredible *problema*—was the requirement that we must reach Mariel by *Oktyabr'* 20th even though we left Sayda Bay on *Oktyabr'* 1st. This was worse than the first proposed timetable, which estimated that we could reach the Caicos Passage, as we approached the Caribbean Sea, by the 26th or 27th of *Oktyabr'*. That had been the original plan until the time was advanced by the high command.

This meant that we needed to achieve an average speed of twelve knots throughout the voyage. A FOXTROT's maximum surfaced speed was sixteen knots, and perhaps twelve submerged. But those are ideal numbers. They assume calm sea-states, all equipment working perfectly, and no reconnaissance aircraft in pursuit.

We were traversing the *Atlanticheskiy Okean* with winter upon us. We were facing heavy seas and we were going to face more as the days passed. And also, after we escaped the heavy gale I told you about, we could only run on the surface in the darkness of the night to avoid detection from aircraft.

Realistically, we were only able to do seven or eight knots underwater.

As my friend Captain Ketov had pointed out back in Sayda Bay, a surface ship might well be able to sail from Pol'arnyi to Mariel in about eighteen days. This would mean steadily cruising above the waves for the entire transit and not being concerned about being detected. In fact, two *Sovetskiy* merchant ships carrying nuclear warheads for the missiles at *Kuba* had done this in *Sentyabr'*—but they had not faced winter weather.

It was another story entirely for a submarine to do this while proceeding with half its transit underwater—and trying to remain hidden. I later discovered that another draft plan had us departing on *Oktyabr'* 7th and arriving on *Noyabr'* 9th. Such a transit—around 32 days—may have been in the realm of possibility. But as you listen to my story you are realizing that is not what actually happened.

In short, for us—or Moskva—to depend upon an average speed of twelve knots was unrealistic. A voyage of twenty days was unrealistic.

Let me be even more clear: it was *nevozmozhno* [impossible].

CHAPTER 21

At the risk of wearing out your patience and losing your interest, Comrade Listener, I must tell you of another problem. I am sorry! I regret having to display to you all these frustrating challenges which we faced.

This other major *problema* was in the realm of trying to communicate with our superiors back in the *Sovetskiy Soyuz*. And within that was our enormous need for *informatsiya* as to what was going on in world events. We also had severe challenges in communicating with the other boats in our *brigada*.

You should know that we had been ordered to conduct daily communication sessions with headquarters. This was not just with the headquarters of the *Severnyy Flot* but with headquarters in Moskva. Each boat was required to surface once per day at a minimum—and the proscribed time was when it was midnight in Moskva.

Well, the old and wise men at headquarters had apparently not realized that midnight in Moskva was mid-afternoon for us when we reached the western *Atlanticheskiy Okean*. Thus, in order to comply we had to surface in daylight. Obviously—well, obvious to you and me, Comrade Listener—daylight surfacing greatly increased the chances of our detection.

But, we had to do it. Otherwise we would expose ourselves to severe reprimand. And, as we soon found out, Moskva was usually not very forthcoming with important *informatsiya* for us. So we greatly feared missing a single session almost as much as we feared detection on the surface. We believed that we had to take the risk in order to hear what Moskva had to say—in case on any particular day they actually said something useful or important!

We did have a very thin whip antenna that, when we were just below the surface, we could raise up through the surface and receive messages—but not transmit. Using this system we were able to harvest some very low-frequency signals. However, the *signaly* had to be very strong for that to happen and that was often not the case. Thus, you are not surprised to know that we were mainly deaf when we were submerged.

We were further challenged in that we had to communicate with the other boats of our *brigada* using the ultra-high frequency net. On board the *B-4* the *komandir brigady*, Captain Agafonov, required daily radio checks. These were to be acknowledged by a coded clicking of the transmission key as each boat came to the surface to charge her *akkumulyatory*.

Thus, the *brigada*'s radio communications checks were extremely brief—radio "bursts" lasting mere *sekund*. But as I learned much later, even these brief bursts were often caught from many interception posts—from Norway to Great Britain to New England.

As I had mentioned earlier, *Sovetskiy Severnyy Flot* ships and submarines usually operated in the Barents and Norwegian Seas. There, almost all communications were done over ultra-short-wave, short-wave, and medium-wave radio frequencies. In those high latitudes the Arctic's magnetic storms and the

Northern Lights caused sporadic radio interference, particularly during the winter. Usually such *interferentsiya* was only temporary. However, those high-latitude communication challenges were nothing—mere trifles—compared to what we had to face in the *Severnyy Atlanticheskiy Okean*.

Of course, Comrade Listener, we were not fools! We certainly knew that the farther we traveled from our *Severnyy Flot* bases the more difficult communications were going to be. However, as we proceeded south from the Iceland-Faroe line, we essentially found ourselves in a radio *vakuum*. We could not reach Moskva on either short or medium wavelengths, leaving us with just long-wave channels of communication. *Severnyy Flot* stations were completely blocked with radio *interferentsiya*. A significant number of days presented us with no audible voices—other than civilian fishermen out of Murmansk! We desperately tried to find ways out of this unsatisfactory *situatsiya*.

Our communications with our Naval General Staff could only be kept *sekret*—or at least relatively *sekret*—using low-power transmissions. Our fifteen-kilowatt transmitter's antenna had to be dried off for fifteen to twenty *minut* before sending or receiving a message. Exposed on the surface of the sea, we just did not have this kind of time! Spending that kind of time in daylight was an impossible option facing the growing NATO and *Amerikanskiy* ASW efforts as they realized something was going on. And sometimes we had to retransmit the same message twenty or thirty times before we achieved success! You can see how this increased the odds that we might be tracked.

Inevitably, as the days passed and as we progressed to the south, the NATO forces obtained multiple "fixes" on our transmissions. They began to develop reasonably good confidence regarding our general position.

After a while we did find a partial solution that helped our sending and receiving radio communications. To a small degree we were able to predict and adapt to the fluctuations of radio *interferentsiya*, finding moments of clear air and sending messages during those "cracks."

Leitenant Orlov and his special OSNAZ group worked on these challenges for many days. They were assisted by *Leitenant* Rodzyenko and his men of *B-59*'s regular Communications Department—*BCh-4*. Thus, I can tell you that while solid progress in communicating with headquarters remained elusive, we did make headway in gaining insights as to *Amerikanskiy* and NATO activity.

In particular, Orlov gathered an enormous amount of *informatsiya* through radio interceptions. This is where the OSNAZ group began showing its worth to the mission and gaining some solid respect from Captain Savitskiy and the crew—and from me, to be frank. They were able to listen-in on NATO ultra-short-wave and short-wave frequencies, translate the interceptions from *Angliyskiy* [English], *Norvezhskiy* [Norwegian], or *Datski* [Danish] into *Russkii*, and then present solid reports to Savitskiy and myself.

This was made easier at this time because—and as we expected—the U.S. Navy and the other NATO navies sent almost all of their radio communications via unencrypted open text. That is to say, "in the clear." This was particularly the case regarding shore-based ASW aircraft guided by on-shore stations, as well as the ships belonging to the ASW aircraft-carrier groups.

Later on, after we reached the latitudes of the Azorean Islands and then moved more directly southwest toward *Kuba*, we started to receive and listen to *Amerikanskiy* commercial radio. When Orlov began to correlate commercial radio news, the communications between ASW units, and then the infrequent communiqués from our own headquarters, we realized we had some good operational intelligence to work from.

To an extent we were able to analyze where and when the NATO ASW assets were deployed. We gained a feel for their activities and routines as well as the directions and orders given to their commanders. We were able to gain some sense of the unfolding *situatsiya* in the Caribbean Sea.

Comrade Listener, this was incredibly helpful to us!

As you know, when *Leitenant* Orlov and his men came on board *B-59* they were greeted with suspicion and, to a degree, open hostility by the captain and crew. They were perceived as members of the KGB or, at the least, as interlopers and outsiders. Needless to say, as time passed they became viewed in a much different light.

I have already told you that we departed Sayda Bay with a scarcity and deficiency of *informatsiya*. We all felt this very keenly on board the *B-59*—particularly *Kapitan* Savitskiy and myself. I have no doubt this was also felt by the *komandir brigady* and the captains of the other boats in the *brigada*. We were all very concerned—may I even say extremely nervous—

that there was a great deal transpiring in the world about which we knew far too little.

In all military organizations, but perhaps the *Sovetskiy* system even more so, *informatsiya* is held very closely. *Secretnost'* often spawns more *secretnost'*. Even those who really need to know something often have *informatsiya* withheld until the last possible moment.

We felt, keenly, not only the lack of tactical *informatsiya* but also our ignorance of the strategic situation. Did I mention that we had actually received no communications from *Severnyy Flot* headquarters for the first fourteen days after we departed Sayda Bay? Incredible, but true.

Our appetite and desire for *informatsiya* was enormous—it was all-consuming. What is going on in the world? What is happening in *Kuba*? Has our mission changed? Has our destination changed? Is war imminent? What if war has actually broken out? Is there actual conflict with the *Amerikantsy*?

Would we not need to know these things—ASAP—as soon as possible, as the *Amerikantsy* like to say?

As each day passed, *Leitenant* Orlov and his men—as well as B-59's *Leitenant* Rodzyenko and his men—felt enormous pressure to fill in the answers.

CHAPTER 22

Enjoying relatively calm seas for a few days, we finally approached the Azorean Islands from the west on *Oktyabr'* 15, 1962. That morning I accompanied *Kapitan* Savitskiy to the Forward Torpedo Room. Dmitriy Konstantinovich Pavlov, our "special weapon officer," had respectfully requested the *komanduyushchiy ofitser* to come forward and he, in turn, asked me to come with him.

As we slid through the small, round watertight doorway and landed on our feet with the grace born of many years of practice, *Kapitan-Leitenant* Pavlov called the compartment to attention and formally greeted us. Savitskiy nodded at the two men working around the equipment and waved at them to carry on with their duties.

"*Dobroye utro, Tovarishch Spetsial'noye Oruzhiye Ofitser.* You wanted to see me?"

"*Da, Tovarishch Kapitan.* Good morning to you! I need to inform you that since we left Sayda Bay none of the crew are bringing cots up here and are sleeping elsewhere. Moreover there is rarely anyone in here doing any work."

"*Interesno,*" replied Savitskiy, "and yet is this not how you and your *starshiy ofitser* wanted it? You wanted to sleep with your prized possession and wanted virtually no other access to it. By your rules only you, myself, *Kapitan* Arkhipov, the *starpom,* my *ofitser torpedy*, and a couple of torpedomen are supposed to enter here for the duration of the mission."

"But *Kapitan*," said Pavlov, "if we have battle stations or a *torpeda* emergency, so few men here at any given moment will adversely impact response time."

"You have a point, *Tovarishch*," said Savitskiy. "But you cannot eat your cake and have it also. For fear of *sabotazh*—or whatever—you have ordered severely restricted access to the compartment. In my assessment, in case of emergency, there are always plenty of men in Compartment Two on the other side of this bulkhead who can quickly respond."

"The other issue," I interjected, "is the fear of possible radiation emanating from your *torpeda*. The men in this boat are untrained in nuclear weapons—or nuclear reactors—but all have heard frightening stories and rumors." I did not mention that, for myself, memories of the actual radiation horror I experienced onboard the *K-19* were still all too fresh.

"*Tovarishch Nachal'nik Shtaba*," Pavlov replied, "the nuclear warhead is completely safe. I myself am unconcerned with sleeping up here."

"How nice for you. But you are not qualified in submarines, Dmitriy," said Savitskiy, "and thus my submariners do not feel any bond with you, nor any confidence in your opinions." He paused, thinking.

"Nevertheless," he continued, "if you can persuade any of my torpedomen that it is safe, and if you lift your security restrictions from this compartment, I will certainly encourage them to repopulate it."

Pavlov, in turn, thought for a moment. *"Da, Tovarishch Kapitan.* Thank you."

Savitskiy met my gaze, and turning away from Pavlov, smiled. *"Tak derzhat'* [Carry on], Dmitriy Konstantinovich." Savitskiy and I bent ourselves double to exit the hatch and then walked back to the CC.

I mentioned that the *B-59* and our *brigada's* other three boats—at least as far as we knew—had now reached the approaches to the Azorean Islands. This actually was a little farther east than we had planned to be, or wanted to be. You will recall that shortly after we emerged from the Faroe-Iceland line and into the northern *Atlanticheskiy Okean* we were particularly concerned about the strong current—which for days steadily pushed on our starboard side. This of course was the North Atlantic Drift which stems from the Gulf Stream. As you may know, once the *Gol'fstrim* flows north up the eastern seaboard of the United States and Canada, it then crosses the *Severo-Atlanticheskiy Okean* in an easterly direction with remarkable strength.

We certainly were aware that this current was working against us and we made efforts to compensate for this eastwards set. Alas, we did not compensate forcefully enough. This is somewhat embarrassing to admit, we being professional sea officers in the navy of a great power. Not to make excuses, Comrade Listener, but people at sea in unpleasant conditions are rarely as efficient as they think they are—or as they might be in kinder circumstances.

So now the *brigada* significantly altered course, essentially west-southwest—as opposed to the southwest-by-south heading we had attempted since passing the Faroe Islands. Now free of the easterly push of the *Gol'fstrim*, we were confident that this heading would efficiently bring us to *Kuba* in a very direct line.

The next morning the officer-in-charge of the Special Purpose Radio Interception Unit, *Leitenant* Orlov, came into the CC and approached *Kapitan* Savitskiy and me.

"*Dobroye utro, Tovarishch Kapitan; dobroye utro, Tovarishch Nachal'nik Shtaba.*"

"Good morning, *Tovarishch Podslushivaniye Ofitser.*"

"*Ser*, starting today I have been monitoring the *Amerikanskiy* "Voice of America" on their *Russkiy* language channel. I have also started listening to the British Broadcasting Corporation's radio programs and the *Amerikanskiy* "Radio Free Europe.""

"Very good! Have you heard anything of *interes?*"

"*Da, Kapitan.* They are reporting that a few days ago a war, or at least an altercation, began between China and India. Chinese troops opened fire on Indian troops along a section of the border. India reported twenty-four initial casualties, while the Chinese admit to thirty. I will continue to search for more *informatsiya* on this issue."

"*Interesno.* What else?"

"Well, *ser*," Orlov began with a smile, "today the *N'yu-York Yankiz* beat the *San-Frantsisko Giganty*, winning the World Series four games to three! The players included Willie Mays, Yogi Berra, Roger Maris, and Mickey Mantle."

"Really, Orlov," I said, laughing. "You are an American *beysbol poklonnik* [fan] it would appear."

"*Da, Kapitan* Arkhipov. Ever since I was a boy living in the United States when my father was stationed there."

"Orlov," said Savitskiy with a sigh. "Was there anything else, political or military, in the *Atlantika* area, or in the *Karibskiy*, or in *Yevropa?*"

"No, *Tovarishch Kapitan*, not at this time."

However, Comrade Listener, something terribly important had just occurred—but it was classified at the very highest levels of the *Amerikanskiy* government, so of course the "Voice of America" had no knowledge of it and certainly we would have no knowledge of it until very far in the future. On the fourteenth of *Oktyabr'*, flying a high-altitude *Amerikanskiy* Lockheed U-2 reconnaissance aircraft, an Air Force colonel named Richard Heyser took 928 *fotografii* over San Cristóbal, *Kuba*. These pictures revealed that at least four *Sovetskiy* missile launchers, capable of firing the *SS*-4 SANDAL medium-range ballistic nuclear missile, had been placed in western *Kuba*. Other flights would soon locate 42 nuclear missiles in ten sites. Mr. Arthur Lundahl, the *direktor* of the *Amerikanskiy* National Photographic Interpretation Center, so informed Mr. John McCone, the *direktor* of the CIA. Mr. McGeorge Bundy, the U.S. National Security Advisor, in turn notified *Prezident* John F. Kennedy. Mr. Kennedy directed thirteen key military, political, and diplomatic figures to assemble as the Executive Committee of the National Security Council—the ExComm—to advise him on what appeared to be a crisis of the greatest magnitude.

On *Oktyabr'* 18th *Prezident* Kennedy and U.S. Secretary of State Dean Rusk met, at the White House, with *Sovetskiy* Foreign *Ministr* Andrei Gromyko and *Sovetskiy* Ambassador to the

U.S. Anatoliy Dobrynin. For his part, Gromyko told Kennedy that *Sovetskiy* operations in *Kuba* were purely defensive and non-threatening. Kennedy did not choose to tell Gromyko that he positively knew that *Sovetskiy* offensive nuclear missiles were in position.

It *was* a crisis of the greatest magnitude. The *Amerikantsy* had finally discovered *Prem'yer* Khrushchev's *Operatsiya Anadyr'*, and thus finally noticed that a hedgehog had indeed been thrown down their pants.

The "Cuban Missile Crisis" had now begun in earnest.

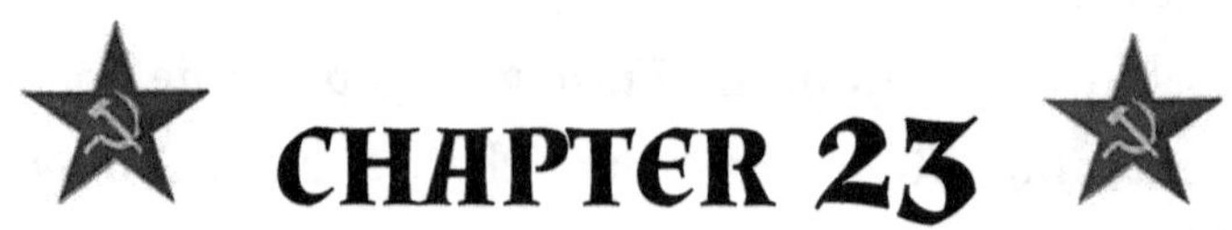

CHAPTER 23

As I just said, hardly anyone in the world actually knew what was going on at that time—and certainly we in the *Voyenno-Morskoy Flot 69 Torpeda Podvodnaya Brigada* were among those ignorant masses. Comrade Listener, I have only told you so that you are aware of the world *situatsiya* and sequence of events at that time.

In any event we shortly came to our new heading of west-southwest and left Azorian waters. We then found an issue presented by Nature that was going to fully occupy our attention for a few days. You already know that we had previously suffered through a Force-Nine gale just to the south of the Faroe Islands. Well now, as luck would have it, we sailed right into part of a Category-Three hurricane.

In the middle of *Oktyabr'*—let us say approximately *Oktyabr'* 14th—an upper-level "low" developed across the Turks and Caicos Islands, which are about 160 *kilometrov* north of Haiti and the Dominican Republic. Then a tropical depression developed and moved northward. A day after forming it intensified into a tropical storm which was officially named *Ella*. It began a track to the northwest, located east of a weakening upper-level trough. On *Oktyabr'* 17th *Ella* strengthened further and became a hurricane. This *uragan* turned to the east-northeast on *Oktyabr'* 19th, and later that day *Ella* attained its peak intensity of

185 *kilometrov* per hour—that is, 115 miles per hour. This made it the strongest *uragan* of the season. It gradually weakened over cooler waters while accelerating to the northeast, and its "eye" grew to an unusually large *diametr* of 150 *kilometrov*. *Ella* became "extratropical" on *Oktyabr'* 22nd over the northern *Atlantika* as it interacted with an approaching cold front. Shortly thereafter its remnants moved over Newfoundland before dissipating on *Oktyabr'* 23rd.

Fortunately we did not bear the full brunt of *Ella*, nor the full duration. But, my friend, what we did bear was bad enough.

We were cursed that this happened to us but blessed that essentially only the hurricane's tail caught us. As a result we did not face the 115 mile per hour winds. However, for several days we did fight winds approaching 100 mph. Similar to the earlier Force-Nine gale we endured, we now encountered seas that were whipped up to amazing heights. Indeed, to heights that had to be called mountainous. As before, we felt it safest—or at least most practical—to ride it out on the surface. You can imagine the boat's motion—continuously swinging, jerking, rocking, rolling, and swaying. The crew struggled to move around, staggering, crawling, pushing and pulling themselves to their duty stations, to their berths, and to their mess compartments. Meals were difficult with the likelihood of losing them on the green linoleum-covered deck—either by spillage or by vomit.

Once again the crew—the hardened *veterany* as well as the fairly new recruits—became very seasick with the terrible and violent motion as the sea leaped, boiled, and foamed. We were all hurled to the deck, tossed up toward the overhead, and relentlessly thrown around. Sleeping was difficult, requiring extensive efforts to wedge and strap oneself into one's bunk in order not to be frequently thrown out.

We all were miserable, but the poor souls on the rotating bridge watch were particularly affected. At one moment the *B-59* was bodily tossed into the air, and then next briefly buried under tons of water. The wind howled, whistled, and whined incessantly. The watch standers were steadily scourged by the stinging *sprey*. Everyone scrupulously ensured his steel safety belt was securely clipped to the boat at all times. The wind and *sprey* tore at our rubber suits, cut our faces, and constantly worked to tear off our goggles.

Occasionally, during the nights, the storm lost a little of its violence—but invariably came back strongly as day broke.

In the passageway one morning, coming off bridge watch, *Leitenant* Andreyev told me that for the first time in his career he had been covered by such huge masses of water his ears actually hurt under the pressure.

"*Kapitan* Arkhipov, how magnificent the ocean is when it is angry! It is all white. I believe I have seen some serious *shtormy* in my life but never anything more incredible and beautiful as this. The sea is not simply all covered in whitecaps—the whole surface is white! It makes me think of Maxim Gorky's *Song of the Stormy Petrel*: 'the valiant Stormy Petrel proudly wheels among the lightning, o'er the roaring, raging ocean, and his cry resounds exultant.'"

"It is quite something, Anatoliy Petrovich," I replied, "the boat looks like a tiny goldfish next to the monstrous waves. There cannot even be any comparison."

Well, Comrade Listener, it was truly terrible. Yet we managed to survive. And though it seemed to be an eternity, it was only three days—thank God!

No one had received any serious injury. The wind and sea calmed themselves and, for the brief moments we could now expose ourselves on the surface in daytime, the sun blessed us with some light and warmth. The crew slowly tried to recover from the ordeal. However, poor *B-59* herself was not entirely as fortunate. Upon thoroughly inspecting the boat we found that the *shnorkel'* had been damaged, several exterior rubber hatch seals were cracked and some even torn, and the *dizel'* cooling systems were caked and blocked with crusted salt from the high-velocity seawater *sprey.* This last item was very serious, for we could not fully deal with it in the open sea, and it began to cause the *dizel'* engines and the *elektricheskiy kompressory* to sporadically malfunction—and periodically break down.

In truth, all of this damage was very serious, and we would very much regret it just in a few days' time.

CHAPTER 24

s I have mentioned to you already, my friend, our *Projekt-641* submarines were designed for anti-surface ship and anti-submarine warfare *operatsii* in northern latitudes. They—and their crews—were not equipped nor prepared for tropical waters. The equipment was not built for high water-salinity nor *tropicheskiy temperatura*.

Sadly, we were truly not prepared to deal with the factors of climate in this more southern region of the *Atlantika*. I have no doubt that the "Department of Navigation and Oceanography of the Ministry of Defense of the Soviet Union" was very knowledgeable of these factors and other hydrographic phenomena— as well as relevant procedures to be used to cope with these conditions. Unfortunately, we were not provided with any written material from them nor any instructions on the subject prior to our departure.

As we approached the Sargasso Sea, somewhat to the northeast of Bermuda, we sharply felt a change in *klimat*. The *Sargassovo More* is a region of the *Atlanticheskiy Okean* bound by four major currents rather than by actual land boundaries. It is distinguished by its characteristic brown Sargassum seaweed and often calm and very blue water. It lies between 70° and 40° West, and 20° to 35° North, and is approximately 700 by 2,000 miles in size. The water is distinctive for not only its deeply blue color but also its exceptional clarity, with underwater visibility as deep as 60 *metry*. Here, the rough weather that had chased us for much of our voyage to date was replaced by calm seas and increasingly high water *temperatura*. Even when we were as deep as 50 *metry* we began to record *temperatura* as much as 83 degrees *Farengeyt!*

As we continued farther into the *Sargassovo More* we got to the point where we were all constantly sweating in the extraordinary heat, humidity, and stuffy conditions. We quickly started to long for the cold of the Arctic and of Pol'arnyi! Such thoughts would have been laughable just two weeks earlier as we looked forward to the warmth of the Caribbean!

Of course, Comrade Listener, this change initially brought us delight. But this was only briefly felt and was rapidly replaced by alarm as we began to struggle against the terrible air *temperatura* inside the boat—and the concurrent exhaustion of the crew. Heat became an enemy instead of a welcome friend—which initially warmed us considering the Arctic beginning of our voyage. You may find this hard to believe, but interior *temperatura* of the boat soon reached one-hundred degrees of *Farengeyt*, with the engine compartments twenty to forty degrees higher. High humidity made conditions very much worse as it reached ninety percent and even more. Men began to present *simptomy* of heat exhaustion. At the same time, the increase of heat and humidity began to affect the performance of some of the boat's equipment.

For fear of the increasing ASW threats being brought to bear by the *Amerikantsy*, we simply could not spend much time on the surface trying to blow cooler air through the boat. While submerged and using our damaged *shnorkel'* we could pull in very little air to cool the aft compartments—most of the *shnor-kel*'s air went directly to the *dizel'* engines. While submerged and running on *akkumulyatory* there of course was no intake of fresh air at all.

I must also mention that none of our boats carried sufficient fresh water for an operation of this length. We had taken on board extra water at Sayda Bay but it appeared not to have been enough. We began to worry we did not have what was needed to reach *Kuba*. Had we been able to reach Mariel by *Oktyabr'* 20th, as our unrealistic orders specified, it might have been "o.k." But, we were not going to make it on that timetable. And, unlike modern submarines, the *tekhnologiya* of the day allowed us to distill very little fresh water from seawater.

Soon conditions became horrible with the heat, humidity, and the stink of many things—but mostly the stink of sweat, *akkumulyator* gases, *dizel'* fuel, and *dizel'* exhaust.

CHAPTER 25

As you very well know, Comrade Listener, each of our boats had one of those special nine-man signals-intelligence teams on board. I am sorry if I repeat myself! Anyway, while we were on the surface, or just below with our masts raised above the water, our team had been monitoring NATO and U.S. Navy radio frequencies—particularly after we reached the latitudes of Bermuda and then the Bahamas. At this point we learned that the *Amerikantsy* were apparently aware of our *brigada*'s existence as well as one or two other *Sovetskiy* boats elsewhere in the *Atlanticheskiy Okean*. We also learned that ASW units were greatly increasing their efforts to find us.

As he was able to collect information and listen to *Amerikanskiy* military and commercial transmissions, *Leitenant* Orlov had begun briefing *Kapitan* Savitskiy and me several times per day.

On the afternoon of *Oktyabr'* 20th he reported to us in the officers' wardroom. Savitskiy mopped his streaming forehead with a handkerchief and motioned Orlov to sit.

"*Tovarishch Kapitany*, I just heard more about the China-India *konflikt* I told you about earlier. A force of 30,000 Chinese troops stopped the Indian invasion and overran the outnumbered Indian force in the disputed area."

"*Interesno, Leitenant*. What else?"

"*Ser*, it appears that the *Soyedinennyye Shtaty* and the *Sovetskiy Soyuz* just conducted high-altitude nuclear weapons tests, both of which apparently had been previously scheduled and announced."

"What!?" Savitskiy exclaimed.

"*Da, ser.*" The *Amerikantsy* tested a weapon 146 *kilometrov* over somewhere in the Pacific Ocean, and we tested one 150 *kilometrov* over Kazakhstan."

"Strange," I said. "But I do not think that has anything to do with the operation in which we seem to be caught."

Orlov's news the next morning was not as exciting. The *Amerikanskiy* spacecraft *Ranger 5*, meant to take and transmit *fotografii* of the lunar surface, apparently malfunctioned and ceased operating when 725 kilometers from the *luna*. And the 1962 "World's Fair" closed in the *Amerikanskiy* city of Seattle after running for six months.

However, *Leitenant* Orlov caught the most incredible news on the evening of *Oktyabr'* 22nd. Finding all *Amerikanskiy* commercial channels clearing their usual *programmirovaniye*, he then heard *Prezident* John F. Kennedy make an extraordinary announcement in a nationally and internationally broadcast address. Orlov brought his notes into the CC and anxiously motioned Savitskiy and me to go forward with him to the captain's stateroom. Savitskiy sat down at his desk, I sat on his bunk, but Orlov was too excited to sit anywhere.

"*Kapitany*, using television and radio, *Prezident* Kennedy told his entire country—and thus the entire world—that 'unmistakable evidence has established the fact that a series of offensive missile sites' have been placed in *Kuba* by the *Sovetskiy Soyuz* 'to provide a nuclear-strike capability against the Western Hemisphere' using 'large, long-range, and clearly offensive weapons of sudden mass destruction.'"

"Kennedy then announced that the *Soyedinennyye Shtaty* was going to immediately impose 'a strict quarantine on offensive military equipment under shipment to *Kuba*,' and warned that any launch of a nuclear weapon from *Kuba* would require 'a full nuclear retaliatory response upon the *Sovetskiy Soyuz*.' Kennedy closed by saying that 'I call upon Chairman Khrushchev to halt and eliminate this clandestine, reckless, and provocative threat to world peace and to stabilize relations between our nations. I call upon him further to abandon this course of world domination.'"

Savitskiy slowly reached out his hand and Orlov gave him the sheet of paper. The *leitenant* said, "*Kapitan*, I can bring you the entire text in a few minutes as soon as I check my *Angliyskiy* and type it up." Savitskiy merely nodded, carefully reading the handwritten notes. Orlov came to attention, slid open the thin wooden door of the stateroom, and headed back to his radio room. I closed the door and looked over at Savitskiy, who now was staring at me. He handed me the notes.

"So, Vasiliy, what a remarkable *situatsiya*," he said. "We just happen to be on a *sekret* mission, supporting some *sekret operatsiya* about which we know almost nothing. We just happen to have a special radio-intelligence unit on our boat, and it just happens to monitor *Amerikanskiy* commercial radio stations as well as their military and naval frequencies."

"And, at least one of our *radisty* just happens to be completely fluent in *Angliyskiy*. Thus, and I am humiliated to think of it, we learn of this incredible thing from *Amerikanskiy* commercial radio—not from our own leaders or our own government. We learn details about a significant deployment of *Sovetskiy* nuclear weapons and troops to *Kuba*, and an imminent forthcoming *Amerikanskiy* naval blokada around *Kuba*."

I had nothing to say. Truly I was as confused, humiliated, and angry as Savitskiy. Well, perhaps not quite as angry, but certainly confused.

In fact, it only got worse the next day as Orlov reported that *Amerikanskiy* news stations were unofficially discussing a possible *Amerikanskiy* invasion of *Kuba*—and that one broadcast mentioned that "special camps are being prepared in the Florida peninsula for Russian prisoners of war." Still another stated that over 200 ships of the U.S. Atlantic Fleet, their many associated aircraft, and perhaps as many as 200,000 *Amerikanskiy* service personnel were preparing for a *konfrontatsiya*.

More than one source informed its listeners that the *Sovetskiy* freighter *Poltava* would be the first ship that would reach the *Amerikanskiy* quarantine line.

Orlov spent some time with us discussing several possible translations of the *Angliyskiy* word "quarantine" and its usage in this situation. We concluded that it apparently did mean a naval *blokada*—which by international definition and agreement was an act of war.

CHAPTER 26

Comrade Listener, another important thing occurred right at this time which had remarkable effects upon our *brigada*. As you know—because I have been complaining to you about it incessantly—we had received virtually no communications from *Severnyy Flot* headquarters since the voyage began, and we had received precious little from headquarters in Moskva. But now we received a message from Moskva—and it was crucially significant!

The message came in as a very low-frequency broadcast, running for several *minut*. Because of the extremely narrow bandwidth this type of signal did not carry audio—that is to say, voice—but rather only *tekst* messages and even that at a very slow rate. When the message had finished printing out on the teletype, the *B-59's* communications officer—*Leitenant* Rodzyenko—brought it forward to *Kapitan* Savitskiy in the CC. Savitskiy skimmed through it, caught my eye, and motioned me to follow him over to the *navigatsiya* station. Once we had pulled the heavy canvas and rubber curtain around us and the plotting table, he handed the Cyrillic-scripted pages to me. The message was addressed to all four of the boats in our *brigada* and had come from the main Navy Staff. It was entitled "Operational Secret: Modification of Orders." After listing page and paragraph numbers of our original orders which we, of course, had carried from Sayda Bay, this *modifikatsiya* quickly got down to business:

> 69 *Torpeda Podvodnaya Brigada* will modify its track from the original orders.
>
> Submarines *B-4*, *B-130*, and *B-59* will now deploy in a barrier due north of the entrance to Turks Island Passage and take up combat positions in the *Sargassovo More*. The named submarines will not, repeat not, proceed through the narrow sea-lanes of the Turks and Caicos Islands.
>
> In the separate case of Submarine *B-36*: It is directed that *B-36* will proceed via the Silver Bank Passage between Grand Turk Island and Hispaniola Island.

I turned the teletype paper over looking for more *informatsiya* and found...nothing. I looked up at Savitskiy in surprise, who met my gaze with a humorless smile. "That is all there is, Vasiliy. What do the *Britantsy* say? *Korotko i sladko* [short and sweet]? This must be in reaction to Kennedy's broadcast and his declaration of quarantine."

"Do you think Moskva knows something specific about the *Amerikanskiy* deployments?" I asked. "Perhaps they believe the ASW risk has become too great in those narrow sea-lanes. But then why send *B-36* into the Silver Bank Passage? According to the chart it is somewhat wider but relatively shallow. It would not be very safe if there is a robust ASW presence in the passage."

"Perhaps we are to escort some of the *Sovetskiy* merchant ships still *en route* to *Kuba*? That was not part of our original mission but it might be now."

"Who knows?" said Savitskiy, smacking the *navigatsiya* table. "I do know that it means we now pull back from where we are. If there ever was a chance, now there is absolutely no chance in hell of reaching Mariel Bay in *anything* like the time specified by orders. We already missed that 'required' date, and now we are going to miss it even more. By many days! And what do they mean, 'take up combat positions!?'"

I paused for a moment, turning it all over in my mind. "Well," I said, "surely there will be more forthcoming."

"Well," Savitskiy replied, "would it not be pretty to think so? Ah, the hell with it, Vasiliy. *Volkov boyat'sa—v les ne khodit* [Just because one fears wolves, is one not to go into the woods]?"

CHAPTER 27

Call it what you will, on the morning of *Oktyabr'* 24th the U.S. Navy's *karantin*, or *blokada*, went into effect. Orlov and his OSNAZ heard—again from *Amerikanskiy* commercial radio—that some of the *Kuba*-bound *Sovetskiy* freighters were altering course to avoid *konfrontatsiya*, while others were proceeding.

We also heard that the *Sovetskiy Soyuz* had launched a space vehicle called *Mars 2MV-4 No. 1*—which the *Amerikantsy* cleverly named SPUTNIK 22—with the intended mission of flying past the *planeta* Mars and transmitting back images to the earth.

As true *sotsialisticheskiye patrioty* we were very proud to hear of this incredible *tekhnologicheskiy* achievement of the *Rodina*. At the same time, as true *sotsialisticheskiye patrioty* and relative to our immediate circumstances, we wished we had more confidence in our military and political leadership.

The *B-59*, obeying orders, had changed course and was proceeding with the best possible speed to where Moskva wanted us—northeast of the entrance to the Turks Island Passage. We had passed the latitude of the Bahama Islands and were approaching the straits between the Greater Antilles Islands.

Thus, this change of course was almost a reverse, essentially taking us back in the direction from where we had already just come. On board *B-59*—and I assume on board our other boats—we were not convinced that this was a good thing. As every hour went by we became more and more aware that the *Amerikantsy* were massing ASW efforts in our area. It appeared that the entire *Nakat* frequency range was filled with *signaly* from surface ship and aircraft radars. You will recall that the *Nakat* was our electronic surveillance measures system?

Moreover, whenever we dared surface, or at least dared to use the *shnorkel'* with our radio masts also above the surface, we intercepted huge quantities of *Amerikanskiy* naval radio traffic. This traffic was increasing by the hour—mostly related to their ASW efforts.

It seemed very clear that the entire area, certainly including the positions to which Moskva had just directed us, was covered with a formidable web of surveillance. *Leitenant* Orlov and his team had positively identified three ASW "hunter-killer" groups having entered the southern *Sargassovo More*. These were centered around the *avianostsy* [aircraft carriers] USS *Essex*, USS *Wasp*, and USS *Randolph*. It appeared each carrier had around six to twelve *esmintsy* [destroyers] in its group, along with many fixed-wing aircraft and helicopters. And as if that were not enough of a threat, a considerable number of larger shore-based ASW aircraft was also systematically searching the area.

This tension and stress, on top of the acute physical *diskom-fort* of the incredible heat, humidity, and pervasive poor air, had us in a pretty miserable condition.

CHAPTER 28

As you might be able to guess, we were heading for an uncomfortable reckoning with the *Amerikantsy*. Comrade Listener, I promise you that I will shortly get to that part of my story, but first I would like to point out to you some *interesno* things you should know—even though none of us in our submarine *brigada* knew them at the time. We only learned of them months later.

By the time of *Prezident* Kennedy's famous television and radio speech to the *Amerikanskiy* people—on the evening of *Oktyabr'* 22nd—his Central Intelligence Agency had told him that they believed several *Sovetskiy* FOXTROT submarines were within six or seven days of reaching *Kuba*.

So then the head of the *Amerikanskiy* navy, Admiral George Anderson, signaled to his *flot* to be alert regarding possible surprise attacks by *Sovetskiy* submarines. I have read that he ended that message with "Good luck, George." Is that not remarkable? *Amerikantsy*! Such strange people. He used his forename in an official communication. It is hard for me to imagine the chief of the *Voyenno-Morskoy Flot* at that time, Admiral of the Fleet Sergey Georgyevich Gorshkov, closing an official message with "Good luck, Sergey!"

As a proud former Soviet officer, I am very pleased to tell you that their electronic discovery of our *brigada*'s incursion into the Atlantic profoundly shocked the *Amerikantsy*. Before this mission *Sovetskiy* submarines mostly operated in the Arctic Ocean, or the Black Sea, but not out in the *Atlanticheskiy Okean*. For that matter, until 1962, *Sovetskiy* naval forces in general rarely deployed beyond home waters. Individual *Sovetskiy dizel'-elektricheskiy* submarines had really only begun intermittent *Atlantika* patrolling in 1959.

Basically, since the Great Patriotic War, the *Voyenno-Morskoy Flot* had restricted its operations and training in support of our huge ground forces in Europe and Asia.

When the *Amerikantsy* realized we were in the greater *Atlanticheskiy Okean*, their surprise and concern was considerable. Admiral Robert Dennison, the *komandir* of the *Amerikanskiy* Atlantic Fleet—and a *podvodnik* [submariner] himself—said that "this was the first time Soviet submarines have ever been positively identified off our East Coast." He also said that this surely meant a "clear-cut Soviet intent to position a major offensive threat off American shores."

I must also tell you that at this time our four FOXTROTs of *69 Brigada* were not the only *Sovetskiy* submarines in the *Atlantika*—and not the only ones tracked by the *Amerikantsy*. For example, the *B-75*, which was a *Projekt-611*—ZULU Class—*dizel'-elektricheskiy* boat, had also been out, tasked to escort the merchant ship *Indigirka*. This she had done and they reached the Navetrenny Straits together at the Cape Verde Islands. The *Indigirka*, loaded with about ninety nuclear warheads, went on to Mariel Bay—arriving on October 4th. *B-75*, cruising to the north, was recalled by Moskva when the *Amerikanskiy prezident* announced his *blokada* around *Kuba*. On October 22nd she was detected by NATO antisubmarine forces while refueling near the Azorean Islands. In any event, by November 10th she had returned to Murmansk.

On the morning after *Prezident* Kennedy announced his *blokada*, Chairman Khrushchev ordered the missile-carrying freighters remaining at sea to reverse course. This left only a few civilian tankers and freighters still heading toward *Kuba*.

So, according to *Amerikanskiy* politicians and historians, we *Sovety* had "blinked"—regarding this "eyeball-to-eyeball" moment. A great many liked to refer to this part of the Crisis in those colorful terms. This was several days before what these same people like to call "Black Saturday"—October 27th—which became the most critical and tense day of the Crisis.

As it turned out it also became the most critical and tense day for *Sovetskiy* Submarine B-59.

However, it actually took the *Amerikantsy* in Washington a while to comprehend what was happening at the *blokada* line. And the course-reversal of such missile-carrying ships did not mean that the Crisis—and the danger—were over.

Oh, no, not at all.

Leitenant Orlov even heard the famous *Amerikanskiy* news man from television, Val'ter Cronkite, worry over the danger. I have since learned that for many years Mr. Cronkite was called "the most trusted man in America." On the evening of *Oktyabr'* 24th Orlov picked up Cronkite's broadcast on radio intercept. The OSNAZ man came up to the bridge and found Savitskiy, Chernyshev, and me. He reported, saying excitedly,

"*Tovarishchi Kapitany, Tovarishch Starpom,* you must listen to this intercept from *Amerikanskiy* commercial news!" Seeing he

had our full attention he quoted Cronkite from his yellow-lined
pad.

'It was beginning to look this day as though it might
be one of armed conflict between Soviet vessels and
American warships on the sea lanes leading to Cuba.
There is not a great deal of optimism tonight.'

CHAPTER 29

Well, Mr. Val'ter Cronkite's *pessimizm* notwithstanding, there was not much *optimizm* in B-59's wardroom that evening either. As it turned out, due to the duty rotations, once again I was having my supper with only my friend *Leitenant* Andreyev coming in to join me. He looked terrible—flushed and sweating with the now-constant high heat and humidity. I do not mean to be overly critical of the young man. We all looked terrible at this point and for the same reasons. However, Andreyev also looked as if he had been crying. He merely picked at his food which tonight was milk and rice *sup*, a huge portion of beef with noodles, some salted fish, caviar, a small can of juice, and some fruit. Terribly thirsty—at this point we were all thirsty all of the time—I focused on my *sup* and drank my juice. But I was not particularly hungry myself so I concentrated on an effort to cheer up Andreyev.

"Goodness, Anatoliy Petrovich, these are *gigantskiy* servings of meat, not to mention all the other things." I thought, since he was the supply officer, I would be on safe ground with this topic of conversation. I am afraid that I was mistaken. Andreyev stared at me for a moment, frustration and unhappiness alternately mixing in his expression.

"*Kapitan* Arkhipov I am so upset—I do not know what to do. As you know, with this horrible heat, we have been having problems with the freezers and refrigerators down below in the hold. This crazy heat is reaching even down there. The *temperatura* has been slowly but surely rising like everywhere else in the boat. The refrigerators are keeping things slightly cool—but not *cold*. And today the freezers are at 47 degrees *Farengeyt* instead of the 30 degrees they should be."

"You have had the *glavnyy inzhener* look at them?" I asked, though I knew very well that Captain Pugachev had worked on them repeatedly.

"*Da, ser.* I asked for assistance from the hold operators and then the *inzhener*. No one has been able to help. The *inzhener* says that higher-quality *mashiny* would be working better, but these units were ordered and installed during the boat's original construction with the idea that she would be kept in cold water environments."

What could I say? I just shook my head and picked at my plate.

"So, *Kapitan* Arkhipov, that is why I have increased the meat rations even though everyone is miserable and no one is hungry. But if we do not eat it soon, it will all be spoiled."

"And that is not the worst of it. When *Kapitan* Savitskiy found out about the freezers he called me to the CC and shouted at me in front of everyone. He said that I must be making the provisions go bad on purpose! It was terrible. He made me feel so low, as if I might be a saboteur or some sort of enemy of the *Rodina*."

"I am very sorry, Anatoliy," I replied. I had not been present for this *intsident* but I knew that it had happened. Savitskiy's nerves seemed to be fraying. In the last couple of days he had publically shouted at and berated a number of people, not just Andreyev. "Of course it is not your fault."

"I know, *Kapitan*, thank you. But what am I to do? The *komanduyushchiy ofitser* has become impossible to deal with. I am angry with him—but I also feel sorry for him."

"Listen to me, *Leitenant*," I said. Fortunately the heavy wardroom curtain was drawn, and we were speaking softly. "You must not criticize *Kapitan* Savitskiy to anyone on the boat. You could get in grievous trouble. You should not even speak to me about this." Andreyev looked startled, glanced at the curtain, and then nodded.

"Of course, *ser*. Forgive me for imposing upon your good will and our unofficial friendship."

"Very well," I replied. "All is good between us. Tell me, what are your other supply and provision concerns?"

"*Kapitan*, as you yourself know all too well everyone is thirsty. That is all everyone is talking about. I am thirsty! Obviously you are thirsty! We do not have enough fresh water so we have now had to severely *ratsion* it."

"I know, Anatoliy. And now that we are heading away from *Kuba* that issue will only become more critical." Two quarts per day per man, for drinking and cooking, was a minimal standard—and it was below minimum for the tropics. We were already far below that.

A diesel-electric submarine uses a lot of fresh water. In addition to being used for drinking it refills the main batteries, cools the main engines, cooks food and washes dishes and, if there is any left, cleans the crew. Of course we carried a great deal from Sayda Bay. We also could make some from seawater using compressor distillers. But the distillers were extremely noisy to run, so we operated them only when we were on the surface—yet even so they did not generate much quantity.

"Fortunately, *ser*, what we do have in fairly large quantity are cans of syrupy fruit compote. The men are drinking it at every meal even if they are not eating much. I have to keep the supply under lock and key for it needs to last us for quite a while longer, it seems."

"Good work, Anatoliy," I said. "*Molodets* [Well done]! You are doing a fine job—in addition to all the bridge and conning tower watches you have been standing. I know that *Kapitan* Savitskiy knows it too despite what he said to you." Andreyev just shrugged his shoulders.

"The Lord only knows how much longer all this is going to last," he replied, staring at the table. "I think the only ones who know are the ones who write the orders."

After Andreyev excused himself and went back to work, I decided to confer with the medical officer. I found him in the Forward Torpedo Room napping on a cot placed on top of a conventional *torpeda*. Apparently the *spetsial'noye oruzhiye ofitser* accepted his company, and apparently the *meditsinskiy ofitser* was not afraid of the special weapon itself.

"*Tovarishch Ofitserskiy Vrach*, may I consult with you for a moment?" Doctor-Major Stepan Yevgenyevich Kuryakin slowly opened an eye and then sat up. He rubbed his fingers through his closely cropped, reddish-blond hair.

"Of course, *Tovarishch Nachal'nik Shtaba*. How may I assist you?" I noticed that the special weapon officer seemed to be asleep on his own cot, so I motioned Kuryakin forward and we sat down in front of the torpedo-tube doors. I also noticed that it was significantly cooler here in Compartment One. Not cool, but cooler.

"Please tell me, *Tovarishch Doktor*, how do you medically assess our situation?"

"Well, *Tovarishch Kapitan*, I assess it as pretty rough," he replied. He took his eye glasses from a case and carefully put them on, considerably enlarging the appearance of his brown eyes. Kuryakin was not a naval officer, but rather a member of the Soviet Military Medical Directorate which served all branches of the armed forces. As a result his uniforms were of a distinctly military rather than naval appearance.

"Obviously the heat and humidity are at dangerous levels due to the high air *temperatura*, the high water *temperatura*, and the constant considerable heat our *mashiny* produce."

"We are all perspiring profusely which is dangerous considering we have far too little drinking water and are on severe rations. We all look as if we had just come out of a steam bath. By necessity most men are wearing nothing but shorts and sandals—although I have noticed that the officer-on-deck wears a uniform jacket for propriety's sake, and you senior officers are wearing your blue shirts." Kuryakin himself was in khaki shorts with a thin undershirt.

"You of course have noticed that most of the men are now shaving, and even shaving their heads, trying to stay cooler.

Obviously this is in contrast to the normal submarine practice of letting moustaches and beards grow out on long missions."

"What about heat exhaustion?" I asked.

"I am seeing cases of it. Just today three crewmen fainted from overheating. I am hamstrung to accurately assess it because there is no damn place on the boat to get good *temperatura*. Since no space is under one-hundred degrees *Farengeyt* all my thermometers read off-scale. By the way, as I am sure you know, the engineering and motor spaces are around 120 degrees. The men have to rotate out frequently."

"Quite a few men have swollen feet, there are *simptomi* resembling hives, and there are various rashes breaking out for which I am applying that bright green ointment you have no doubt seen on some of them."

"The other great *problema* is the air."

"*Bozhe moi!* Oh, my God, yes!" I exclaimed. "My head is bursting from the stuffy air and I am occasionally feeling dizzy, and I suppose everyone else is the same. On top of the damned heat and humidity, the compartments are incredibly stuffy. I assume that it is a combination of low oxygen and high carbon dioxide—with high CO_2 actually the greater *problema* of the two."

"*Da, ser*, most certainly," replied Kuryakin. "Even here in Forward Torpedo—where it is strangely somewhat cooler—the CO_2 is too high." I thought about that for a moment. Most people believe that the danger to a submerged submarine's crew is running out of oxygen. Very true, but a greater danger is the buildup of CO_2, which can be fatal in and of itself.

"So," I finally said, "you paint a dismal picture. In your opinion, what can be done to mitigate any of this?" The medical officer smiled while shaking his head.

"Come into port? Or surface for a long period of time, fully ventilate the boat, and allow the crew to frolic in the sea?" He actually laughed. "*Nyet, Kapitan*? Probably not? Well, I just do not know. And there is the acute fresh water problem which truly does require getting into port or replenishment from a supply ship."

"None of that seems at all possible in the foreseeable future," I said, "as we move away from *Kuba* and the *proklyatyy* [damned] *Amerikantsy* increase their ASW efforts by the *minut*."

"*Ser*, the only thing I can think of is for every man to sit still or, better yet, lie down when not actually working. And I know to surface the boat right now is to court *katastrofa*, but if we possibly could—even for short periods—to try and ventilate, it would be an incredible blessing."

I clapped Kuryakin on the arm and proceeded aft, entering Compartment Two. As I passed Savitskiy's stateroom on the boat's port side I noticed, through the partially open sliding door, that he was sitting on his bunk with his eyes closed. I rapped on the door and he motioned me in.

"*Chto novogo* [What's new], Vasiliy?" he said, rubbing his hands over his wet face. "Please sit at the desk."

"Well, Valentin, I had something to talk to you about. But *chto novogo* with you?"

"*Leitenant* Orlov just left. He brought me some cheery news." I looked at him expectantly.

"This morning the *Amerikanskiy* destroyers *Joseph P. Kennedy, Jr.* and the *John R. Pierce* boarded the *Sovetskiy*-chartered ship *Marcula* on the *Amerikanskiy* 'quarantine' line—640 *kilometrov* from *Kuba*. Apparently finding nothing on board that was *kontrabanda* in their eyes, they kindly allowed it to proceed."

"No actual shooting or sinking seems good," I replied. He looked at me blankly. Then he said, "One of Orlov's men thinks that the *Joseph Kennedy* is named for *Prezident* Kennedy's brother, who was killed in the Great Patriotic War."

"That is an *interesno* coincidence," I replied, "if it is a coincidence."

"Orlov also reported that there was a meeting of the United Nations Security Council. The *Amerikanskiy* ambassador, Stevenson, confronted our ambassador, Zorin, with *foto* of missile sites in *Kuba*. Stevenson asked, 'Do you, Ambassador Zorin, deny that the USSR has placed medium- and intermediate-range missiles in Cuba?' Stevenson then badgered Zorin. 'Answer me, yes or no? Do not wait for the translation—*da ili net?*'"

"Then what happened?" I asked, amazed.

"Orlov says Zorin apparently laughed and replied, 'I am not in an *Amerikanskiy* courtroom, *ser*, and therefore I do not wish to answer a question that is put to me in the fashion in which a prosecutor puts questions. In due course you will have your reply.'"

"Well, good for him," I laughed. "Zorin sounds like a great patriot."

"Maybe, Vasiliy, maybe," replied Savitskiy. "What did you want to talk about?"

"I was just speaking to the doctor. He has some *problemy* about the crew…"

"Yes. Yes, Vasiliy, I know about the doctor's *problemy*. He gave me a report earlier this morning. Even though I am afraid I was rude to him and cut him short, I agree with everything he says."

"*Tak* [So]. What are you thinking of doing?" I asked.

"As much as I fear it, we need to surface and ventilate. We are running too hot with the *shnorkel'* and getting no fresh air anyway. And perhaps the *radisty* can pull some communications from the *Rodina*. It is all very well to shape our world view and tactical decisions based on *informatsiya* that we glean from the *Amerikantsy*, but it would be nice to know if our own leaders want to share anything with us." I nodded in agreement.

"And, Vasiliy, the *akkumulyatory* are pretty well drained. We desperately have got to recharge in order to operate—or hide— while submerged."

Comrade Listener, I could only nod again.

CHAPTER 30

"*Trevoga! Trevoga!*" screamed the port-side lookout. "Aircraft! *Boyevaya tre—vo—ga* [Battle alarm]! Airplane dead ahead!"

"Clear the bridge!" shouted Captain Savitskiy. "Dive! Emergency dive!" The alarm bell rang and pealed with ear-splitting *intensivnost'* all throughout the boat. "Fifteen degrees angle—take her deep!"

We had only been on the surface for about an hour. During that time we had been able to ventilate the boat—but we had not cooled her *inter'yer* temperature worth mentioning.

And, critically, we had not been able to recharge the *akkumulyatory* to any significant degree.

Within seconds Savitskiy, the watch keepers, and the lookouts all leaped down the hatch, barely touching the steel ladder as they came down. They smacked the conning tower's deck plates with a frightful clatter, with most of them then continuing on down into the CC.

"Flood negative! Hard dive on the planes!"

The intercom suddenly came to life with a breathless voice from the radio-electronics compartment.

"*Vnimaniye* [Attention] Control Center! Detecting surface-search radar, believe it to be an *Amerikanskiy* AN/APS-44. Impulses bearing one-two-zero, getting stronger."

Seawater poured into the buoyancy tanks with an enormous roaring and gurgling. *Starshiye ofitsery* [Petty officers] hung from the valves' hand-wheels using their full body weights to speed the action. Other men frantically spun other wheels and closed and dogged water-tight hatches.

The boat started down, sharply, with other men grabbing for unsecured items which were falling about. Comrade Listener, you would not think that—after the violent storm and the hurricane which we had already been through—we would have anything left to break. Apparently we did, judging from the crashing noises coming from seemingly everywhere.

"Take a depth sounding and report," ordered Captain Chernyshev.

The sound technician flipped a couple of switches and then listened intently.

"*Ser*, the sea floor is at 5,140 *metry* below," he called out. Well, we certainly had no need to worry about being trapped in shallow water!

Once again the sound-powered phone came alive with the *radisty*. "Radio to CC—we must assume that the aircraft will activate a magnetic anomaly detection system against us, probably the *Amerikanskiy* AN/ASQ-8."

Well, Comrade Listener, what was going on?

Of course it was not known to us then, but now I can tell you that a U.S. Navy Martin *Marlin* SP-5B seaplane had sighted us. Based out of their *aerodrom* on Bermuda, this aircraft— amusingly named "Woodpecker Five"—was one of several belonging to their Patrol Squadron 49. Not only had it sighted us visually, with radar, and with its MAD system, but it now was going to maintain MAD *kontakt* with us for quite a while. We were not really concerned about its weapons *sistemy*—in fact we did not believe it had any. However, what this aircraft could do, and what it did do, was instantly report to the Bermuda ASW Task Group as well as the USS *Randolph*, flagship of the nearby Hunter-Killer ASW Task Group 83.2.

The Randolph was an *avianosets* [aircraft carrier] that we had detected a few *minut* ago while we were on the surface. I think I have already mentioned to you that we knew it was in our general vicinity. Unfortunately it was now sending several of its destroyers as well as a considerable number of its aircraft to our exact position.

Comrade Listener, we had just begun what was going to be an extremely unpleasant forty hours in the history of Soviet Submarine *B-59*.

Suddenly the boat dipped—violently. I grabbed a piece of railing to keep from falling down the conning tower hatch into the CC.

Just as suddenly, over the sound-powered phones, there was a scream from the bow. "*Kapitan!* The forward torpedo room hatch has not sealed! We are taking aboard water—*a lot of water!*"

In fact, *B-59* was not diving, she was sinking—bow first and very rapidly—with a thirty-degree angle. Captain Pugachev, the chief engineer, left the CC and darted forward.

Then there was another shout from the bow, this time on the intercom. "We are trying to stop the flow! Water volume considerable!"

The boat continued to go down. "Bow planes up!" Savitskiy shouted. "Hard rise on planes! Stand by to blow tanks."

Well, this was a terrible choice, Comrade Listener. Were we to sink and drown, or were we to "emergency surface" and face the *Amerikantsy*? I knew Savitskiy would attempt to surface only as a last resort. We could try some other things first.

You might remember that several rubber hatch seals had cracked and some had even broken during our extreme ordeal with Hurricane *Ella*. We had made replacements and repairs as best as we could and they had seemed to be sufficient—until now.

The needles on the depth gauges—one in the CC and one in the conning tower—continued their frightening sweep marking our descent: 50 *metry*, 60, 80, 110 *metry*. Then, suddenly, the bow rose and we momentarily attained an even keel.

But then the bow dipped again, jerked up, rose slightly and then radically dipped. Once more *B-59* sank! We were absolutely sinking out of *kontrol'*. We were catapulted toward the sea bottom almost five *kilometrov*—that is to say three miles—below! Water gushed into the boat and splashed over the linoleum-covered deck plates, then dropped into the bilges. It seemed that our chances to recover were diminishing with every second that passed.

But wait, my friend—you do know that we would never actually reach the bottom. Do you not? Once we passed the limit of her design the *B-59's* hull would crumple and implode, crushed by the frightful pressure of the sea. *Projekt-641* submarines had an official "tested" maximum depth of 300 *metry*.

What their collapse, or "crush," depth might actually be was unknown. Pray God we were not going to find out this day!

Speaking of God, there is an old *Russkaya* saying, "*Grom ne gryanet, muzhik ne perekrestitsya* [Unless thunder strikes, a man will not cross himself]." Well, I have to tell you that I saw several members of the crew—theoretically good, scientific, atheist *kommunisty*—making the sign of the cross right then. Needless to say, no one admonished them.

Now, tilted at an angle of almost forty-five degrees, we continued to *spiral'* down, much like an airplane falling toward the earth in an unrecoverable spin. Once again things slid and fell toward the bow—boxes, cans of food, tools, personal belongings. No matter what else they were doing, every man was using one hand to grip something, anything, solid—trying not to slide and fall. In the CC the ballast and trim tank operators did in fact slide off their seats, hanging desperately onto their wheels, trying not to fall into the hydroplane *kontrol'* station. The CC was filled with shouting, with cursing, with orders, and with countermanded orders. Frantically working with the *starpom*, the *pomoshchnik inzhener* [assistant engineer], and the hydroplane *operatory*, Captain Savitskiy seemed to now be having some success in stabilizing the fall. Bow and stern planes were forced into the "full rise" position, with each *kontrol'* lever double-manned, as we desperately struggled to halt our descent. *Kapitan-Leitenant* Volkov, the assistant engineer, worked the trim-tank controls. The *starpom* released some compressed air into the forward buoyancy tank.

Then the overhead loudspeakers gave a click and *Glavnyy Inzhener* Pugachev's voice—deep, calm, reassuring—came over the intercom. "Forward Torpedo Room to Control Center. I am happy to report that the application of crowbars and sledgehammers, some extra sealant, the pressure of the sea, and the God of my *babushka* all together have reseated and resealed the hatch and stemmed the flow of water. There is a trickle, but the hatch is essentially secure."

We had fallen to a depth of about 300 *metry*, which coincidentally was the boat's maximum "test" depth. We now began to level off. Perhaps, today, we would not discover our crush depth! Now *B-59* lay quietly, the sounds of shouting and cursing, of breaking glass and crockery, and of stores and equipment falling from shelves, were all gone. We slowly drifted to starboard, neither sinking nor rising, while the *starpom* and the *pomoshchnik inzhener* worked to trim the boat and establish true level.

Every man slowly regained his composure, feeling his bunched muscles relaxing and his heart-rate slowing. The boat continued to drift virtually silent in the silent water.

For some reason I suddenly thought of the great French author, Jules Verne. You have read him, Comrade Listener? His Captain Nemo's motto was *Mobilis in Mobili* [moving within the moving element] describing his submarine *Nautilus*. Well, moving around under the water is one thing, but I do not remember Nemo's *Nautilus* sinking—or rising—totally out of *kontrol*!

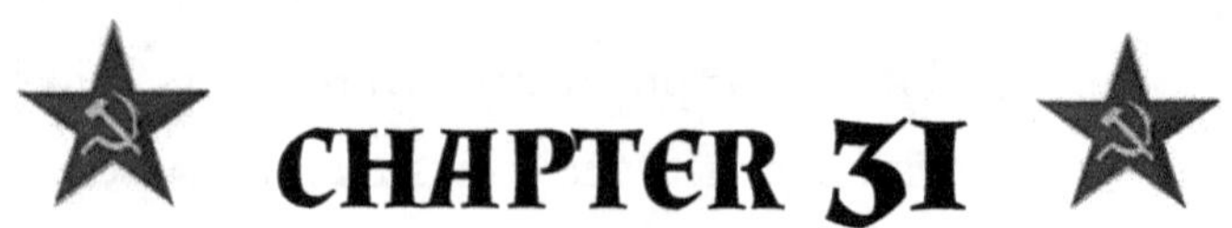

CHAPTER 31

Well, my friend, this unplanned diving crisis had consumed considerable time—time which we knew the *Amerikantsy* had used to their advantage by rushing toward our position. During the short period that we had been surfaced we had triangulated the positions of that nearby aircraft carrier—the *Randolph*—and her brood of destroyers. They were very close, unfortunately! We had done this with our QUAD-LOOP direction-finding *elektronnyy* equipment as well as listening to and tracking their increased radio "chatter." We also learned that two *Sovetskiy* freighters were within a few miles of the *Amerikanskiy* quarantine line, and that there was a submarine with them. The freighters were the *Yuri Gagarin* and the *Kimovsk*. To the *Amerikantsy* that submarine—actually she was the *B-130*, belonging to our *brigada*—seemed to be escorting the ships. In reality *B-130* was not escorting—her proximity was essentially a coincidence—but it scared the *Amerikantsy* none the less. This was about 480 *kilometrov* east-southeast from our position.

Hearing the *radisty*'s earlier reports Savitskiy had remarked, "You know, any *minut* now I expect orders from Moskva directing us to commence combat operations. I hope it doesn't come to that."

"Actually, it is almost funny. For twenty-five days I have been complaining about the lack of communications from headquarters. But right now I am dreading any message which begins '*Gavorit Moskva* [This is Moscow speaking]!'"

Well, having survived our aborted fall to the sea floor, and now moving slowly and quietly away from where we had executed that crazy emergency dive, we contemplated what was coming next. We did not have long to wait.

"Sonar to CC, hydrophone effects, port quarter, bearing three-three-zero, multiple *Amerikanskiy* surface ships, high speed, closing rapidly."

Of course, Comrade Listener, the sonar operator was listening on his passive sonar equipment. From now on we would carefully avoid using our active sonar. It was not useful in this type of *situatsiya* and using it would show the enemy exactly where we were. To be frank, active sonar has limited value since by sending out impulses it advertises the sender's precise position. However, from a tactical point of view, passive sonar—just listening—can give you a very accurate picture of what is going on in your immediate vicinity.

You will forgive me for now using the word "enemy" in regard to the *Amerikantsy*. As far as we knew we were as yet not in a "shooting war," but that could change at any *minut*. In any event the tactical *situatsiya* we were in seemed very warlike.

"*Starpom*, let us get ready," said Savitskiy. "Sound 'battle stations.' Rig for depth charges. Make everything secure. Ensure all water-tight doors are closed. Get the emergency oxygen bottles out, clear, and ready for use. Check the CO2 absorbers and break out the individual potash cartridges."

"Yest', Kapitan."

Indeed, we were just about to have quite a bit of uninvited company. Right then I recalled an old *Russkiy* saying. You will remember that I had jokingly mentioned it to Savitskiy when he first welcomed me on board. *"Nezhdanny gost' khuze Tatarina* [An uninvited guest is worse than a Tatar]." Certainly, some unwelcome *Tatary* were rushing to come *vizit* us. From listening to unencrypted *Amerikanskiy* radio traffic when we were on the surface, the OSNAZ team believed our guests to be the U.S. destroyers *Beale, Murray, Cony, Bache,* and *Eaton.* Perhaps even others would approach if we were truly unlucky.

These were upgraded "Fletcher Class" destroyers built during the Great Patriotic War. They may have been twenty years old but they were nothing to be trifled with. Each was 2,000 tons, 115 *metry* in length, and moved by two *propellery* with a maximum speed of 35 knots. Most important, they had advanced sonar equipment including the SQS-23 and were armed with five 5" guns, six depth-charge projectors, two depth-charge racks, and ten 53-cm *torpeda* tubes.

In addition, my friend, by now we were certain that the sky above us was full of ASW aircraft. Even if they came from nowhere but the USS *Randolph,* what she carried would be more than enough to defeat us. She would have as many as thirty Sikorsky SH-3 *Sea King* helicopters, each armed with a small number of *torpedy* or depth charges. These helicopters would have AN/AQS-13 "dipping" sonars, various models of sonobuoys, ASQ-8 Magnetic Anomaly *Detektory,* data-processing *komp'yutery,* and data links for the rapid dissemination of collected sonar information to other *Amerikanskiy* units. All very sophisticated equipment for 1962!

The *Randolph* would also have perhaps fifteen Grumman S-2F *Trackers*, which were twin-propeller ASW airplanes. They were armed with *torpedy* and depth charges. They would have the AN/APS-38 radar, the MAD, a smoke-particle *detektor*, JEZEBEL passive sonobuoys, and JULIE active-sonar equipment.

Forgive me for overwhelming you in a lot of detail, but I want to make sure that you understand we were up against very many and very formidable anti-submarine assets!

As the destroyers approached, Captain Savitskiy ran his fingers through his damp crew-cut hair.

"Level off at 200 *metry*," he ordered. "Rig for silent running. Secure all *mashiny*. No unnecessary moving about or loud talking. No dropping of wrenches on the deck!" He paused for a moment.

"*Leitenant* Andreyev!"

"*Ser!*"

"Go through the boat with a couple of men and make sure all loose gear is stowed and secure. With all we have been through I cannot imagine there is anything left to fly around or break, but let us be sure."

"*Yest', ser.*"

As Andreyev moved past me, he whispered, "*Kapitan* Arkhipov, we are indeed in the enemy's lair. Though we shall try not to reveal our presence to them, they sense our closeness and are searching for us." I had to smile at his formal and almost poetic assessment, but there really was nothing to say in return.

Soon—too soon—the sound of the destroyers' *propellery* could be heard inside the *B-59* even without sonar earphones. The noisy throbbing of fast-rotating propellers was seemingly everywhere.

Now it was certain that the enemy had made *kontakt* with us—the sharp metallic pings of their active sonars were also becoming audible within the boat. It was a new experience for almost all of us on board. Of course the destroyers had no qualms about using their active sonars. It would certainly help them in their efforts to pinpoint us while they were unconcerned if it helped us pinpoint them. We were really in no position to do anything about them other than try to avoid them.

We slowly descended—this time under total *kontrol'*—while we listened to the unnerving pounding of the destroyers' engines, the whine of their *turbiny*, and the cavitation of their many *propellery*. The noises rapidly increased, seemingly to deafening proportions. Of course it was not really that loud but to our nervous ears it seemed that way. Most of our crew seemed frozen in position, awaiting—what?

CHAPTER 32

The sea resonated with an enormous "boom," followed by several more. A spread of six depth charges had bracketed the *B-59*. While this was loud and frightening, it was also puzzling. I say that because the booms were not as loud as we had expected, and the subsequent jolts hitting the boat were relatively mild. As you may know, water does not *kompress*, so an underwater explosion displaces the water around it with considerable force. It normally is the violent *shok* of such displaced water hitting a submarine that damages it. Thus, a depth charge does not have to actually strike a submarine's hull to badly hurt it, and in fact rarely does.

Savitskiy and I looked at each other. "Vasiliy," he said, "is that not strange? The detonations seemed all around us, and sounded reasonably close, but we did not feel much force. No severe rolling to the side, no knocking and shrieking of the steel, no valves thrown open or leaking."

"Yes, it is strange," I repeated. Chernyshev ventured a thought.

"The *Amerikantsy* sometimes drop hand grenades on our boats. Actually, I have heard that we sometimes drop grenades on *their* boats when they poke around outside of our harbors."

"But would not a *granata* go off before it sank very deep?" interjected my young protégé, Andreyev. He and his men had quickly completed their inspection of the boat's *inter'yer* and had returned. "*Ser*, how could they reach our present depth?"

"There's a *tekhnika* where you pull the pin, jam the grenade into a roll of toilet paper while keeping the safety lever from releasing, and then drop it. By the time the sea water softens the roll to the point the lever can fly away, it has sunk pretty deep."

"There is another possibility," I said. "The *Amerikantsy* have an 'exercise' or practice depth charge which they call a 'PDC' in abbreviated form. Their detonations are a fraction of a full charge. Our navy has observed them being used in NATO exercises. In such exercises the ASW aircraft usually drop them, while surface ships usually drop the grenades. Depending on how long this keeps up today we may be able to differentiate the sounds."

I was interrupted by the phone talker. "Sonar to CC! Distinct splashes at the surface!"

A *minut* went by, another, then another. Then it came. Twenty charges detonated in quick succession. Again, the noise of the explosions rattled our *nervy* but the physical concussions only slightly disturbed the trim of the boat. Was it merely some 'sound and fury, signifying nothing?' This confirmed to us that at this point our tormentors were just that— *demony* of torment but not *angely* of death—riding in chariots painted haze-gray.

Let me be clear; the noise was significant. It was like we were sitting in a *metall* barrel which someone was repeatedly striking with a sledgehammer. But we could bear these attacks of grenades and *praktika* charges. What was harder to bear was the thought that the next detonation—or the next, or the next—could be full-charge, conveying not just noise but also boat-crushing force.

Captain Savitskiy mopped his streaming forehead with his perspiration-soaked handkerchief. We all had such wet rags in our hands, desperately trying to keep the sweat out of our eyes in the boat's one-hundred degree heat. Most of us were breathing with our mouths open, not really because of the bad air—that problem would be coming soon enough—but because of the high heat and humidity. The staggering humidity, which had already been terrible for several days, continued to condense on the steel bulkheads, drip from pipes, drip on us, and ultimately work its way down to the bilges.

"So, this is how it is," Savitskiy said. "I wonder how many of the damned charges they carry. *Starpom*, have every man not specifically on duty lie down in his bunk or somewhere out of the way. I know the Forward Torpedo Room is the coolest space on the boat but do not let the men overcrowd it—and ensure the racked *torpedy* and loading gantry remain clear."

"*Yest', Tovarishch Kapitan.*"

"At the last report the *inzhiniring* spaces had reached 120 degrees. God in heaven! Make sure the men standing watch there are rotated every thirty *minut.*"

"*Yest', Kapitan.*"

"*Ofitser Torpedy!*" Savitskiy called down into the CC.

"*Da, Tovarishch Kapitan?*" Senior Lieutenant Sluchevski called back up into the conning tower.

"Get to the Aft Torpedo Room. Make sure the vertical launch tube is clear and ready. Also make sure there are plenty of the chemical canisters ready for use. Lastly, check the noisemaker *torpedy*—I have a feeling we may soon need to use them."

"Yest', Kapitan."

The chemical canisters to which Savitskiy referred could be launched from the vertical tube in Compartment Seven. They were important in defense against ASW tracking. When the chemicals were ejected from the submarine they instantly mixed with seawater creating a thick cloud of hydrogen bubbles. These bubbles interfered with the enemy's active sonar and were reasonably effective in masking the submarine's actual position.

I believe that I have already told you that the noisemaker *torpedy*—of which we had only two—carried defensive *elektronnyy* packages instead of high-explosive warheads. These *elektronika* generated noises which mimicked the sounds of the submarine, only louder. When fired, such a torpedo moved off at fifteen knots in a different direction than the boat's base course. With any luck the *torpeda* would act to decoy the enemy, drawing attention away from the boat.

In his tiny compartment across from the commanding officer's stateroom, with headphones covering his ears and his eyes closed in *kontsentratsiya*, our primary sonar operator heard more charges splash into the water above us. We heard his report and then patiently waited as the damned things floated down to us. Did we have any choice? At this point we took no measures to evade them. Would it have done any good? This time there were twelve detonations—loud, frightening, but again causing no damage.

The destroyers regrouped, no doubt trying to figure out an *effektivnoye* pattern and establish a routine. With five of them thrashing about up there they wanted to keep us pinned but likely had no desire to ram each other in the excitement of the chase. We all could hear them but of course not in the full detail with which our sonar men could. Most of the time our *operatory* could actually differentiate each individual destroyer from the others.

A fourth barrage bracketed the *B-59*. Then, with no discernible change in their *propellery* noises, another spread arrived.

"*Glavnyy Inzhener!*" Savitskiy called down into the CC.

"*Da, Tovarishch Kapitan,*" replied Captain Pugachev.

"I am almost fearful to ask. What is the current condition of the *akkumulyatory?*"

Pugachev climbed up the steep steel ladder until he could see his *komandir*. "*Ser*, when we surfaced we were essentially depleted. Even after putting all three *dizeli* on *akkumulyator* recharge we only achieved twenty-five percent before we were forced under."

"Not enough."

"No, *ser*, not nearly enough. We needed at least six hours for full charging."

Savitskiy thought for a moment. "We have no idea how long this ordeal may last. I estimate it will last ... too long."

"*Ser*."

Aft of the three main *elektricheskiy motory*, below deck in Compartment Seven, was a fourth, smaller motor. Infrequently used, this "economy" motor would consume a minimum of *elektrichestvo* while moving the boat very silently at two to three knots. It would drive only the center propeller. Unsurprisingly, Savitskiy was thinking along these lines.

"Bogdan Tarasovich, stop the main electric *motory* and engage the economy motor. If we move slowly, *yesli povezet* [with any luck] we may have as much as three days before the *akkumulyatory* completely die."

"*Yest', Kapitan.* And, *yesli povezet*, the oxygen will last that long, and the carbon dioxide will not build too high."

Savitskiy dug his knuckles into his eyes, trying to push the heavy perspiration out of them.

"Let us consider," he said. I was not sure if he were talking to himself or to the group in the conning tower. "What is the goal of the *Amerikantsy?*" No one responded, but he smoothly went on as if he had not really expected an answer.

"Well, they apparently are not trying to kill us—at least right now. The explosive charges they are dropping—whether grenades or the practice depth charges—are not really hurting us. *Psikhologicheski*, perhaps. But not physically. The same for their damned sonar pulses which relentlessly penetrate the hull and hit every crewman in the head and heart." He paused, looking at nothing.

"So, *Kapitan*, what are they doing?" dared young Andreyev.

"Until war actually breaks out, I think they hope to drive us crazy. They are going to *bombardirovat'* us with sonar pulses and explosions. They are going to keep us under water until the heat and humidity and the stink are more than we can stand. They hope to run us out of *elektricheskiy* power so we drift blind and out of *kontrol'*. And they count on us running out of oxygen and being suffocated with excessive carbon dioxide."

"But, *Kapitan*, to what end?"

"So that we are driven to a complete and utter state of *bezras-sudstvo* [desperation]. So that we are broken as sailors and as men. So that we are forced to come gasping to the surface with our spirits crushed. So that our professional demeanor is destroyed along with our self-esteem. And so our offensive spirit is so completely obliterated that we will no longer be able to function as an effective fighting unit."

I have to admit, Comrade Listener, that I found Valentin Grigorievich's analysis logical and completely sound.

"Moreover," I added, "if we should surface under these conditions—weak and desperate—it would be easier for them to board us. Easier to try to seize the boat if they have that kind of action in their minds."

"*Kapitan*," asked Chernyshev, "do you have a plan?"

"*Da, Starpom*. We shall play a bad hand as well as we can."

"*Ser?*"

"We will try to get away from the wolf-pack circling above, and at the very least we will not come to the surface or display any weakness. The *Amerikantsy* are not *patsiyent* people. If they get no quick results it is possible that they might lose *interes* in us. Or for some reason they may be called to deploy elsewhere. I do not think our chances of those things happening are very good, but they could happen." He paused for a moment.

"We will *konservirovat' elektricheskiy* for as long as we can. As we have already ordered, all hands not specifically on duty must lie down and conserve air as much as possible. When the time comes we will employ all the CO_2 counter-measures we have at our disposal." We all nodded as one, as if on cue.

"In fact," Savitskiy continued, holding out his hand, "I need to address the crew." The telephone-talker stretched a handset over to him. He thought for a moment and then thumbed the buttons. The usual metallic click sounded throughout the boat.

"*Vnimaniye!* Attention in the boat. This is the captain speaking. *Tovarishchi* [Comrades]! Officers and men of *Sovetskiy* Submarine *B-59.* I do not need to tell you that right at this moment we find ourselves in an uncomfortable *situatsiya!* When we began our voyage I told you that it was vital to the success of our mission that we maintain the *sekretnost'* of our deployment. We have done very well for some twenty-five days, eluding the ASW efforts of the NATO countries and particularly the *Amerikantsy.*"

"But now, obviously, they have found us. We have hidden well in the depths but an *Amerikanskiy* aircraft-carrier, her aircraft, and five of her destroyers are above us and clearly have a very good notion of who and where we are."

"*Tovarishchi,* at this time they are not attempting to destroy us. The detonations we hear appear to be hand grenades and practice depth charges. We can thus deduce that no state of war currently exists between the *Soyedinennyye Shtaty* and the *Sovetskiy Soyuz.*"

"I believe they are assaulting us psychologically while hoping we soon run out of air and *elektricheskiy.* I believe they hope to force us to the surface, which is to say to humiliate us. This we shall not do! We shall hold out as long as possible and, of course, we shall attempt to escape from them."

"So, *Tovarishchi,* much is still expected of us. This *situatsiya* demands our best efforts. Keep alert! As always, instantly obey the orders of your superiors. We shall show the *imperialisty* what mettle the men of the *Voyenno-Morskoy Flot* are made of. Good luck! Remain strong, and remember that *distsiplina* is the mother of victory! That is all."

So with that, Comrade Listener, Soviet Submarine *B-59* began in earnest her *danse macabre* with the United States Navy. The *minut* became hours, and indeed one day blended into the next. We grimly fought for our sanity against the steady rain of explosive detonations, against the thrum-thrum-thrum of the destroyers' engines, and against the swish-swish-swish of their many *propellery*. The incessant "pings" of their multiple sonars hit *B-59*'s hull like so many arrows, then penetrated through the steel and then through our heads almost as if they were arrows—or perhaps drill bits.

We also fought against the excruciating heat. Even with many equipment systems shut down and only using the *ekonomika elecktricheskiy* motor, *B-59* still generated considerable internal heat. As you already have heard, most of the boat was measuring around one-hundred degrees *Farengeyt*, with the *inzhiniring* spaces reporting around one-hundred twenty. And the *temperatura* continued rising. We had not been at all successful in cooling the boat's *inter'yer* during our last brief time on the surface. In addition, though you may find it hard to believe, the sea did not help cool the hull. Even at a depth of fifty *metry* the water *temperatura* was—incredibly—around eighty-five degrees!

Intertwined with the terrible heat was the extremely high humidity. Depending upon which compartment you might be in, it was measuring ninety-five to one-hundred percent.

Then there was the air. It was very hot, and flat—which I know sounds strange considering the heavy humidity. It was dense with the odors of *dizel'* fuel and hot oil. There was the strange smell of *ozon* emanating from brushes scuffing the *armatur* in the myriad *elektricheskiy motory* on board. There was the pervasive stench of sweat—old as well as fresh—and old cooking smells. There were the smells coming from the heads. Remarkably, the odors of hot rubber and linoleum were fully discernable, mixed together with decaying food stores.

As discussed, we had ventilated the boat fairly well before our last perilous crash dive so at least the oxygen level was reasonably good and the carbon dioxide reasonably low. But, as we all knew, that balance was changing with every *minut* and hour that passed—and we knew that in the forthcoming hours this might be the greatest threat to our ability to stay submerged.

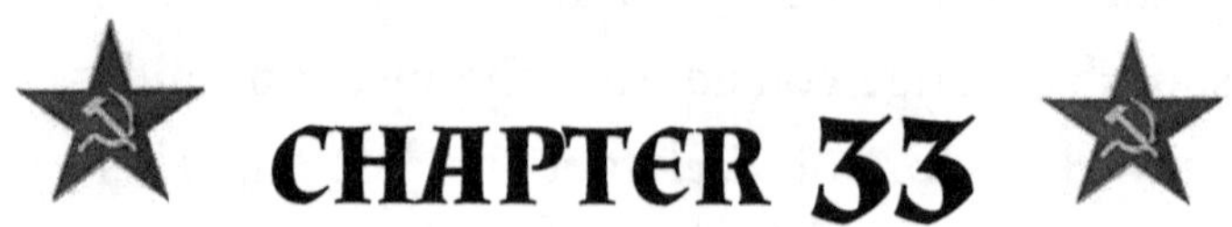

CHAPTER 33

Time seemed to move terribly slowly, yet I suddenly real-ized that fully eight hours had passed. The *Amerikantsy* had been dropping at least a half-dozen charges on us every twenty *minut*. It was so regularly done that we could have almost dispensed with our clocks!

Virtually silent, the *B-59* floated in a great arc at about two-hundred *metry* depth. Though night had fallen on our tormen-tors above they steadfastly continued their routines. This, of course, included that cycle of dropping charges—the concus-sions of which continued to crash around the boat.

Slowly we descended, approaching a layer of colder and thus denser water. We had been hoping for it and looking for it. Now, just below us, our bathythermograph was showing we had found one and we entered it with great hopes. The tone of the destroyers' sonar pulses changed a little and they became less audible. The sound waves were being refracted by the dense layer of colder water now above and around us.

As you might guess, spirits rose in the conning tower and the CC! We carefully moved further into the depths. We had gained a protective cover with this layer of different thermal density, and it seemed the destroyers had lost *kontakt* with us. For a blessed moment the destroyers' engine and propeller noises grew distant, and the high-pitched sonar pings grew less intense.

In fact it became very quiet. In that silence everything else seemed greatly amplified—droplets of moisture dripping on the deck, drops falling into the bilges, the coughing of men feeling the rise of the CO_2. I could even hear the *starpom*'s wristwatch ticking although we were not sitting side-by-side. The silence actually seemed to hurt our ears! At this moment it was only the sonar *tekhniki* who could hear the enemy through their equipment.

For about two hours the *Amerikantsy* scoured the area where we had been and then searched in outward circles, dropping random charges, hoping to re-acquire us.

Unfortunately, they did. This was when we accidentally came to the edge of the cold-water layer. The nerve-wracking swish-swish-swish of multiple *propellery* once again grew louder, and the brain-piercing pings doubled, then tripled, and then quadrupled. The sonar technician duly reported that the destroyers were fast re-approaching, but our naked ears had already told us the story. They were indeed back, no doubt embarrassed and irritated that they had briefly misplaced us. It seemed that the fresh *bombardirovka* came with a renewed—and savage—*intensivnost'*.

Attentively listening, I could picture their "attack" in my mind while I sat in the conning tower, but it would have been gratifying to be on the surface and actually see it. In apparent fine *koordinatsiya* they sped in *kontcentricheskiy* circles, suddenly stopped, listened to their own sonars as well as the "dipping" sonars of their accompanying helicopters, dropped more explosives, reorganized, charged ahead, stopped, reversed, charged forward again, and dropped more charges. Once again the *inter'yer* of B-59 became a torture chamber.

We hoped there might be a collision among the destroyers with all that erratic maneuvering, but we had no luck on that score.

Captain Savitskiy changed our course time after time, one direction and then another, to no avail. After reflection we decided not to dare any bursts of speed along with these turns, for we were desperately worried about our dwindling *elektricheskiy* reserves—and in any event our pursuers were neither amateurs nor incompetent.

Their methodical attacks went on hour after hour. Occasionally one of the destroyers would break out of the pattern, but this never gave us any actual *rel'yef*. We did have some hope on a couple of occasions, however.

"Sonar to CC! One ship appears to be breaking off and moving away."

"What course!?"

"Two-eight-five."

"Helm, steer two-eight-five!" I wondered if it would be worth bringing the larger three *elektricheskiy motory* back on line and trying a burst of speed—and I could see in Savitskiy's face he was thinking the same thing. But it would take two or three *minut* to do so and it might create too much noise.

Savitskiy reached to the instrument *panel'* behind him and grabbed a set of earphones that were tied to the sonar feed. He closed his eyes, listening intently. A *minut* passed, then a few more. Suddenly he opened his eyes and shook his head. "Left full rudder—steer due south."

He looked around the conning tower, his face without expression. Taking off the phones he said, "Unfortunately, it did not work. They may have guessed we would try something because two other destroyers quickly filled the gap left by the first."

We tried similar efforts two more times with the same *rezul'tat*.

We also tried another ruse. You will recall that we earlier had prepared a number of chemical canisters in the Aft Torpedo Room. Through the vertical launch tube in that compartment, over a period of hours, we shot out several of these which created great masses of hydrogen bubbles. These *massy* formed screens which effectively reflected sonar impulses, appearing to the enemy like large, solid forms. Three times the enemy chased these decoys but they soon realized the truth and came back toward us. In any event, at least one ship always stayed right above. Had we been dealing with one or two destroyers it might have been successful, but it was difficult to fool five of them and their helicopter friends.

After the last such attempt Chernyshev asked Savitskiy, "*Kapitan*, what about the decoy *torpedy*?"

"*Nyet*. We only have two of them. If the *proklyatyy* [damned] *Amerikantsy* start to drop real depth charges—a change I fear is coming—I want to save those *torpedy* for that actual combat *situatsiya*."

The eighteen-hour mark passed. The air in the boat had become incredibly foul. All of the *inter'yer* lights appeared to be shining in fog. Every man was periodically gasping as breathing was becoming more and more difficult.

On and on it went. The charges kept coming down upon us. We changed course frequently, we stopped, we moved forward, and we searched for more cold-water thermal layers. Nothing helped our *situatsiya*.

The heat was unbearable. The humidity was staggering. All hands were totally fatigued, many were feeling dizzy, and most were becoming mentally numb.

At twenty-four hours Savitskiy ordered another technical *analiz* of the air. After a moment the telephone-talker reported the results.

"*Tovarishch Kapitan*, the carbon dioxide is at two point five percent." I had feared it was going to be that bad. At three percent most of the men would actually pass out. At four percent—even if there were some oxygen still present—the CO_2 would suffocate us. Savitskiy bowed his head.

"Open the remaining oxygen bottles," he ordered, "and spread out the CO_2 *absorbiruyushchiy*."

We had a good number of canisters containing lithium hydroxide in dry powder form. It removes carbon dioxide from air by producing lithium carbonate and water. One *gramm* of lithium hydroxide can remove 450 cubic *santimetr* of CO_2. The *glavnyy inzhener* mustered a working party which went through the boat spreading the powder on flat surfaces—excluding the deck which was too wet due to the considerable *kondensatsiya* steadily dripping on it.

The hours continued to pass. Breathing got more difficult, the heat and humidity got impossibly even worse, the stench

became practically unbearable, the unmerciful sonars rang our
ears to distraction, and the explosions abraded and dulled our
senses.

CHAPTER 34

Comrade Listener, forgive me. I could go on and on but you are numb with listening to this terrible part of my story. And, my friend, I frankly grow miserable with the memories. So let me bring us to the early evening of Saturday, *Oktyabr'* 27th, 1962.

At now roughly thirty-six hours submerged most of the crew lay in their bunks, on mess tables, or on the filthy and wet deck. Those on watch, operating the boat, were slumped on stools or on the deck in front of their controls. Everyone was profusely perspiring and routinely gasping.

A report came in to the telephone-talker, startling him out of his stupor.

"*Kapitan, atmosfera* tests at two point eight percent."

Savitskiy merely nodded. The *starpom* keyed his handset and issued orders for the individual chemical oxygen generator packs to be distributed to the crew. When activated—which is to say heated up with chemicals—these devices generated a quantity of oxygen. Not a lot, but some. Soon most crewmen— who were conscious—had the packs on their chests and were fiddling with the attached rubber hoses which ended in mouth- pieces. Biting the mouthpiece and resisting the *impul's* to breathe through his nose, a man drew hot air through the potash cartridge in the packs—and fought the urge to retch and cough. There was some good oxygen to be obtained, but it came at a price! Most of us in the CC and conning tower put on the packs but were using them sparingly.

I was studying Captain Savitskiy through the sweat in my eyes. *What is he thinking? How desperate is he? Has he reached his limit? What is he going to do? And—what would I do if I were in his place?*

Savitskiy looked up from his seat at the *periskop*. He stared at the overhead and began speaking.

"The *akkumulyatory* are almost completely drained and are reduced to mere containers of water. The carbon dioxide threatens our lives. Several men have fainted. In fact we are falling like dominoes. We have had it. We are done for." He thought for a moment.

"We can surface and surrender. Or we can go below the boat's safe depth and dive down to her crush depth—which likely would hide us from the enemy but would just as likely kill us." He paused again.

"There is another option," he said, very quietly. He paused for a moment.

"We have the *spetsial'noye oruzhiye*," he said, again very quietly.

Oh, I thought to myself. Oh, no.

CHAPTER 35

"No, Valentin," I said, "that is not an option."

He looked at me as if startled. As if he were surprised I had heard him.

"The *ad* [hell] it is not, Vasiliy." He worked his jaw for a moment. "*Ad I smert'* [Hell and death]! I believe that it is the only real option we have at this point."

"*Tovarishch Kapitan*," I replied. "It is not an option. The conditions which would allow for that have not been met." I paused to think.

"The only real option is the first one you stated," I continued. "We must surface and face the *Amerikantsy*. Of course it is not a pleasant scenario. But it is not a foregone conclusion that we will have to surrender to them, or that they will do anything hostile on the surface. Who knows what they will do? At this time there does not appear to be an actual state of war so they have no right nor reason to demand that we surrender. They have no right to attempt to board us. After all, we are a warship of a powerful sovereign state in international waters."

"They have been *agressivno* prosecuting us!" he replied.

"Oh, I grant you that," I said, "and it does seem beyond reason. Perhaps they think their *prezident*, by declaring a *karintin*, gives them extraordinary rights—extra-legal rights! But they have not damaged our boat and they have killed none of our crew. So our actions must be measured, and they must be in proportion. The use of the special weapon right now is inappropriate."

Savitskiy abruptly stood up and slapped the *periskop* housing. "Bah! Do not speak to me of reasonable measures or what is appropriate, *Tovarishch Nachal'nik Shtaba.*"

With a dismissive gesture towards me, Savitskiy turned to a *figura* leaning against the bulkhead and fiddling with his oxygen generator pack. The captain spoke to him very pleasantly in a calm tone of voice.

"Well, what do you think, *Tovarishch Zampolit?*" The political officer involuntarily started, then looked around the conning tower as if seeking the answer posted among the dials and gauges.

"Yes, *Kapitan Tret'yego Ranga* Maslennikov," I butted in. "You must tell us your opinion for you have an important vote in this decision." Maslennikov turned to me, wide-eyed but still silent.

"Ivan Semonovich," I pressed, "please speak up. You are the *Zamestitel' Komandira po Politicheskoy Chasti.* You take up space, breathe a lot of oxygen, and eat a remarkable amount of food. It is time to earn your keep. An official decision of this magnitude requires your concurrence—as it also requires mine."

Before this discussion went too far in what I greatly feared would be the wrong direction, I wanted to intimidate the political officer and, if I could, try to achieve some sort of dominance. I did not want him to take the very easy path of passively agreeing with his emotional captain, or blindly falling back on his conservative political training.

You might also be able to tell that I did not particularly like the *zampolit.* Oh, do not feel sorry for him. It is not the lot of a

Sovetskiy political officer to be liked by professional military and naval *ofitsery.*

"*Tovarishch Kapitan,*" he began. He glanced between me and Savitskiy, but then closed his mouth and frowned.

"*Tovarishch Zampolit,*" I said, trying to push him along. "According to the regulations of the Navy of the USSR, what is the political officer's role in the case of *yadernaya voyna* [nuclear war]?"

Maslennikov seemed relieved to be asked a simple question to which he knew the answer. He drew himself to military attention and, as if reciting in *schkola,* he delivered the lesson to me.

"*Tovarishch Kapitan,* when conducting combat actions with *yadernye* weapons, the most important tasks in *politicheskaya* work are as follows. One, ensure all measures are taken to repel an enemy nuclear attack. Two, ensure the precise execution of the order to deliver our own nuclear strikes. Three, use the results of such strikes in support of the combat task. Four, mobilize personnel to protect themselves against the enemy's weapons. Five..."

"*Khvatit* [stop]!" I shouted. "Do you really believe that the *Amerikantsy* are truly—that is, within the next few *minut*—about to launch a nuclear attack? I mean specifically on us, or upon the *Rodina?*"

Maslennikov shot right back, all his previous hesitation gone, and with the full confidence of a veteran and arrogant political officer.

"*Da!* It is very possible, *Tovarishch Kapitan* Arkhipov! For the last several days all that we have heard on the *Amerikanskiy* radio are reports that tensions are incredibly high. Their news to their public hardly speaks about anything else. We stand toe-to-toe with them over this damned *Kuba konfrontatsiya*—whatever the hell it is all about!"

"*Radi Boga* [for God's sake]," he continued, "we hear from their broadcasts that in Florida they are preparing prisoner-of-war camps for *Russkiye*! As to us, specifically, their damned destroyers and aircraft prosecute us unmercifully! It feels like we are a rabbit in a small cage, with five slavering hounds continuously banging and rattling it—with ten hungry hawks circling above with razor-sharp beaks."

"*Ya ponimayu* [I see]," I replied. "Very colorfully put, *Tovarishch*. But your second article of the regulation stated you are to engage in the execution of an order to deliver our own nuclear strikes. As you know, we have had no such order. So, *Tovarishch*, what are you engaging?"

"*Ser.*" Maslennikov paused for a few seconds. "It is *der'mo* that we have had no recent *instruktsiy* on any subject from Moskva—or even the smallest communication! It is *der'mo* not to know what is going on! What if war has already begun, or begins any *minut* while we are submerged—as we run out of air and *elektrichestvo*? We will have no idea! But they will, with their radio *antenny* always in the air and in constant communications with their superiors. They will. And if they get the word to fight, then in our ignorance of such news, they will kill us whenever it suits them. We are apparently on the front line in this *chertovski* [f--king] mess, regardless of what our original mission might have been."

"But we cannot forget that we are *Zashchitniki Rodiny* [the Motherland's Defenders]." His voice softened a little.

"Thus, I think we should take action and it seems to me there is only one action which we can take that will make any sort of difference. We are now bound by honor and duty to strike at the aircraft carrier that leads the attack on us. We must use the *spetsial'noye oruzhiye.*"

"So, since you insist that I 'vote,' *Tovarishch Kapitan,* this is how I cast my ballot."

All the while, as Maslennikov was speaking and warming to his subject, Captain Savitskiy became more and more agitated—nodding his head in an exaggerated *manera* and smashing his fist into his palm as the *zampolit* made his points.

"That is right," Savitskiy said quietly. "The *zampolit* is right. We have no choice. We must defend ourselves and other *Sovetskiy* forces from this or any other attacks."

As unobtrusively as I could, I nudged the *glavnyi starshina* [chief petty officer] seated at the *kontrol' panel'* to my right. This motion in the small compartment was not as obvious as you might think. It was somewhat dark because at this point only the emergency lights illuminated the boat as we tried to conserve *elektrichestvo.* Keeping my voice down, I gave him an order.

"Slowly, carefully, and without drawing attention to yourself, get up and go find the *glavnyy inzhener.* Tell him he is needed up here right now."

"*Yest', Tovarishch Kapitan,*" he whispered back.

"And then," I continued, still speaking as quietly as I could, "go find the *meditsinskiy ofitser* and tell him the same thing." I was not sure what help Doctor-Major Kuryakin might be, but I had an unhappy thought that the *situatsiya* would continue to deteriorate. In that case perhaps the doctor could possibly declare Savitskiy somehow unwell and perhaps medically unfit to command.

"*Yest', ser*," the *glavnyi starshina* replied and then quietly slid off his stool and dropped down the ladder.

His head had hardly disappeared when—suddenly—Valentin Grigorievich swung around and shouted at me.

"Vasiliy, this is war!"

"Valentin," I replied, startled, "if the *Amerikantsy* were trying to sink us we would already be dead!"

"They are incompetent! And we have been taking good evasive action!"

"I am not sure they are incompetent, Valentin," I said, "and in any event, they are not trying to kill us. You know as well as I do they have not as yet dropped any fully-armed depth charges."

Savitskiy turned back to the telephone-talker and actually snarled.

"Get the Special Weapon Officer up here, NOW!" Shrinking from the *komanduyushchiy ofitser's* fiery eye, the talker looked away and spoke quietly into the phone's padded mouthpiece.

It was really only two *minut* before *Kapitan-Leitenant* Pavlov's cap-covered head appeared rising up the ladder, but it seemed an eternity. No one spoke during that eternity and, aside from the ever-present heavy *kondensatsiya* dripping loudly onto the deck, even the conning tower's normal sounds seemed subdued. All eyes but mine were on the deck plates, fearful to meet Savitskiy's frightful glare.

Pavlov paused to catch his breath, having run a third of the length of the boat while opening and shutting two heavy water-tight doors. He gulped the oxygen-thin but steamy air in the compartment. It was far hotter in the conning tower than in the Forward Torpedo Room. Pavlov wiped sweat from his eyes and drew himself to attention, barely avoiding banging his head on one of the emergency light fixtures.

"Da, Tovarishch Kapitan?"

"Tovarishch Spetsial'noye Oruzhiye Sotrudnik! Listen very carefully to me. I know you are very attached to your 'baby,' and will doubtless have difficulty in seeing her leave, but you will nevertheless arm and load her into Tube Two." In a softer voice he continued, almost as an aside, "When it comes to it, only you know how to do the arming—but my *torpeda* men will help you load and carry out all the other necessary procedures."

Pavlov opened and shut his mouth twice, looking very much like a guppy—just like in a *komediya* motion-picture but, I assure you, it was not funny. The tension was palpable, as Westerners like to say. Pavlov looked at the *zampolit*, and then at me. Seeing nothing useful in our expressions he at last nodded.

"Nyemedlenno' [at once], *Tovarishch Kapitan!"* Pavlov disappeared back down the ladder into the Control Center. I could hear his shoes clattering on the deck as he ran forward.

I knew that when Pavlov arrived back into the Forward Torpedo Room he would see red ready lights glowing on five of the six *53-santimetr* diameter *torpeda* tubes. Each cream-painted breach door had a large, red, five-pointed star neatly stenciled on it, on top of which was a brass medallion displaying the tube's number. As I have told you, these tubes contained conventionally armed *torpedy*—560 kilograms of high-explosive in each warhead—loaded and combat ready in conformance with the mission.

The sixth tube—Number 2, low on the port side—was empty, held in reserve for the "special weapon."

"Valentin," I exclaimed, "for God's sake! What are you doing? What are you thinking? I say again, this *Amerikanskiy* prosecution of us is not an actual attack! They are only harassing us—no doubt trying to make us surface. Rescind your order to Pavlov. Tell him to not load the torpedo. Tell him to keep it in its stored position, and to not touch the protective devices."

Savitskiy pushed his cap up, running his hands across his forehead and then over his face with its damp beard. He then shook his head, perspiration flying everywhere, and looked directly at me.

"*Chert voz'mi* [damn it], Vasiliy! What if they are just about to attack us!? What if Ivan Semonovich is right? Maybe the war has already started up there while we are turning somersaults and suffocating down here!" He was now shouting. His face twisted with *emotsiya*. "*Chert voz'mi! Chert voz'mi!*—I think it has!"

"Valentin..."

"*Nyet!*" he interrupted. "We cannot take this anymore! We cannot wait and let them strike us first when the war begins!

We are going to blast them now! We will perish ourselves but we will sink them all! We will not disgrace our Navy!"

I was running things through my mind, wildly, trying to marshal some argument—any argument—that might change the direction of his thinking. I nerved myself up to reengage the conversation. *"Tovarishch Kapitan* Savitskiy..." I began, a little desperately.

"Tovarishch Kapitan Arkhipov!" Shouting, Savitskiy again interrupted, mocking me. He had reached a conclusion and apparently had reached it some time ago. The wrong conclusion.

"I am the *komanduyushchiy ofitser* of this boat! When you came on board you said you would never forget that!" he spit the words out. "Who are you to interfere with my command, *mister bol'shoy vystrel* [mister big shot]?" He took a breath and then slowly let it out.

"I have made my decision. *Ponyatno* [Got it]? Now kindly *zatknis'* [shut up], you *sukin syn* [son of a bitch]!"

"Valentin! Think of your family!" I shouted. "Think of all our families!"

"I do not have time to think! I told you to shut up!"

Everyone and everything in the conning tower seemed to freeze, certainly including me. Except for the soft ticking of the *instrumenty* and drip of *kondensatsiya*, the ensuing silence was, as it were, deafening. Even the *Amerikantsy* were for some reason momentarily silent—giving us just now a break from the explosions of practice depth charges. Curiously, the "pings" of their active sonars also seemed diminished.

All eyes alternately focused upon Savitskiy and me. Perhaps that was good for no one seemed to notice the chief engineer, Captain Pugachev, as he quietly rose up the ladder from the CC and entered the conning tower. Thankfully he did not then move across the small compartment toward me to see why I had summoned him. Instead he pressed himself against the closest bulkhead, intently looking around as he tried to assimilate what was going on.

Early in the voyage I had gained the impression that the *inzhener* was a man of maturity and reason. He actually was the same naval rank as were Savitskiy and I—this is because *glavnyye inzhenery* were and are crucially important and highly skilled figures in the submarine service. Beyond that I had observed that he seemed to have a good relationship with Savitskiy. With any luck he might be an influence of reason in this horrible *situatsiya*.

Just then Savitskiy tore his gaze from me, spun on his heel, and pushed the telephone-talker aside. He snatched the handset from its cradle.

"Forward Torpedo Room, this is the conning tower. *Kapitan-Leitenant* Pavlov, there! This is the *komanduyushchiy ofitser*. Arm the *spetsial'noye oruzhiye!*"

After a moment the speaker clicked and Pavlov's distant voice filled the compartment. *"Yest', Tovarishch Kapitan!"*

Savitskiy thrust the handset to Maslennikov who took it and forcefully jammed down the talk button.

"Kapitan-Leitenant Pavlov, this is the deputy to the commanding officer for political issues. Arm the *spetsial'noye oruzhiye!*"

"Yest', Tovarishch Zampolit!" Pavlov replied through the speaker, a little more rapidly and louder than the first time.

Maslennikov held the handset out to me but I slapped it out of his hand, earning shocked looks from him and almost everyone else. The *zampolit* recovered the handset from where it dangled from its cord. He cradled it in his arms as if it needed soothing.

I stared at the commanding officer. *"Kapitan* Savitskiy, I do not concur. I can not concur."

Once again the conning tower grew awkwardly silent. No one moved. It was so hot it was difficult to breathe properly; even so it appeared that some of the men were holding their breaths—as unlikely as that might be.

"Proklyat'ye [God damn it] *Kapitan* Arkhipov, repeat the arming order!" Savitskiy exploded, literally stamping his foot on the deck plate.

"With respect, *Kapitan,* no," I replied.

"You WILL repeat the order!" he said, his knuckles white as he gripped the back of the telephone-talker's seat. His voice rose to a scream. "YOU WILL REPEAT THE GOD-DAMNED ORDER!"

"Ser, I cannot."

I knew that even without my order, thirty meters away in the Forward Torpedo Room *Kapitan-Leitenant* Pavlov was already arming the nuclear torpedo. *Sovetskiy* military and naval officers were steeped in a *kul'tura* of strict discipline and slavish obedience to orders. So, what else could he do?

Pavlov knew that leaders at the highest levels of the *Sovetskiy* government had made a deliberate decision to place the special weapons on the *brigada*'s boats. Surely that decision encompassed their possible use?

Ultimately, the Special Weapon Officer knew that he had to obey the *komanduyushchiy ofitser* and the *zampolit*. He had to take for granted that they had good reasons for giving these orders. And they had authority under the law. D. K. Pavlov was a good *kommunist* and a loyal *ofitser* of the *Rodina*. I pictured him, in my mind, efficiently unscrewing a cover on the weapon to check the *elektricheskiy* connections that married the detonator and the warhead. He would then remove the green "safety connector plug" and replace it with a red "arming plug."

Besides, Pavlov was probably telling himself that my coming to agreement would probably happen. And, arming the weapon did not mean the commanding officer was actually going to shoot it.

At that point Savitskiy snatched the handset from Maslennikov and clicked the talk button.

"*Kapitan* to Forward Torpedo Room! *Kapitan-Leitenant* Pavlov, load the *spetsial'noye oruzhiye* into Tube Two!"

Again, Pavlov's voice filled the conning tower. "*Yest', Tovarishch Kapitan!*"

I calculated that step would take only five *minut*. Longer, if I were lucky. Perhaps the *B-59*'s torpedomen assisting Pavlov would be nervous and handle the necessary procedures with an excess of caution. The special weapon had to be pulled slightly inboard on its storage rack until it was in line with Tube Two. Then the *torpedisty* would pick it up with the overhead-mounted gantry crane, using its pulleys and chains. Carefully they would guide it into the tube. I could clearly see it all, in my mind's eye, as if I were there with them.

In the conning tower Captain Savitskiy continued his death-grip on the talker's seat, looking around wildly.

"I am going to shoot," he said, his voice almost normal. "I can. I will! Our air is gone. The *akkumulyatory* are dead. What else can I do!?"

Suddenly his eyes opened very wide. "Well. I'll tell you WHAT I WILL NOT DO!"

Savitskiy let go of the seat long enough to strike it with his fist. "I will not surface and surrender to those *svolochi* [bastards]!" His voice climbed back up into a virtual scream.

He struck the seat again. "I will not surface and be humiliated by the GOD-DAMNED *AMERIKANTSY!*"

And again. "I WILL NOT DISGRACE THE *VOYENNO-MORSKOY FLOT!*"

Then, sooner than I had hoped, we heard a click which heralded Pavlov's voice once again filling the compartment.

"Forward Torpedo Room to *Kapitan*. *Spetsial'noye oruzhiye* loaded in Tube Two. *Torpeda* power *kabel'* connected. Breech door shut and locked."

"Very well, Dmitriy Konstantinovich," replied Savitskiy, nodding his head. "Turn on power and commence *torpeda* warmup. Set run depth to seven meters."

"*Yest', Kapitan.*"

"Valentin..." I began, but broke off as he vehemently 'shushed' me with forefinger to his lips. Speaking again into the handset he said "*Kapitan* to Forward Torpedo Room. Flood Tube Two!"

"Yest', Tovarishch Kapitan."

In my mind I pictured water rapidly pouring into the tube from the forward trim tank with the displaced air venting into the boat. Air from the tubes was never vented into the sea because a large bubble, rising to the surface, would give away a submarine's exact position to enemy destroyers or aircraft above. I then imagined Pavlov—or one of *B-59's torpedisty*—opening the equalizer valve to match tube pressure with the ambient sea pressure. He then would wait for the order to open the tube's outer, or muzzle, door.

Pavlov's voice filled the compartment again.

"Forward Torpedo Room to CC. Tube Two flooded. Depth set to seven meters."

Savitskiy clenched his jaw and spoke again.

"*Kapitan* to Forward Torpedo Room. Open the tube's outer door."

A pause.

"Forward Torpedo Room to CC. Outer door open. Load completed. Tube Two, containing the *spetsial'noye oruzhiye*, is ready to fire."

Savitskiy's eyes gleamed with satisfaction. Then, in a relaxed, almost conversational tone he looked at me and said, "*Tak* [So]."

He picked up the telephone-talker's handset and thumbed the intercom switch. The usual metallic click sounded from speakers throughout the boat. In the same relaxed voice he began to speak.

"*Vnimaniye*. Attention in the boat. This is the *Kapitan* speaking. *Tovarishchi*. Officers and men of *Sovetskiy* Submarine B-59.

As you very well know we are going through an incredible *situatsiya*. A horrible *situatsiya*. The *Amerikantsy* continue to hound us unmercifully."

"*Tovarishchi*, I know what those bastards—in their sleek destroyers and dashing airplanes—are thinking up there. They think we are part of an *operatsiya* leading to an attack on their country. If we were on the surface in a destroyer, and they were down here in a submarine, we would draw the same conclusion. So, thinking that, they are fully determined to thwart our purpose. Any *minut* now such a war may begin. If that happens, when the word reaches them that a war has started, they will strike first and destroy us. They certainly have that capability and that advantage." He paused, rubbing his bristly beard.

"But until that happens they are committed to the next best thing. Hunt us down. Lock us in and blast us with their sonar beams. Harass us mercilessly. Starve us of power and of air. Scare us with their practice depth charges and grenades. Fray our *nervy*. Drive us to madness until we break. They will do all of these things until we are forced to surface in their full view. Forced to face their *triumf* and their glee. Forced to face their laughter. If they do not get to kill us, then they intend to make us slink home with our tails between our legs—there to report defeat, disgrace, and humiliation. And doubtless we will face punishment for our failure."

"*Tovarishchi*, on my honor as a *Sovetskiy ofitser*, I *obeshchayu* [pledge] to you that I will not allow any of this to happen! They do not know that we have a nuclear weapon. Can you imagine their *syurpriz*! HA!" Savitskiy paused for a moment, relishing the thought, apparently suppressing a laugh. "Before they destroy us we shall strike them ten-fold. Before they humiliate us we will kill them all. This I promise you."

"Officers and men of *B-59*, one way or another this will soon be over. I may not be able to speak to you again. So, I congratulate you now on your fine service and on your stamina, fortitude, and admirable devotion to your *patrioticheskiy* duty to the *Rodina!*"

Nodding to himself, Savitskiy clicked off the intercom and rehung the handset. Raising his voice he called, "Activate the *torpeda* firing circuit switch!" I do not know why he raised his voice; the *Ofitser Torpedy* was now up in the conning tower and only a few feet away. The reply came—after a long pause.

"*Yest', Kapitan. Torpeda* firing circuit switch activated."

"Valentin," I said, quietly.

He spun on me with a shout—his momentarily relaxed demeanor entirely gone and fire in his eye. "WHAT!?"

"Valentin, you must calm down."

"I am calm!" he shouted. "God damn it! I AM CALM!"

"Valentin, you are not calm. You are in pain. You are in pain due to the unrelenting tension we have been under for the past twenty-seven days—and especially the horrible stress of the last thirty hours." He continued to glare at me with an unsettling *intensivnost'*. Aside from the overarching *problema* in which we were immersed, I feared for him individually. He had been under terrific pressure. That, combined with oxygen starvation, heat exhaustion, and the breathing of too much CO_2, was severely clouding his judgement.

"You feel it more than the rest of us, since you are the *komanduyushchiy ofitser* and bear the full weight of responsibility.

We—you—are drowning in frustration and uncertainty. There may be no blood as yet, but it is *agoniya*, to be sure."

As if to prove my point, Savitskiy screamed, *"STARPOM!"* and slammed his fist against the seat one more time. This time he struck the metal frame rather than the padded surface. Blood welled from his knuckles.

Chernyshev had been standing with his back to the bulkhead, trying to keep out of the fray. Startled, he stepped forward and then came to attention. *"Ser!"*

"Kapitan Arkhipov is relieved of duty! Remove him from the conning tower! Go get your God-damned *pistolet*! If he *rezisty*, shoot him!"

Chernyshev was clearly wishing himself back in Pol'arnyi— or anywhere else, for that matter. He cleared his throat, shifting his gaze from Savitskiy to me, and then back to Savitskiy. I decided to try to distract everyone by pressing my argument and giving Chernyshev time to think. I hoped I would not merely be giving him time to go find his *pistolet*.

But then Savitskiy leaned over and called down the CC hatch. "Chief warrant officer of the watch!"

"Ser!" came the instantaneous reply from that *ofitser*, standing at his post at the base of the ladder.

"Find some cord and get up here."

Thirty seconds later the *michman* came up the ladder with a length of light rope. In the face of all this insanity my mind ridiculously wandered into trivia: where could he have possibly found rope in the CC? Maybe from the shelves in the small toilet compartment, next to the ladder on the port side?

"Tie *Kapitan* Arkhipov's hands behind his back."

The *michman* just stared at Savitskiy, doubting he had heard correctly.

"Are you f—king deaf?" shouted Savitskiy. "Do what I tell you!"

"*Yest'*, *Kapitan!*" Looking frightened and confused he came up to me and grasped my left arm. "Your pardon, *Tovarishch Kapitan.*" I put my hands behind my back. I thought that there was no point in physically fighting the poor man and making a crazy *situatsiya* even worse. I was grateful that he tied the cord loosely.

Well, I have to tell you, Comrade Listener, I was in a *panika!* This was a bad turn of events. I was beside myself, groping for *idei* and searching for words to stop this madness. All it was going to take now was a simple order to close the firing switch and with a massive blast of compressed air the *spetsial'noye oruzhiye* would burst out of Tube Two—with absolutely no way to call it back or stop it!

Then, for one brief moment a hopeful thought entered my mind. While the *torpeda* indeed could be fired right now, in theory and in *protokol* it still needed to be fed the bearing and range of the *Amerikanskiy* aircraft carrier!

Of course you do know that is what Valentin Grigorievich intended to shoot at, versus any of the smaller destroyers? The *zampolit* had already suggested that. But it would take some time to make those inputs—time I needed to *puskat' pod otkos* [derail] this horrible scenario.

In fact, right next to our SNOOP TRAY radar display in the CC we had a computing machine—an *elektromekhanicheskiy analogovyy komp'yuter*—which was essential to the effective firing of *torpedy*. Of course, it was crude and unsophisticated in regard to current, modern equipment, but for 1962 it was state-of-the-art and incredibly useful. Once fed data from radar, sonar, or *periskop* readings, it would calculate a target's course, speed, and position. It would then send accurate *giroskop* angles and other *informatsiya* to the *torpedy* as they waited patiently in their tubes. You may be aware of such *machiny* from books or motion pictures. We called it the "Weapons Control Center." The *Amerikantsy* called their machine the "Torpedo Data Computer." But, right now, ours was not even powered up.

Unfortunately, my hope for more time died in my thoughts almost as soon as it appeared.

What is it that the *Amerikantsy* like to say? "Close only counts in horseshoes and hand grenades?" Well, my friend, you know "close" also counts with nuclear weapons. I suddenly realized that Captain Savitskiy needed neither precise analysis nor sophisticated solutions from the WCC. He did not need the "perfect" or even the "better" solution. He only needed a couple of pencil calculations from the "torpedo attack crew," which is to say the fire-control party. All that was really necessary was to release the weapon in the approximate direction and distance of the carrier, and it would be good enough.

Unquestionably good enough.

As if he were reading my mind, Savitskiy turned and shouted down the ladder into the CC.

"Fire Control! Have you been plotting the enemy?"

We had taken note of the bearings and ranges of the *Amerikanskiy* ships as of when we last dove. The executive officer and *torpeda* officer were up in the conning tower, but the rest of the fire-control party—the navigator, a sonar *tekhnik*, and the idle WCC operator—were packed around the navigator's plotting table in the CC, pouring over its chart with dividers, *parallel'no* rulers, and colored pencils. At this moment the OSNAZ Radio Interception Officer, *Starshiy-Leitenant* Orlov, was also in that group.

"*Da, Tovarishch Kapitan,*" replied Tsezar Sutulin, whom you already know was the senior navigator. He called up the conning-tower ladder, which was easy as its foot was immediately adjacent to the plotting table.

"Do you have an estimate for the God-damned carrier?"

"*Da, Kapitan.* Based on her last observed position, and assuming she has not significantly changed course or speed, *da.*" That was a fair assumption. To facilitate her aircraft *operatsii*, the *avianosets* would likely be cruising steadily and relatively slowly. In contrast, we were not sure where all her destroyers were as they were dancing around everywhere on the sea looking for other *Sovetskiy* submarines. Well, of course, we did know about five of those destroyers—they were directly above us!

"And, *ser,*" added the sonar technician, "we have periodically been hearing her on the passive *Feniks* system. I am confident that we know where she is."

"Excellent! Distance?"

"*Ser,* estimate three point seven *kilometrov.*"

"Bearing?" Savitskiy almost snarled.

"*Ser,* estimate target bearing two-nine-two degrees." This response was from *Leitenant* Orlov. While Sutulin was carefully plotting the movements of the *B-59*, Orlov was employing the skills of his original naval career *spetsializatsiya* as a navigator and was tracking the *Amerikanskiy* ships.

As you already know, the kill radius of the weapon was just approximately eleven or twelve *kilometrov*. The carrier, her destroyers, her support ships, most of her aircraft—and the *B-59*—were all going to die together.

Savitskiy clapped his bloody hands together, apparently not feeling any pain. "Officer on Deck, make your course two-nine-two, speed four knots!"

"*Yest', Kapitan!*" This would point the *B-59*—and her forward torpedo tubes—at where we estimated was the *Randolph's* current position.

The navigator handed a scrap of paper to the telephone-talker, who then passed the distance and *giroskop* data to the Forward Torpedo Room. There the *torpedisty* would manually enter that data into Tube Two's guidance *sistema*, which was part of a *kontrol' panel'* mounted in between Tubes Five and Six.

The *Ofitser Torpedy*—Leitenant Sluchevski—then asked, "*Kapitan*, shall we make a final shooting observation?"

"*Nyet! Konechno nyet* [Hell no]! We shall not come up to *periskop* depth. We shall not raise the scope! For the same reason we shall not employ the active sonar. We would betray our exact position. The destroyers would pounce on us before we could shoot. We have enough *informatsiya*, Sluchevski! They cannot escape. The *spetsial'noye oruzhiye* will destroy them all!"

O Gospodi, I said to myself. Oh God of my sainted *Babushka*!

Comrade Listener, do you see? If Savitskiy now merely called out "Shoot" it was done! Was he going to forget that he needed my agreement? Or was he just going to ignore me? If he gave the order, would the torpedo officer refuse—or at least hesitate? Would he forget that I needed to agree? Or would *Leitenant* Sluchevski obediently reach over to the instrument *panel'* just at his eye level? Would his fingers close onto the *torpeda* firing circuit switch? Would he then turn it?

"*Tovarishch Kapitan*," I said, loudly, desperately. I took a step toward Savitskiy. Raising his arms while simultaneously stepping toward me, he slammed his bloody fists into my chest. Thrown off-*balansa* with my hands tied behind me I slipped on the wet deck and fell down, hitting my head but able to keep my nose from smacking into the *periskop* housing. But as Savitskiy moved, so did the *glavnyy inzhener*. Pugachev leapt forward and threw his arms around his captain from behind.

"*Kapitan*," Pugachev said quietly, in the stunned silence of the conning tower. "Valentin Grigorievich."

Savitskiy tried to shake him off. "Let me go!" But Pugachev held on firmly. I had hoped that bringing Pugachev up into the conning tower would be helpful. *O Gospodi*, he was being more helpful than I could have imagined.

"God damn it!" Savitskiy screamed, continuing to shake, "why is Arkhipov still in my conning tower? GET HIM BELOW AND OUT OF MY SIGHT!"

Bogdan Pugachev continued to hold his *kommanduyushchiy ofitser* in a bear hug. I shakily got back to my feet, helped by Chernyshev. Despite Savitskiy's order, no one seemed interested in moving me down the ladder and out of the conning tower, so I started speaking again. I was desperate to get Savitskiy thinking rather than fighting.

"*Tovarishch Kapitan*, the rules of engagement for this mission are clear." Savitskiy stared past my shoulder, saying nothing. Thus encouraged I went on.

"We are authorized to fire the special weapon if we are attacked—either on the surface or under the water—and if, as a result of such attack, our pressure hull is damaged. We may also fire it if we are so directed by signal from Moskva. But as of right now, Valentin, none of these conditions have been met!" With my arms tied behind me, I unsuccessfully tried to shake the pouring sweat out of my eyes.

"Moreover," I continued, "we can fire the special weapon—and let us be clear about this—*Kapitan*, gentlemen." I glanced around the compartment, finding all eyes on me once again. And I really hoped that the *ofitser torpedy*, standing so close to the damned firing switch, was listening to me. "Let us be clear—it is a *torpeda* tipped with a nuclear warhead. Once again, we can fire it only if you, and the *zampolit*, and I, all agree. All three of us. This is no mere bureaucratic mumbo-jumbo to which we can pay attention, or not. These rules are inviolate. We can not release a nuclear weapon outside of this *protokol*. Those rules came clearly and directly from *Admiral Flota* Sergey Gorshkov and were relayed to us by *Kontr-Admiral* Leonid Rybalko."

"If we violate these rules we would be subject to courts martial. We would doubtless spend the rest of our lives in a *gulag* in Siberia. Of course, that is if we live to get home—and if there remains a home to go to. Neither of which are likely." I paused for a moment and tried to catch my breath. For me, and everyone else, it felt as if all the oxygen molecules had been boiled out of the air.

"Again, Valentin, any *komanda* on your part to fire the special weapon absolutely requires *Tovarishch* Maslennikov's assent and my assent." I paused for a few *sekund* to give my words emphasis. Again, I was speaking to the *zampolit* and the *starpom* as well as the *kapitan*, hoping that all three were turning the issues over in their minds. I was hoping that *Glavnyy Inzhener* Pugachev was also carefully listening. As I already told you, so far he was playing a wonderful part. I needed him to continue!

"You have the *zampolit*'s assent. But, I say again, *Tovarishch Kapitan*, as clearly as I can—I do not give mine!"

Savitskiy was staring at me so intently that I feared his eyes might pop out of their sockets. He drew a deep breath and violently shook his head, scowling. He had been relatively still for the last few *minut* but now resumed struggling against Pugachev's "hug." They both actually slid down onto the deck, with the *inzhener* holding fast.

"*Starpom*," Savitskiy muttered, "what are you waiting for? Arrest that *ofitser*! Get him below." His voice became almost a whimper. "*Radi Boga*, Zakhar Yanovich!"

"*Kapitan*," Chernyshev began slowly. I had my heart in my mouth. What was the executive officer going to say? What was he going to do? Thankfully he had not gone to find his pistol. He took a deep breath of the horrible air.

"*Ser*, with respect, I believe that *Tovarishch Nachal'nik Shtaba* Arkhipov is correct. You must not fire the *spetsial'noye oruzhiye* unless he concurs. That is a clear *direktiva* from the *komandir* of the *Voyenno-Morskoy Flot, SSSR*." He thought for a moment.

"And you cannot relieve him of duty on the grounds that he will not concur! Such an act would wrongfully and illegally defeat the intent of the *protokol*. In fact, it seems to me that we should not have even armed or loaded the weapon in the face of *Kapitan* Arkhipov's stated *oppozitsiya*."

Savitskiy flinched from the words as if he had been slapped in the face. He bowed his head down, almost touching the deck.

"*Chert voz'mi* [Damn it], *Starpom*." He was almost sobbing. "Your *kapitan* is asking for your help and for you to do your duty to the *Rodina*." Then, in almost a whisper, he said, "Will you not help me? Will you not do your duty?"

I interrupted before Chernyshev had a chance to respond. Sensing a slight change in Savitskiy, I was hoping to further push reason in the midst of the confusion and high *emotsiya*.

"Valentin," I said, quietly. "We have the *potentsial* here to make a mistake beyond all imagination." I paused for a few *sekund*, groping for words.

"Valentin, put yourself in the shoes of *Prezident* Kennedy, his *konsul'tanty*, and his *generaly* and *admiraly*. As we speak there is incredible *diplomatichnyy* tension between our two countries. Tension over this God-damned *Kubinskiy* thing." I paused.

"So, in the middle of this extreme *politicheskaya* tension, a completely unexpected nuclear explosion is detected—just off Kennedy's quarantine line not far from *Kuba*. The explosion vaporizes the damned *Amerikanskiy* aircraft carrier which relentlessly pursues us—just as Ahab pursued his white whale! It vaporizes the double-damned *pak* of ravenous destroyers which so ruthlessly hounds us. But, before the *spetsial'noye oruzhiye* destroys them, they will detect it. They will instantly report to Washington that they see it and that it came from a submarine. A submarine, *Tovarishch Kapitan,* which the U. S. Navy has already identified as a *Sovetskiy* FOXTROT." I paused again, listening to the water vapor dripping on the deck in the otherwise silent conning tower.

"What will Kennedy and his *konsul'tanty* think?" I continued. "Valentin, let me tell you. They will *panika!* They will think that the *Sovetskiy Soyuz* has actually launched a nuclear attack against them—and that it is just the beginning of a *full* nuclear attack. They will think that, in order to survive, they must immediately *strike.* Not at us; oh, no, not at us—at this short range we will already have died in our own *T-5 torpeda*'s nuclear explosion."

"No, Valentin, they will strike at the *Sovetskiy Soyuz* with everything they have. I have read that the *Amerikantsy* have more than three-thousand nuclear weapons which they can hurl at the *Rodina* from bombers, land-based missiles, and sea-launched missiles."

"Then, the *Sovetskiy Soyuz* will doubtless launch everything *we* have at the *Amerikantsy.* Of course we will. Our leaders will not merely stand still and be vaporized! Despite the propaganda of our leaders to the contrary, we all know that we do not have nearly as many weapons as the Main Enemy. But we have many—and our leaders in the Kremlin will certainly use them."

Savitskiy was still slumped over, staring down at the deck, his face in his hands, nodding his perspiring head. It appeared now that Pugachev was holding him up, keeping him from completely collapsing onto the green linoleum.

"Valentin, hundreds of warheads will cross past each other in the air and in outer space, and hundreds of warheads will fly east and west in the bellies of jet bombers. When all those nuclear warheads reach their targets the *Rodina* will be utterly and totally destroyed. The seven countries of our Warsaw Pact will be totally destroyed. Western Europe will no doubt be destroyed. Much of the United States—one-third? Maybe one-half?—will be destroyed. And on top of that, thick clouds of *radioaktivnoye* dust will encircle the earth. It will be a holocaust beyond imagination."

"Tens of millions of people will be killed, and tens of millions more will have radiation poisoning." I paused as tears welled up in my eyes. I did not do it for *dramaticheskiy* effect. It just came over me.

"I know about radiation poisoning, Valentin Grigorievich," I continued, trying to get tears and sweat out of my eyes. "As you know, I was on board *Sovetskiy* Submarine *K-19* when her *reaktor* accident occurred. Men died horribly on that boat, right in front of me. Other men died, horribly, later in hospital. The rest of us—including myself—got very sick, and only miraculously recovered." I paused, again not for effect, while emotion fully swept over me.

"Valentin, our infallible leaders may start such a war. The damned *kapitalisticheskiye Amerikantsy* might cause such a war. It could very well happen. But that is beyond our *kontrol*.

As an *Amerikanskiy* author, Emerson, once wrote, 'Things are in the saddle, and ride mankind.'"

"That may well be the case today. 'Things' may get out of *kontrol* and ride the world to nuclear war over this *Kuba* issue."

"However I do know that we, standing here in the conning tower of this submarine right now, on our own, we can *kontrol* one thing. We can ensure that *we* do not trigger such a horrendous event."

Savitskiy slowly stopped struggling. He took a deep breath of the terrible air and, coughing, slowly let it out. Almost a minute passed. Then, looking down and addressing the linoleum on the deck he said quietly, almost conversationally, "Before we left Sayda, Admiral Rybalko did implore us, '*Tovarishchi*, do try to keep us out of total nuclear war.'"

Taken fully by *syurpriz* by that remark I groped for something useful to reply, but with no success. Then Savitskiy surprised me again.

"You can let go," he said to Pugachev. The engineer relaxed a little, but kept his arms in place around his captain. Savitskiy looked up at me.

"I understand. I understand you, Vasiliy," he said quietly—actually to my amazement—and thus he raised my hopes. Risking another deep breath of the moist and foul air he continued, reviewing the points of my argument.

"A war might not have already begun between the *Soyedinennyye Shtaty Ameriki* and the *Sovetskiy Soyuz*. In that case, if we fire a nuclear weapon we will start a war—perhaps even a full *yadernaya voyna* [a nuclear war]."

"Oh, not just a nuclear war, Valentin," I replied softly, not really wanting to interrupt him but I felt I needed to underscore the point. "A *yadernaya istrebleniye* [nuclear holocaust]."

Savitskiy, still looking down at the deck, slowly nodded his head.

"You can let go," he said to Pugachev. "You can let me go, Bogdan Tarasovich."

The *glavnyy inzhener* looked over at me and I quickly nodded. He let go of his captain and sat back. Savitskiy climbed back up onto his feet, shaking. He steadied himself, and relaxed the bloody fists with which he had struck me a while ago. He raised his eyes and focused on me.

"O.K., Vasiliy, O.K. *Ty pobedili menya* [You have beaten me]."

I shook my head and started to reply, but he had more to say.

"More important, *Tovarishch Kapitan*, you are right."

What could I do? What could I say? I merely nodded, thankful. Incredibly thankful.

"*Bol'shoye spasibo* [Thank you very much], Valentin." I paused for a moment.

"Do you think it might be time to get some decent air, and make contact with the *Amerikantsy?*"

Savitskiy nodded and mopped his face. "Yes. *Ofitser Torpedy!* Deactivate the Torpedo Firing Switch. Carefully!"

"*Yest', Kapitan!*"

"Stand by to surface. Lookouts to the bridge."

Then Savitskiy jumped, holding out a hand to steady himself. Actually, we all did! Two explosions detonated alongside *B-59*. Despite the sound, they apparently were not too close since we heard them without really feeling them.

It seemed that the *Amerikantsy* had chosen to *dramatichno* reenter the conversation! Say what you will about them, Comrade Listener, it was interesting timing.

EPILOGUE

So, that is my story of *Sovetskiy* Submarine *B-59*. And the story of how I—V. A. Arkhipov—perhaps "saved the world." I very much hope I have held your interest. But perhaps we should now, as they say in the West, tie up some "loose ends."

As the *B-59* slowly came to the surface, breaking through to air and life, *Kapitan-Leitenant* Pavlov carefully disarmed the special weapon. He and the torpedomen reversed their earlier procedures and safely returned the torpedo to its storage rack.

As we came up we listened intently to our passive sonar, trying to ensure we did not come up directly under one of the American destroyers. They no doubt were listening to us for the same reason, and apparently moved out of our way. We immediately raised our radio *antenny* and sent a message to Moskva describing what had happened and giving our position. Those of us who first came onto the bridge were staggered by the oxygen-rich air, almost to the point of collapse. My young friend *Leitenant* Andreyev nearly fell overboard from the wild sensation of gulping the fresh sea air! We engaged the boat's powerful intakes and blowers and she was ventilated in very short order—accompanied by considerable laughter and cheering from below.

Even though it was past nightfall, the whole ocean was brilliantly lit by the five destroyers' searchlights and the searchlights of several helicopters. And the sea was full of many score sonobuoys which the *Amerikanskiy* aircraft had dropped in their hunt for us—all visible due to their small, flickering *navigatsiya* lights. It certainly was not needed, but several S-2F *Tracker* aircraft also dropped powerful flares, further illuminating the scene.

While the *Amerikantsy* immediately attempted to communicate with us there was no indication of any desire for us to surrender, and there was no effort on their part to board us. Captain Savitskiy ordered a large, red *Sovetskiy* state ensign raised on the conning tower—rather than the smaller and more conservative blue and white flag of the *Voyenno-Morskoy Flot*. He wanted to ensure that the *Amerikantsy*, and all their cameras, clearly saw that B-59 was a warship of a strong superpower. One destroyer was able to send a readable message by a flashing signal light asking if we needed any assistance. Savitskiy replied by saying, "This ship belongs to the Union of Soviet Socialist Republics. Cease your provocative actions."

Early the next day *ofitsery* on board the destroyer USS *Lowry*, which had come close alongside, attempted more conversation. Valentin Savitskiy was having none of it. Through miscommunication or deliberate obfuscation we did not even give them the satisfaction of learning B-59's number or designation. Giving up, the *Lowry*'s captain assembled his ship's small band on deck and had them play various *melodii* to either celebrate the U.S. Navy's "victory"—or to entertain us *Russkiye*—or both. Some of the *Amerikanskiy* sailors tried to toss bottles of *Koka-*

Kola and packs of *sigarety* over to us, but most fell short and into the sea. Captain Savitskiy, noticing one of his sailors enthusiastically tapping his foot to the American band's music, gruffly sent him below.

After two days of close company, while charging our *akkumulyatory* to the maximum, we submerged and dove down to 150 *metry*. We changed course and slowly moved away towards the northeast. At this point the *Amerikantsy* either lost track of us or lost interest in us. Regardless, they did not pursue. We eventually and fairly uneventfully returned home per instructions, arriving at Sayda Bay on December 23rd.

* * *

Let me also tell you of the fates of the other boats in our *brigady*.

Soviet Submarine *B-4*: Only one of our four FOXTROTs, the *B-4*, avoided the intense professional humiliation that the other three boats underwent. *B-4*, as you already know, was commanded by my good friend Ryurik Ketov and carried on board the *komandir brigady*, Vitaliy Agafonov. Though *B-4* was detected more than once, she managed to evade and escape each time, and never was forced to surface in front of any *Amerikanskiy* warships. She ultimately arrived back at Sayda Bay on December 16th.

Soviet Submarine *B-36*: As you already know, Moskva had decided against sending three of our FOXTROTs through the narrow sea lanes of the Turks and Caicos Islands. However, headquarters had directed *B-36* to explore the Silver Bank Passage between Grand Turk Island and Hispaniola Island. The admirals thought it might be reasonably safe due to the channel being 130 *kilometrov* wide, which might reduce the chance of detection. But this turned out to be an unfortunate decision—at that time the *Sovetskiy Soyuz* was unaware that on Grand Turk Island there was a new and operational U.S. Navy SOSUS facility!

Alerted by that facility regarding a "reliable contact," *Amerikanskiy* aircraft spotted *B-36* on the surface at 0819 hours on Friday *Oktyabr'* 26th, 120 *kilometrov* east of Grand Turk. She of course dove and tried to remain invisible to the many sonobuoys which were dropped above her. Apparently the aircraft were not able to pin her down precisely, but this intense activity nevertheless put her under great stress.

Captain Dubivko became fearful that war might have broken out while he was submerged and under prosecution, and the thought of using his *spetsial'noye oruzhiye* in order to survive also crossed his mind. After two and a half days of relentless pursuit, on *Oktyabr'* 31st the *B-36* was forced to the surface by the destroyer USS *Charles P. Cecil* and several P2V-7 *Neptune* aircraft. Later on, after getting away from the *Amerikantsy*, *B-36* returned to Sayda Bay, arriving on December 25th.

Soviet Submarine *B-130*: I later found out that my colleague in the *B-130*, *Kapitan* Shumkov, caused the *Amerikanskiy prezident* his worst moment during the Crisis. On the morning of Wednesday, Oktyabr' 24th, *B-130* found herself the center of attention as a P5M *Marlin* aircraft—from U.S. Naval Air Station Bermuda—spotted her *shnorkel'* about 800 *kilometrov* south of that island.

Then, on the morning of *Oktyabr'* 26th, the SOSUS system detected *B-130*. SOSUS aided several aircraft, the aircraft carrier USS *Essex*, and the destroyer USS *Blandy* to pinpoint her. To the *Amerikantsy* she seemed to be escorting the merchant ships *Kimovsk* and *Yuri Gagarin* in the Sargasso Sea. In fact, the *Amerikantsy* were moving to intercept the *Kimovsk* with a destroyer while also preparing to exert extreme "pressure" on the *B-130* with ASW helicopters. This was to force her away from the merchant ships. But, as you have already realized, the close proximity of *B-130* to these merchant ships was essentially a coincidence. Our *brigada* of submarines was never intended, nor ordered, to escort any surface ships.

Comrade Listener, you may find it *interesno* to know that the *Kimovsk* was carrying a dozen *R-14* intermediate-range ballistic missiles, and the *Gagarin* carried critical missile refueling equipment.

The historical record shows that *Prezident* Kennedy was "okay"—as the Westerners like to say—about boarding or even destroying a merchant ship. But, for some reason he was extremely uncomfortable about attacking a *Sovetskiy* submarine!

He said to his *konsul'tanty*, "At what point are we going to attack him? I think we ought to wait on that today. We don't want to have the first thing we attack be a Soviet submarine. I'd much rather have it be a merchant ship."

But then he was told by his *Sekretar'* of Defense, Mr. Robert McNamara,

> "The plan is to send antisubmarine helicopters out
> to harass the submarine. And they have weapons and
> devices that can damage the submarine. And the plan,

therefore, is to put pressure on the submarine, move it out of the area by that pressure, by the pressure of potential destruction, and then make the intercept. But this is only a plan and there are many, many uncertainties."

At that point, according to Kennedy's chief *konsul'tant*—his brother Robert—the president turned very pale.

Prezident Kennedy might have turned even more pale had he known that the *B-130's* captain, Shumkov, had flooded four of his *torpeda* tubes—including the one which he had loaded with his "special weapon."

After we returned to Pol'arnyi, Shumkov told me about this. However, he said that he had no real intention to use the purple torpedo. He merely wanted to impress his own *zampolit* about how zealous Shumkov was for our important socialist mission! You might recall that it was Shumkov who was the only one of our captains who actually had fired real nuclear-tipped torpedoes in test exercises.

B-130 also suffered from many *mekhanicheskiy problemy* during the mission, and frankly should never have been certified to depart. Her *akkumulyatory* were malfunctioning and would not take full charges. There were also flaws in two of the *dizel'* engines' auxiliary drive gears which ultimately failed. She generally trailed behind the rest of the *brigada*, at one point by 640 *kilometrov*.

B-130 was ultimately forced to surface by destroyers controlled by the carrier *Essex*. She then—with enormous humiliation—had to be slowly towed back to *Rossiya* by a *Sovetskiy* ocean-going tugboat.

* * *

All four submarine commanders, and the *komandir brigady*, received stringent reprimands for the failure of the mission.

I was not reprimanded for I was serving as a staff officer and held no command responsibility in the *brigada*. Neither was I praised, for no one reported my tense *konfrontatsiya* with *Kapitan* Savitskiy in *B-59*'s conning tower.

The unhappiness of the high command was conveyed to us by *Kontr-Admiral* Rybalko, who appeared visibly embarrassed. Rybalko also said that he thought it was "criminal" to have sent our *brigada* on the mission fundamentally "blind" regarding the full *strategicheskoye situatsiya* and the parameters of Operations Kama and Anadyr.

We were censured because of our exposure to the *Amerikantsy* against the requirement of our mission to remain covert. And, of course, because three of our boats had been forced to surface, which humiliated the *Sovetskiy Soyuz*. No thought was given about FOXTROT boats being technically poor choices for this kind of mission. Even if they were in short supply at that time, nuclear-powered submarines would have been far superior to meet the speed and stealth requirements which were put on us. But in typical fashion, the high command saw no fault in its own planning or *strategicheskoye* thinking.

However, also in the fashion all too typical of the *Sovetskiy Soyuz*, the reprimands were almost immediately overlooked. The subsequent rapid expansion of the submarine force in the next several months and years demanded large numbers of good and experienced *ofitsery*, so there were none to be wasted.

Thus, my colleagues—and I—all shortly received new commands with greater responsibility and with our careers apparently unaffected. For example, Captain Ketov was immediately given command of a new nuclear-powered boat. Later, Captain Savitskiy was given command of a nuclear-powered submarine armed with cruise missiles and torpedoes—all tipped with nuclear warheads (a *Projekt*-670M CHARLIE II Class). Captain Agafonov was soon promoted to *kontr-admiral* and then commanded a division of Northern Fleet nuclear boats.

* * *

How bad could the *situatsiya* really have been? What do you think, Comrade Listener?

Over the years I have read much and given it a great deal of thought. Just as I emphasized to Captain Savitskiy on that fateful day on board *B-59*, one nuclear detonation in that area—against either nation's military forces or territory—would certainly have sparked a full nuclear war. This would have been a war for which the *Soyedinennyye Shtaty*, the *Sovetskiy Soyuz*, the NATO countries, and the *Varshavskiy Dogovor* [Warsaw Pact] countries had been preparing.

I ask you, though, how can you prepare against total annihilation?

It was certainly within the power of Valentin Savitskiy—or any of the other three captains—to instantly turn the Cuban Missile Crisis into World War III. Do you appreciate this, Comrade Listener?

Let us look, for a moment, at nothing other than the U.S. Air Force's Strategic Air Command. We will not consider the *strategicheskoye* forces of the U.S. Navy or of the United Kingdom. In 1962, the S.A.C. had almost 3,000 nuclear weapons. It had 1,500 bombers, 1,000 refueling tanker aircraft, and almost 200 ballistic missiles. There were 220 targets in the USSR which were designated "first priority." Many of these targets were scheduled for *more than one strike*—to absolutely ensure total destruction!

At that time, the *Sovetskiy Soyuz* and the *Varshavskiy Dogovor* were not as powerful as the West regarding nuclear strike ability. We had far fewer warheads than did the United States. Moreover, we did not have nearly as many accurate, long-range missiles. Indeed, we eventually *would* have them, but that would come a few years later! However, having said that, even at that time we certainly had enough to wreak deadly havoc.

In 1962, in a total nuclear war, it is likely that all of the *Sovetskiy Soyuz* would have been obliterated, much of the *Soyedinennyye Shtaty* would have been destroyed—and much of Europe would have been as well. Clouds of radioactive material would have encircled the Earth.

It truly would have been, Comrade Listener, the end of the world.

 # AUTHOR'S AFTERWORD 

Did this Cold War high-seas event really happen? Apparently it did.

Did Captain Valentin Savitskiy almost start a nuclear World War III? It seems so.

Was Captain Vasiliy Arkhipov really the individual who stopped him? Evidence says yes.

Was the Savitskiy-Arkhipov debate a dramatic confrontation—or was it calm, reasoned, and polite? Well, on this point, I'm really not sure!

What I am sure of is this: Saturday, October 27th, 1962, became known as "Black Saturday" around the John F. Kennedy White House. During the Cuban Missile Crisis—what historian Arthur M. Schlesinger, Jr. named "the most dangerous moment in human history"—the 27th was in many ways *the* day of the Crisis. It was the day that found the world within a hair's breadth of nuclear Apocalypse.

On top of all the other palpable stresses of October 27th, a U.S. Air Force U-2 aircraft of the 4080th Strategic Reconnaissance Wing was shot down by Soviet forces using an S-75 *Dvina* (NATO designation SA-2 GUIDELINE) surface-to-air missile. This was over Banes, Cuba. The pilot, Major Rudolph Anderson, Jr., was killed. To the Americans this action made it appear that the USSR was deliberately escalating the Crisis.

In addition, on this same fateful day, another U-2 "spy plane" accidentally (if you can imagine) intruded into Soviet air space for over an hour before recovering its proper course. Piloted from Alaska by Captain Charles Maultsby, the mission was to fly north to collect high-altitude radioactive air samples from Soviet nuclear weapons testing. The mission was totally unrelated to the Crisis. However, as Chairman Khrushchev later said, during these moments of incredibly high tension some Soviet officials feared that this aircraft was an American nuclear-armed bomber. This certainly escalated the Crisis from the Russian point of view.

On that day, "eyeball-to-eyeball," President Kennedy and Premier Khrushchev, in a manner of speaking, stared hard at each other, pushing and shoving. Foreign correspondent and eminent historian Michael Dobbs has written that Black Saturday was the defining moment of the Crisis—just as the Crisis was the defining moment of the Cold War.

All of that is true. And, it stands true even with no accounting of the crisis on board Soviet FOXTROT submarine *B-59*. In fact, it would take the passing of almost forty years before anyone in the West would even learn about *B-59*'s nuclear torpedo, Captain Savitskiy, and Captain Arkhipov.

By the way, do you think that the U.S. Navy would have prosecuted the Soviet 69th Torpedo Submarine Brigade so aggressively if they had had any inkling that each boat carried a nuclear weapon? I rather doubt it. Ignorance is bliss, I suppose.

Thus, annihilation that day was even closer than anyone—including the Soviet leadership—realized. On that day, had Savitskiy fired and detonated a nuclear weapon off the coast of Cuba—obliterating himself and at least six warships of the United States Navy—what would have happened?

Such an action would have occurred precisely when the U.S. and the U.S.S.R.—John Fitzgerald Kennedy and Nikita Sergeyevich Khrushchev—were cautiously groping their way back from "the abyss." Such a cataclysmic event—a nuclear explosion unexpectedly coming from left field, as it were—would have instantly changed everything.

I believe that there's no question that the U.S. would have interpreted the event as the beginning of a Soviet "first strike" and would have immediately and fully responded, hurling the two countries into the full nuclear war which, that day, both were desperately trying to avoid.

I probably should point out that such a "left field" event might not have been totally unexpected. A few days earlier U.S. Secretary of Defense Robert McNamara and his deputy, Roswell Gilpatric, had kicked around a similar scenario:

McNamara: "The President asked for our views on how we should respond if the Cubans launched a missile, "authorized" or not.

Gilpatric: "We wouldn't know if such a missile actually came from Cuba."

McNamara: "Right. *It could come from a submarine.* I think we should tell the Soviets that if that should happen we will hold them responsible and will fire missiles in retaliation."

That said, the reality of such an event would have been a shocking surprise. During a time of war, disaster, diplomatic turmoil, or other crises, the greater the likelihood is of an unforeseen event happening which might radically change the course of history.

Well, as far as we know, the Cubans did not come close to launching a nuclear missile from Cuba or anywhere else.

But a mid-grade Soviet naval officer apparently did come close to launching a nuclear torpedo from his submarine.

Was Valentin Savitskiy overwhelmed by complex and challenging tactical circumstances, unreliable communications, malfunctioning equipment, and the stress of command? Was he physically smashed by the heat, humidity, and foul air? Was he really pushed beyond his ability to persevere? Beyond his ability to endure? Had he really reached his breaking point?

And did Vasiliy Arkhipov boldly and skillfully talk Savitskiy back from the brink—in so doing "save the world?" Was the debate an emotional, heated shouting match—or was it a calm and dispassionate discussion? We don't really know, frankly, and we will likely never know. Documents and witnesses are sparse and what there are seem at times contradictory.

The main source of the "discussion" is Captain 2nd Rank, Retired, Vadim Pavlovich Orlov, who brought it up at a 40th "anniversary" Cuban Missile Crisis conference held in Havana. The *B-59*'s former OSNAZ radio-intelligence officer spoke about and later wrote about events during the mission, but he was not precise on the nuances of that day.

Moreover, some of the other 69th Brigade officers have questioned Orlov's version of events. But there don't seem to be any other eye-witnesses forthcoming with detailed confirmatory or contradictory information. Savitskiy and Arkhipov are both long deceased—prior to making any unclassified statements. Thus, it's impossible to know their exact words or how tense the situation really was. And, while the fall of the Soviet Union in 1991 opened a lot of government archives and made available considerable material, most Soviet ministry of defense archives are still closed.

One of my writing mentors, author of a bucketful of critically acclaimed high-adventure best sellers, found this story implausible. "If JFK had known those four boats had nuclear weapons," he said, "he would have crapped his pants." No argument from me; I'm quite sure he would have. "Apparently," my friend continued, "the Kremlin passed the somewhat important decision on whether or not to have a full nuclear war with America to four submarine commanders and their embarked political officers. Khrushchev was a real moron if he did that. It's a miracle the world isn't a radioactive cinder." Boy howdy. I don't think Khrushchev was a moron, but my friend's point is well made. What the hell were Khrushchev and the Kremlin thinking? *Anadyr* and *Kama* were incredibly risky operations in and of themselves—without any craziness such as this added to the scenario.

Why did they do it? I have no idea, nor have I been able to find anyone else really able to explain it. Even Khrushchev's son Sergey, who often speaks to American audiences about the Cold War and who was a Senior Fellow at the Watson Institute for International and Public Affairs at Brown University, has shed no clarity on this—other than the boats did have nuclear torpedoes and did have the authorization to use them. It will remain a puzzle until those archives mentioned above are opened—if even then. We do have a good amount of credible evidence that these decisions were made and these weapons were deployed; we just don't know exactly why. Fortunately, for this story, it doesn't matter. I've concentrated on what a handful of mid-grade naval officers did while in possession of those weapons and how they dealt with their authority to use them.

So for the sake of drama, I chose to paint the shoot-don't shoot argument in *B-59*'s conning tower with the bright colors of heat and desperation. I've also stretched the length of time concerning the "battle" between the *B-59* and the *Randolph*'s destroyers for dramatic effect. I'm perfectly comfortable with all of that. This is historical fiction, not academic history—though I promise you I've stuck to the known facts quite a bit.

I do have one concern. I may have unfairly tarnished Captain Savitskiy's reputation as a competent, reliable, and prudent officer. I've always thought it was unfair and wrong for Charles Nordhoff and James Norman Hall to have so incorrectly painted William Bligh as a monster in their best-selling 1932 novel "Mutiny on the Bounty." If I've done something similar to Savitskiy, I am sorry for it.

It's tough and unfair to judge a person unless, as it is said, you've walked in their shoes. During this mission, being on board any one of those boats was extremely unpleasant and incredibly stressful, and to carry the burden and responsibility of command made it much more so. At least one of the other commanding officers felt it—strongly—and, if we only knew, they all probably did. On board the *B-36* (where he really was assigned, not the *B-59*) Lieutenant Andreyev actually wrote this, about Captain Aleksei Dubivko, in his serial letter to his wife:

> The worst thing is that the commander's nerves are shot to hell. He's yelling at everyone and torturing himself....He doesn't understand that he should be saving his strength, and the men's too. Otherwise we are not going to last long. He is already becoming paranoid, scared of his own shadow. He's hard to deal with. I feel sorry for him, but at the same time angry with him for his rash actions.

Well, regardless of whether the Savitskiy-Arkhipov debate (and it is clear that there *was* some sort of debate) was of fire or ice, in the end *Kapitan Vtorogo Ranga* Valentin Grigorievich Savitskiy chose peace versus Armageddon, and that unquestionably goes to his credit. Moreover, *Kapitany* Dubivko, Ketov, and Shumkov all made the same excellent choice.

By the way, you might be interested to know that in real life Captain (or rather Vice Admiral) Vasiliy Arkhipov received significant though very late recognition for his actions on Saturday, October 27th, 1962. Nineteen years after he passed away at age 72, Arkhipov was recognized posthumously with the "Future of Life" award from the U.S.-based Future of Life Institute. This was the first award of this prize. The intent of the program is to highlight a heroic act that has greatly benefited humankind, done despite personal risk and without being rewarded at the time. The $50,000 prize was presented to Arkhipov's daughter Yelena and grandson Sergey.

Well, when it's all said and done, I find this recognition for Arkhipov extraordinarily fitting.

And I, for one, am very grateful that the little boy and his mom mentioned on this book's dedication page (and tens of millions of other people), survived Black Saturday.

 # ACKNOWLEDGEMENTS 

I very much appreciate the extensive technical advice and background information supplied by an old friend, former Interior Communications Electrician 2nd Class (Submarines) Barry Walsh, who in the early 1960s served on board the diesel-electric boat USS *Quillback* (SS-424). Additionally, I want to mention another old colleague, Engineman 3rd Class (Submarines) Noel Defosset, who similarly served on board the USS *Remora* (SS-487) and whose remarks were invaluable. I'm also thankful for the insights of a new acquaintance, former Electrician's Mate 2nd Class (Submarines) Randy Ackerman, who was on board the USS *Blenny* (SS-324) in Cuban waters at the time of the Crisis.

I further appreciate the outstanding language and cultural help of Lt. Col. David Humpert, USAF, Ret., another new friend and former human intelligence [HUMINT] officer, Soviet expert, and Russian translator. Similarly, I'm indebted to my old friend Col. Carl DauBach, USAF, Ret., who brought his Ph.D.-level knowledge of Russian history—and his 1960s-era Chief Boatswain's Mate experience—to polish the manuscript (which he read twice). I can't overlook the nautical advice and suggestions of my long-time mentor and friend, Capt. Richard Woodman, LVO, award-winning novelist, naval historian, and consummate seaman—who is an Elder Brother of the Trinity

House (the British lighthouse authority, pilotage authority, and maritime charity). A formal salute is due to Vice Adm. John Poindexter, Ph.D., USN, Ret., national security advisor to President Reagan, who also read the manuscript twice and found this "what if" story to be exciting and plausible—and who handed me a number of excellent comments and suggestions. Moreover, I appreciate the analysis of Lt. Cmdr. Kurt Schick, Ph.D., USN, Ret., a superb intelligence officer and current professor of writing and rhetoric. Likewise, I salute my long-time friend Cmdr. Suzanne Brannon, USN, Ret., a remarkable career intelligence officer, for her valuable comments and critiques. I greatly appreciate my Rocky Mountain Navy colleague, Rear Adm. Richard Young, USN, Ret., for his enthusiastic help and hand on my back as I approached publication.

I'm indebted to my son, 2nd Lt. Micah Maffeo, (Military Intelligence), USAR, who spent hours with me on board the FOXTROT submarine *B-39* at the Maritime Museum of San Diego, California; there we poked, prodded, measured, and photographed everything we could, trying to capture the feel and texture of these impressive boats. *B-39* was built seven years later than was *B-59*, but she was built in the same place— Sudomekh Shipyard (Yard 196) in Leningrad—and essentially to the same plans, and thus bears considerable familial resemblance. Obviously I'm thankful for the Museum's acquisition and maintenance of this remarkable boat.

I'm also greatly indebted to a number of writers who, through their books, lent me considerable World War II submarine expertise—expertise very relevant to my story as it was drawn from diesel-electric experience from less than twenty years earlier. From the Allied side these include Capt. Edward L. Beach, USN; Capt. Robb White III, USN; and Rear Adm. Ben Bryant, RN. From the German side, *Herr* Wolfgang Ott; *Oberleutnant zur See* Lothar-Günther Buchheim; and *Oberleutnant zur See* Herbert A. Werner. (I might mention that the design of the Soviet *Projekt*-641 boats was influenced by the German Type XXI U-boat.) Thanks also to the published insights of Cmdr. Bruce J. Schick, USN, Ret., whose diesel-electric boat USS *Irex* deployed to the Greenland-Iceland-UK Gap for 53 days during and after the Cuban Missile Crisis.

While working on this novella I read or thumbed-through some twenty-five books, at least that many print and electronic articles, and about four short video presentations. Regarding the specific story of the four FOXTROT submarines which comprised the Soviet 69th Torpedo Submarine Brigade, I found the following sources particularly helpful: *One Minute to Midnight* by Michael Dobbs; *October Fury* by Capt. Peter Huchthausen; *Red November* by W. Craig Reed; and *The Submarines of October* edited by William Burr and Thomas Blanton. In addition to seeing and listening to him in several video interviews, Capt. 1st Rank Ryurik Ketov's lengthy 2005 article in the *Journal of Strategic Studies* was invaluable. Similarly—also in 2005 and in the same journal—a 26-page article by Svetlana V. Savranskaya was pure gold. And, Joseph Allbeury's and Nguyen Tran's very informative and pictorially rich booklet on FOXTROT *B-39* was spectacular.

I can't overlook the unwitting contribution of retired Captain 3rd Rank Anatoliy P. Andreyev. He was a lieutenant on board FOXTROT *B-36* during the operation, and he kept a diary—or rather a serial letter—intended for his wife Sofia and little daughter Lyalechka. While others on board the four submarines undoubtedly maintained diaries or notes, Andreyev's diary is apparently the only one to be discovered and publicized in modern times, and he provides the only known substantial written record of events from inside any of the boats.

Well, in this book, I've taken the literary liberty of "transferring" Lieutenant Andreyev to the *B-59* for the mission, and having him befriended there by Captain Arkhipov. As a result, at various times, many of his journal entries become parts of their conversations. His remarks are to be found in a number of sources, but it appears they were originally translated by Svetlana Savranskaya for the *National Security Archive*.

Thanks to my stepmother, Dolores Owens Maffeo, a retired librarian, grammarian, and voracious reader, who gave the manuscript a solid going-over. Same to my financial advisor, Jeffrey Stotler—a former destroyer/cruiser officer, lawyer, eagle-eye, and all-around sharp thinker whose suggestions greatly enhanced the dramatic presentation. Thanks also for several helpful ideas coming from nautical writers Linda Collison, Alaric Bond, and Rick Spilman.

Huge appreciation goes to my wife, Rhonda, a retired programmer and software project lead. She pulled me off the electronic rocks, where I had run helplessly aground while trying to transfigure my original manuscript into a format desired by the publisher.

A salute has to go to Tony Mauro who developed several incredible designs for the book's cover—making it very difficult to choose among them.

Many thanks go to Commanders Stephen Phillips and Claude Berube, old shoremates as well as the co-owners and managing editors of Focsle Publishing, who fearlessly joined me under the sea for this voyage.

As always, I greatly appreciate the staff of the U.S. Air Force Academy's McDermott Library. Risking grave danger that I'll overlook someone, I want to mention Joseph Barry, Carol Becker, Jeffrey Houchin, Lynn Keskeny, Jill Ponti, Tracey Roman, David Hooker, and Frances Scott.

I found a considerable amount of relevant information in that Library's print stacks. I might also mention that the print and microform holdings of that Air Force library have supported my naval research and writing endeavors amazingly well over the past twenty years!

☭ Personazhi Dramy ☭

On board the Soviet "FOXTROT"-Class Submarine **B-59**

Valentin Grigorievich **Savitskiy**
Captain (2nd Rank), *Voyenno-Morskoy Flot, SSSR.*
Commanding Officer (*Komanduyushchiy Ofitser*).
Commands the ship; has ultimate authority over, and ul-
timate responsibility for, the ship and its crew.
Operates with wide latitude within the boundaries
of law, regulations, and the assigned mission.

Vasiliy Aleksandrovich **Arkhipov**
Captain (2nd Rank), *Voyenno-Morskoy Flot, SSSR.*
Chief of Staff (*Nachal'nik Shtaba*), 69th Torpedo Submarine Brigade.
Not one of the ship's company; temporarily attached on board the *B-59.* Plans and directs all
administrative, financial, and operational activities
for the brigade's commanding officer; acts as an
advisor to the CO, and is responsible for the man-
agement of the brigade's support staff. Actual
duties will commence when the brigade reaches its
new base at the final destination.

Zakhar Yanovich **Chernyshev**
Captain (3rd Rank), *Voyenno-Morskoy Flot, SSSR.*
Executive Officer (*Starpom*).
Head of the Command and Control Department
(*Boyevaya Chast' Upravleniya*) and the Operations

Department (*Boyevaya Chast' 7—BCh-7*). Second
in command, under the commanding officer. Allo-
cates crew duties, maintains discipline, ensures
operational readiness, maintains overall fighting
efficiency; specifically ensures the boat's "trim"—
balance and stability—when diving, surfacing, or
in combat.

Bogdan Tarasovich **Pugachev**
Captain (2nd Rank), *Voyenno-Morskoy Flot, SSSR.*
Chief Engineer (*Glavnyy Inzhener*). Head of the Engineering Department (*BCh-5*). Ensures proper
function and maintenance of the engines, motors,
and all other machinery; oversees the entire technical operation of the vessel including engineering,
electrical, and mechanical divisions.

Ivan Semonovich **Maslennikov**
Captain (3rd Rank), *Voyenno-Morskoy Flot, SSSR.*
Deputy to the Commander for Political Issues /Political
Officer (*Zamestitel' Komandira po Politicheskoy
Chasti,* or *Zampolit*).
Outside the regular naval chain of command. En-
sures that the crew and officers obey orders and
conform to Communist Party ideology; provides
political indoctrination and education.

Stepan Yevgenyevich **Kuryakin**
Doctor-Major, *Voyennaya Meditsinskaya Sluzhba, SSSR.*
Medical Officer (*Ofitserskiy Vrach*). Head of the
Medical Department (*Meditsinskaya Sluzhba*).
Maintains the health of the crew, treats sick and
injured personnel, works to prevent disease, and
promotes good health ship-wide.

Maxim Nikolayevich **Volkov**
Captain-Lieutenant, *Voyenno-Morskoy Flot, SSSR.*
Assistant Engineer (*Pomoshchnik Inzhener*). Assists the Chief Engineer in all aspects of his duties
and responsibilities.

Dmitriy Konstantinovich **Pavlov**
Captain-Lieutenant, *Voyenno-Morskoy Flot, SSSR.*
Special Weapon Officer (*Spetsial'noye Oruzhiye Ofitser*).
  Not one of the ship's company; temporarily attached
  on board the *B-59.* Ensures maintenance and readiness of the single torpedo carried by the submarine
  which is equipped with a nuclear warhead; arms and
  prepares the weapon for launch if and when so ordered.

Tsezar Romanovich **Sutulin**
Captain-Lieutenant, *Voyenno-Morskoy Flot, SSSR.*
Senior Navigator (*Starshiy Navigator*). Head of the
  Navigation Department (*BCh-1*). Maintains awareness
  of the ship's position at all times; plans the journey,
  recommends courses, estimates timing of destinations;
  ensures hazards are avoided; maintains charts, publi-
  cations, and navigational equipment; oversees
  meteorological equipment and communications.

Egor Danilovich **Rodzyenko**
Senior Lieutenant, *Voyenno-Morskoy Flot, SSSR.*
Radio Electronics / Communications Officer
  (*Radiovedushchiy / Ofitser Svyazi*). Head of the Communications Department (*BCh-4*). Organizes,
  operates, maintains, and repairs all signal flags, signal
  lamps, and electronic communications equipment and
  systems onboard; ensures all incoming and outgoing
  message traffic is processed accurately and in compli-
  ance with existing regulations.

Vadim Pavlovich **Orlov**
Senior Lieutenant, *Voyenno-Morskoy Flot, SSSR.*
Radio Intelligence/Interception Officer/Translator.
  (*Radioinformatsiya/Podslushivaniye Ofit-
  ser/Perevodchik*). Not one of the ship's company;
  temporarily   attached on board. Supervises the ten-
  man Special Purpose Radio Interception Unit assigned
  to the *B-59* for this mission; expert in radio intercep-

tion, surveillance, and intelligence; fluent in English; encrypts and decrypts secret message traffic. Will have duties with the permanent 40-man signals-intelligence net to be established when the brigade reaches its final destination.

Kirill Lavrentyevich **Sluchevski**
Senior Lieutenant, *Voyenno-Morskoy Flot, SSSR.*
Mine and Torpedo Officer (*Ofitser Shakhty i Torpedy*).
  Head of the Mine/Torpedo Department (*BCh-3*). Ensures the maintenance and readiness of the submarine's torpedoes and torpedo tubes which are its primary offensive weapons; would have similar responsibilities if naval mines were placed on board for a specific purpose.

Viktor Sergeyevich **Mikhailov**
Junior Lieutenant, *Voyenno-Morskoy Flot, SSSR.*
  Assistant Navigator (*Pomoshchnik Navigator*). Assists the Senior Navigator in all aspects of his duties and responsibilities.

Anatoliy Petrovich **Andreyev**
Junior Lieutenant, *Voyenno-Morskoy Flot, SSSR.*
Supply Officer (*Ofitser Snabzheniya*). Ensures efficient food service and crew pay disbursement; runs the boat's laundry and small stores; stocks spare parts for underway maintenance and repairs.

 # Others of Note 

John Fitzgerald **Kennedy**
>President of the United States of America. Head of
>state of the U.S.A. Commander in chief of the
>armed forces of the United States.

Robert Francis **Kennedy**
>Attorney General of the United States. *De facto*
>chief advisor to President Kennedy, his brother.

Robert Strange **McNamara**
>Secretary of Defense of the United States. The ci-
>vilian head of the U.S. Department of Defense.

Curtis Emerson **LeMay**
>General, U.S. Air Force.
>Chief of Staff of the Air Force. Top military officer
>in the Air Force. Formerly commander of the Stra-
>tegic Air Command.

Nikita Sergeyevich **Khrushchev**
>First Secretary of the Communist Party of the So-
>viet Union; Chairman, or Premier, of the Council of
>Ministers. Head of state of the U.S.S.R.

Sergey Georgyevich **Gorshkov**
>Admiral of the Soviet Union, *Voyenno-Morskoy Flot,*
>*SSSR.*
>Commander in Chief of the *Voyenno-Morskoy Flot.*

Vitaliy Alekseyevich **Fokin**

Admiral, *Voyenno-Morskoy Flot, SSSR.*
First Deputy Commander, Soviet Navy. Second in command of the entire *Voyenno-Morskoy Flot* (under Admiral Gorshkov). Also a member of the Central Committee of the Communist Party of the Soviet Union.

Anatoliy Ivanovitch **Rassokho**

Vice Admiral, *Voyenno-Morskoy Flot, SSSR.*
Chief of Staff, Soviet Northern Fleet.

Leonid Filippovich **Rybalko**

Rear Admiral, *Voyenno-Morskoy Flot, SSSR.*
Commanding Officer, 20th Operational Submarine Squadron, Soviet Northern Fleet.

Vitaliy Naumovich **Agafonov**

Captain (1st Rank), *Voyenno-Morskoy Flot, SSSR.*
Commanding Officer, 69th Torpedo Submarine Brigade (for this mission, embarked on board FOXTROT *B-4*).

Aleksei Fedoseyvich **Dubivko**

Captain (2nd Rank), *Voyenno-Morskoy Flot, SSSR.*
Commanding Officer, FOXTROT *B-36*.

Ryurik Aleksandrovich **Ketov**

Captain (2nd Rank), *Voyenno-Morskoy Flot, SSSR.*
Commanding Officer, FOXTROT *B-4*.

Nikolai Aleksandrovich **Shumkov**

Captain (2nd Rank), *Voyenno-Morskoy Flot, SSSR.*
Commanding Officer, FOXTROT *B-130*.

 # Images 

John F. Kennedy (22 October 1962 TV speech)

Nikita S. Khrushchev

Vasiliy A. Arkhipov

Valentin G. Savitskiy

A. F. Dubivko, N. A. Shumkov,
V. A. Arkhipov, R. A. Ketov

Vadim P. Orlov and SIGINT operators

Soviet Submarine *B-59* (28 Oct 1962)

USS *Cony*, Fletcher Class destroyer

Sikorsky SH-3 *Sea King* with "dipping" sonar

Grumman S-2F *Tracker*

Martin SP-5B *Marlin*

Lockheed P2V-7 *Neptune*

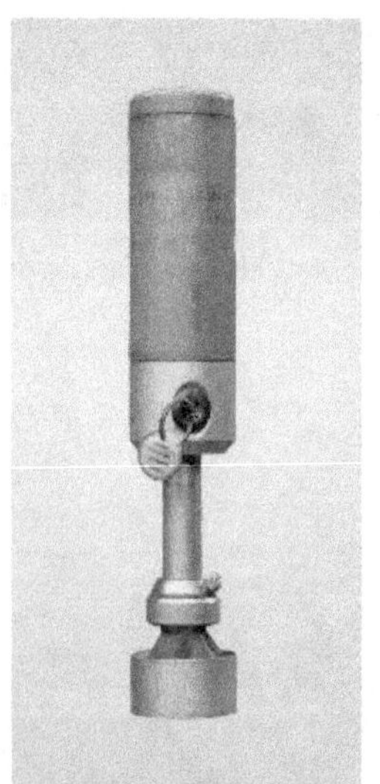

USN "practice depth charge"

USS *Randolph* (CVS-15)

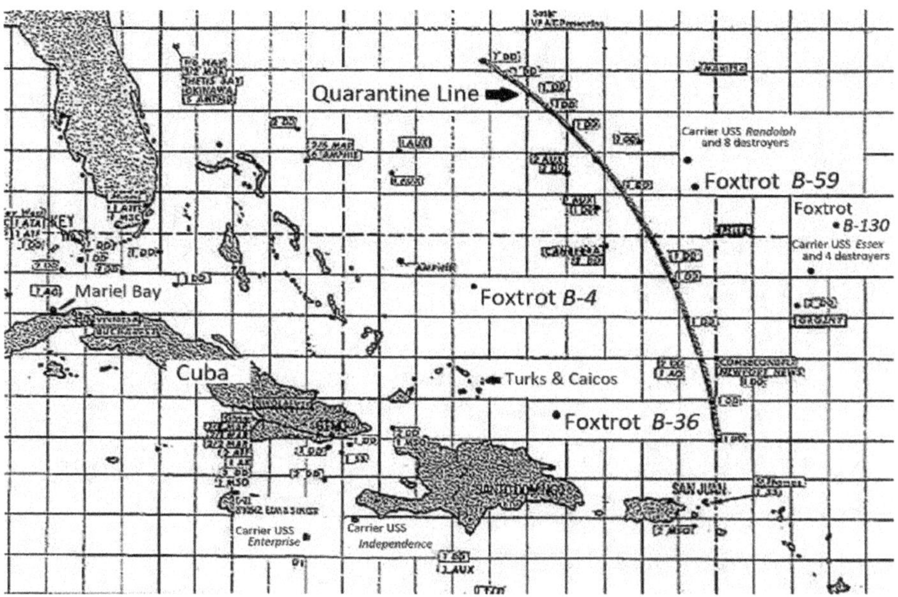

U.S. Navy CNO Flag Plot Chart (modified), 27 Oct 1962. Although not very legible, the plot also shows a considerable number of U.S. Navy warships, particularly destroyers, as well as several Soviet merchant ships. Note also the large aircraft carriers *Enterprise* and *Independence* to the south of Cuba.

IMAGE CREDITS

Blog "Deano in America": FOXTROT submarine drawings

Soviet Navy: V. Arkhipov, V. Savitskiy, A. Dubivko, N. Shumkov, R. Ketov, V. Orlov

U.S. Government, The White House: John F. Kennedy

U.S. Navy: *B-59*, USS *Cony*, SH-3 *Sea King*, S-2F *Tracker*, SP-5B *Marlin*, P2V-7 *Neptune*, practice depth charge, USS *Randolph*, CNO Flag Plot Chart

Wikimedia Commons: Nikita S. Khrushchev (Bundesarchiv, Bild 183-B0628-0015-035/Heinz Junge/CC-BY-SA 3.0)

ABOUT THE AUTHOR

Steve Maffeo is formerly the associate director of the academic library at the U.S. Air Force Academy. He is a graduate of the University of Colorado (B.A.), the University of Denver (M.A.), and the Joint Military Intelligence College (M.S.). In 2008 he retired, in the grade of captain, after 31 years in the U.S. Army National Guard (Signal Corps), the U.S. Navy, and the U.S. Naval Reserve. Steve commanded three reserve shore-based naval and joint-service intelligence units in Salt Lake City, Denver, and Washington, D.C. His final reserve assignment was as an instructor, and the director of part-time programs, at the National Defense Intelligence College in Washington. Steve tinkers with his two '60s muscle cars, is a recreational shooter, and is a volunteer 'commissioner' at the local Boy Scout summer camp. He lives in Colorado Springs with his wife, Rhonda, a retired computer programmer and software project lead; their son, Micah, is a military intelligence officer in the U.S. Army Reserve.